Christina Debi

When Life Walks on Bare Soles

First published November 2014 by Bent Banana Books.

Visit www.bentbananabooks.com
Bent Banana Books *email*
bentbananabooks@gmail.com
24 Lorraine Court Lawnton, Australia, 4501.

A CiP catalogue record for this book is available from the Australian National Library
ISBN 978-0-9872784-6-3
Cover design: Dhrupod
Cover photograph: Pete Markham
http://www.flickr.com/photos/pmarkham/5378230259/

For

Matt
Michelle
Michael
Gabrielle
Francis
Barry
Kai
Kaitlyn
and
In memory of Mum

When Life Walks on Bare Soles

Christina Debi

'Have you guessed the riddle yet?' the Hatter said, turning to Alice again.
'No, I give it up,' Alice replied: 'what's the answer?'
'I haven't the slightest idea,' said the Hatter.
'Nor I,' said the March Hare.
Alice sighed wearily. 'I think you might do something better with the time,' she said, 'than waste it in asking riddles that have no answers.'

Lewis Carroll, *Alice in Wonderland*

Chapter 1

SOME women figure out how to grow old gracefully. Others, like my friend Josephine, make the announcement *we're going to be friends with benefits* sound as simple as *we're going to Sushi Train for dinner. Maria*, she told me, *you only get to be single once. Enjoy it while you can.* I could never quite figure out what being single *once* was about. Some people got to be single at least twice. Once before you got married. And once after you were divorced.

I had been ticking the singles box for twenty years after a ten-year marriage and still the thought of having sex with someone who was only a friend seemed too much. It was like the hot water system in my garage. It didn't provide a continuous supply and the temperature varied based on the consumption. If the flow increased it cooled off completely.

On the other side of the argument, the idea of sex with a stranger was tantalizing but seemed you'd be more likely to get burnt than by the good old loyal benefits-friendship. There was no solution except to find someone who wanted to share his life with you, someone who would love you and most importantly someone who you would fall hopelessly and gloriously head over heels in love with. How about a Japanese love doll for women?

Most times you ended up having sex with strangers because they held the potential of turning into a relationship partner. And of course when they didn't, that only proved that even, or especially, with online dating, the likelihood of meeting someone who was mature and ready to commit was as remote as finding the legendary place called Woop Woop. To me sex without commitment was like garlic without odor, nachos without sour cream, a German without a beer. That's where Dirk came in.

The first time I met Dirk I was in a little bar in Brisbane on a Friday night with Josephine who was not only my friend but also my work buddy at South State Legal and my soon-to-be self-appointed relationship counselor. She'd made a bee line for the ladies' room and had kindly left me to find somewhere for us to become invisible for a few hours of girl talk after work. Simultaneously Dirk and I lurched for a newly vacated table in one corner of the room. He stopped and motioned for me with the same hand holding his beer to go ahead and sit down. Josephine lamented in a whisper after I had my journey to the ladies' room that *suggesting he join us was possibly the poorest decision of your mid-life crisis yet, Maria.*

'But opposites attract,' I finally insisted as I was getting ready in Josephine's ensuite for my first date with Dirk a week later.

'German men have been rated the world's worst lovers,' Josephine announced as she threw herself onto her bed. She sounded like a newsreader on CNN. 'And do you want to know why Maria?' Her green eyes, framed by large black-rimmed glasses, peered at me with intent.

'I'm sure you'll tell me.' I caught sight of her in the reflection of the mirror as I stroked gloss over my bottom lip. She rolled off the bed and stood behind me. All I could see were her eyes peering over my shoulder.

'Because they smell,' she proclaimed.

'No one could smell as much as my ex-husband,' I scoffed, brushing my collar-length hair back and catching the side sections for one last burn through Josephine's Remington hair straightener. 'My ex could make a bar of soap last until it was no bigger than a quarter of an inch square. And still use it.' I switched the straightener off and swept my hair behind my ears.

'All the more reason for passing on this one,' Josephine warned. 'Don't come running to me when his B.O. gets too much for you. You're letting that German accent suck you in. It's all cute and lovely now but it won't make up for bad sex. Don't say I didn't warn you.'

I pulled my jeans on and slipped my feet into my red Diana Ferrari sling-backs. 'Josie do you still think that sex is all there is to a relationship?' I stood up. I could now look down onto the top of Josephine's carrot-red hair.

'It may not be all there is.' She looked up at me with eyes full of warning. 'But,' she said as she headed back to her bedroom, 'if you're in a relationship and sex is bad, it becomes all there is.'

Josephine was right of course. Good sex in a relationship disappears under the comforter but bad sex sticks out like bad vibes at a birthday party. Still, I ignored her comment and instead threw my things into my bag with a smile on my face. 'Thanks for having me. I feel like a teenager after a sleepover.'

'Just remember you're not a teenager Maria. You're a grown woman. An old grown woman. And you don't have time to waste on smelly men.'

'Fifty-five is not old Josie. And I don't feel old. Forty, that's when I felt old, that's when I began my fitness regime. I started with gym twice a week. I've been doing that and more ever since. I'm fit, not old.' I flexed muscles. 'Look I can make my boobs flex.'

'Oh spare me.' Josephine rolled her eyes. 'You're right it's not old, it's ancient. And you have a twenty-year-old daughter who would agree.'

'The thing is that Julia has not yet come to understand that old age is a figment of the imagination,' I answered. 'And unfortunately she won't learn that until it's almost too late.'

'Age is not imaginary Maria. It's deceitful, acts likes it's not there, sneaks up on you like an ant at a picnic but it's not make-believe. My mother always told me to grow old gracefully.' She let out a burst of laughter. 'That's why I only choose graceful men.'

'Age is over-rated, under-rated, X-rated and obscene,' I pitched. 'No one wants it but unless you take an early exit everyone gets it. Trouble is we haven't identified what it really is. Is it a number? Is it a state of mind? Is it the third act? Is it ill-health? I don't know Josie, and I'm not going to sit around knitting socks while I find out.'

'You might do better with that than dating a German,' she scoffed.

'What's wrong with a German?'

'Everything. My father was German-born. '

'Your father is German Josie? I didn't know that.'

'There's nothing to know. My mother left my father years ago. So I don't really know him. And my sister's husband is German too. He left her as soon as he found out he had to share her with her family.'

'Josie you can't judge people by your father or your sister's husband. German people are beautiful. They are brilliant. I've had wonderful German friends at times.'

Josephine ignored my praise. 'And the German you're dating is younger than you are. They have a name for women who date men ten years younger,' she scoffed playfully.

'It's thirteen,' I corrected. 'And that name is best kept for women who actually seek younger men out and use them. I'm not one of them. I like Dirk and it's not like he's twenty, he said he's . . .'

I was interrupted by Josephine who had swung around and was doing an exaggerated imitation of surprise. 'What?'

'I'm fifteen years older than you are Josie. It's okay to be older than a best friend but not older than someone I'm dating? How does that work? And anyway do I have to start acting like I'm no longer a person because I live in a society which worships youth?'

'How on earth are you going to tell him?' Josephine gasped, ignoring my questions. 'As if he'd understand you anyway. *Ya, apologize me,*' she impersonated, rolling her head from side to side. 'That's about the only English the man can speak Maria.'

'You didn't make any effort to talk to him Josie, you wouldn't know. And anyway Hugh Jackman is thirteen years younger than his wife and Joan Collins married a much younger man,' I snubbed, ignoring her criticism. 'It's all very acceptable. And there is no reason why Maria Valance can't date someone younger as well.' I went towards the door.

'If Maria Valance was an actor or some kind of celebrity it would be acceptable, but I don't think you've quite reached that status yet,' Josephine said as she followed me.

'I feel like I'm acting most of the time. I'm always acting happy and responsible and mature when in fact deep down I'm just a vulnerable woman looking for love.'

'Wait.' Josephine jabbed her index finger in the air above her. 'We're going to need some music.' When she reappeared she was playing the first notes of the theme from *Schindler's List* on her violin.

'Have you always got that thing hanging around?' I laughed, thinking of her amateurish efforts the previous night when she'd managed to play through the first third of the sheet music. I was surprised that it had been vaguely recognizable. It had brought tears to my eyes.

'Not always, only when I'm practicing.' Josephine laughed. 'Or when the mood dictates.'

I ignored her antics and blew her a kiss. 'Have a great trip.' I'd almost forgotten she was on leave and going to be in Europe for the next month. 'Stay safe. Stay in touch.'

'Dirk might not be the one for you Maria,' were her only words as she dropped the violin from her chin and planted a kiss on my cheek.

'You have a good night too,' I replied.

My phone rang as I stepped outside. It was my daughter on the other end and her screech sounded like a reaction to a mouse that had run up the inside of her skirt.

'Where are you, Mum?'

'What's wrong?' I got into my car and braced myself. 'Julia what is it?'

'He's done it again.'

'Who's done what?'

'Jamie's broken down on the highway. Can you pick him up?'

A queasy feeling entered my stomach and began its ascent into the guilt department. 'Julia, can't his own mother pick him up for goodness sake?'

'She's gone out. Can you get him?'

I removed the phone from my ear and checked the time. It would take me half an hour to get to where I was meeting Dirk. I didn't have time to turn off onto the highway, pick Julia's boyfriend up, drive him home to Julia at Woody Point and still arrive in time.

'I can't,' I insisted as the guilt logged into the database. 'I have a date.'

'You have to, he's stuck,' she begged as if her own life depended on it.

'He'll need a tow truck anyway.' I tried to shut down my guilt default system. 'He can get a lift in that. I've done it, it's a good view from up there.'

'Thanks,' she replied in a flat voice and the call cut out.

My mother, bless her soul, had warned me against having a child late in life. I could hear her voice in the car with me saying *I told you so Maria*. It only added to my feelings of guilt which had now set up a blog in my mind. The topic was about the downside of not staying in touch with my sister and long-lost brothers and pointed out the pluses that could have been added to my life if only I had tried to save my relationship with them after our father's death. It extended to listing the benefits of having family and how that would help Julia if only that were the case. My mental discussion went on to highlight how guilty I should feel for not being there for my daughter given all of the above and how the blog would not have had to be written if I had been able to have a father figure in her life because he would be there for her at times when cars broke down. And after the blog was complete my feelings of guilt took a couple of screen shots of the latest episode of me being a bad mother so I could look at them from time to time and wallow in self-pity. But Julia is twenty, I argued with my inner self. And planning to move with her boyfriend into an apartment. Surely I don't have to treat her like a child. She doesn't need me around all the time.

The battles we were having over the move were enough to make me want to forget my pride and take up pole dancing. That might give me a better perspective, I thought, or at least get me out of the house a couple of nights a week. Julia's questions came one after another as if she was a three-year old asking about sex. I had to constantly appraise my mood so that I wouldn't end up yelling at her to chill and reminding her she shouldn't be moving until she had her degree and full-time work. I shuddered every time I thought of the debt she and Jamie would end up in but no amount of coaxing or bribing seemed to be working towards changing her mind about leaving. Every time I had that overwhelming desire to walk out and leave the house to her while I took up residence on a deserted island I soothed myself by thinking that my Gold Lotto numbers might come up and instead I'd go to live on an island in the Mediterranean. After that she'd come to her senses, get a degree in psychology and figure out the reasons why she was pushing so relentlessly and at any cost, for what Jamie wanted.

A message from Josephine arrived as I was about to start the engine. *Enjoy ur date. Oh is that u still in my driveway? Go woman ur late.*

I looked up to see her standing at her lounge room window. I did a thumbs up. One of the things I liked about being single was the immense amount of freedom I felt in being myself. Actually that was the only thing I liked. And I suppose when I think about it, being myself was all I could ever be. I just wasn't sure who that self was anymore. It was being *by* myself that I didn't like so much.

Divorce and the resultant single life are under-rated as contributors to loneliness and mid-life crises. To those who haven't tried one, divorce is just something that sits with a little box beside it waiting to be checked off by someone who's recently been granted one as opposed to other options like married or single. I was pregnant with Julia when her father decided to put a tick in the *single* box. We never saw him again so I presume he had no misgivings or lack of courage about being single. It was much the same for Josephine except she had never wanted a child and felt comfortable ticking that box along with her ex-husband. In fact Josephine was the only woman I knew who would turn up at a singles' party looking for a play-mate rather than a life-mate.

But for me divorce was traumatic. For months it left me feeling like a wild woman running up and down the middle of Queen Street in the end-of-work traffic every day. I couldn't see where I was going and I kept getting knocked over by unforeseen large objects that looked like buses but were really letters of demand from the bank that said if I didn't make the next mortgage payment by tomorrow there would be a bigger bus along soon. I was getting nowhere. Finally after I stopped the madness I settled into feeling as if I'd been pulled out of the Whirlpool front-loader after the spin cycle. At least I was clean.

It wasn't only the bills that made me tear my hair out, it was the loss of everything I had dreamed of. I couldn't find anyone who understood or was prepared to admit that the end of a marriage also meant the end of the future I had mapped out. I felt as if I'd hit a brick wall. The path just stopped and I had to fuddle around looking for another path. And there wasn't one. I had to cut one out, push all those bushes and thorns and boulders out of my own way. But the grief made that difficult.

That was another thing that was underestimated. Friends spent most of their time trying to work out who was to blame in the break up so they could take sides and feel good about being on the right side. No one, including society at large, seemed to realize that the loss of a marital partner through divorce was akin to loss by death and that grieving was very real.

But once I worked through all of that and the sensation of being single, and the realization that I could now choose which television channel to watch on Saturday night took hold, I decided I didn't want to be at home alone on Saturday nights in front of a flat screen. That's when the internet dating kicked in. It kicked out a year later when it dawned on me that dating sites were actually in the business of keeping their customers single. Those men couldn't resist the next match offered to them. Emails arrived every day with pics of men and women who had recently joined the site. I terminated my account and went back to the Saturday night footy. And I didn't even like football. So when I met Dirk I was ready to try a new journey.

Josephine only referred to Dirk as *the German*. She reasoned that as every English word he tried to pronounce was either indecipherable or out of context it would be impossible for me to be serious about getting to know him unless I learned to speak German. He could be a spy. And she said he was most likely a Communist. She tried to make me understand that our backgrounds were out of sync, that while I was making my confirmation in the Catholic Church at age fourteen he was taking a pledge to the socialist state at that age. How could the differences be wider than that? As far as Josephine was concerned our backgrounds were like Anne Frank to Lady Gaga. What she failed to notice was that I remained poker-faced throughout her monologue.

My date with Dirk had to be better than any I'd had till now. The chemistry between Dirk and I was palpable. No more potential, this was going to be genuine.

Chapter 2

NOT far from where you turn off the Houghton Highway at Clontarf, about twenty-four kilometers north of Brisbane, if you follow the bay on the right, you come to Woody Point. A search of Wikipedia comes up with information that Woody Point is a residential suburb of the Moreton Bay Region.

Woody Point is where families have picnics and people retire into oblivion. It's where you can look over the water and see the lights of Brisbane and be thankful that not only are you still sane but you also live in paradise. It's also where relationships start and end. It's where I pulled into the car park for my first date with Dirk. Wikipedia doesn't say any of that though.

I caught sight of him, waiting on a bench, fidgeting with his car keys. When he noticed me approaching he stood up, took a few steps toward me and only had time to call 'hallo' before he tripped, stumbled and regained his posture as if nothing had happened, all within the same split second. I rubbed the back of my neck, shaded my eyes with my hand and looked across the water. But when he stood beside me I felt jolts of excitement gather together in my stomach. It was as if I'd never noticed him look so embarrassed.

Without a word we absentmindedly led each other along the path beside the beach's edge and moved onto the jetty. When I was a kid I used to worry that I'd fall between the spaces in the board-walk if I looked down. With trepidation lingering in the back of my mind and taking a tentative peek at the water splashing underneath, I hobbled along beside Dirk while yanking out the heels of my shoes which kept getting caught between the boards.

A few people had begun to set up lanterns near their little bundles of fishing gear, rods leaned against posts, and a hand-held line reflected golden light. Dirk and I tiptoed through bait and fishing lines to a vacant corner at the far end of the jetty, weighted our arms onto the railings and silently admired the pink-gold tinge of the sunset reflected on the water, only a yard from where we stood.

'Do they catch somethink here?' Dirk asked.

'I think so, it smells like they do.'

His laughter was a muffled chuckle, his eyes communicated humor.

'Look, see this metal trolley.' I pointed. 'It's for scaling fish.'

'Ya,' he confirmed tracing the point of welding. 'This is as I make in my job.'

Josephine was right, it was definitely the travesty of the English language that attracted me to Dirk. My auditory receptors swooned at every German-accented syllable that flowed out of his beautiful mouth. I felt as if I was floating with my feet off the ground. No more rickety heels, I could fly back along the jetty.

Sliding his finger across the join in the metal, neck stretched and head back, lips set together to become a mere line, Dirk's look of pride reminded me of the

Roadrunner after he outsmarted Coyote. As he went ahead and recounted fifteen years of welding throughout the world, I was lost gazing at the gold tinge on his arms. The setting sun directly behind him was romancing a moment I wanted to snap on my Samsung. Little did it mean to me whether he had welded in Thailand or Timbuktu, his words were simply background music beating to the rhythm of my heart. Or were my sinuses throbbing? The smell of putrefied fish distracted me and instead of clicking a picture I pinched my nose and raised my eyebrows. We went back along the jetty with Dirk holding me up as I pulled my shoes off. That was another trait I noticed in him: courtesy.

We walked along the footpath as far as the empty boat ramp and stepped down onto the beach.

'And what for you? You must be the same age like me?' Dirk asked.

Josephine's words sounded in my ears like the horn of the cruise ship she was last on. My heart sank into the sand with my feet as I wished I hadn't confirmed his age. Goosebumps spread down my arms. I expected that at any moment Josephine's big green eyes would appear from around the side of Dirk's arm and her finger would wiggle in disgust as she called me a meretricious cougar for what I was about to do.

I knew if I subtracted the years to make our ages the same I could have pulled it off and I would have been tempted to do that but I'd never been a successful liar. It was one of those moments when you decide to go with your limitations. I crossed my fingers behind my back and hoped I wouldn't get found out.

I figured that if Dirk couldn't guess I was older just by the worried look that I'd developed over the years why should I disappoint him? And he was still one of those strangers not yet morphed into a potential. He hadn't yet earned the right to have this woman reveal her age. I came up with all kinds of reasons why it would be best to remain hushed on the subject. And I was comfortable with them all. But rather than lie I decided to act my way out of it.

My feet had sunk until the sand was around my ankles. I balanced on Dirk's arm and I think he blushed. His eyes appeared darker than the light blue they really were but I saw him lower them at my touch. I noticed the light sheen on his black hair and a few grays glistening. I felt as if I'd been caught in a time capsule. There seemed to be a feeling of tightness around me and it was difficult to break my gaze. Our eyes met for a moment as they do in love stories. But instead of something wonderful Dirk sighed and asked, 'Is this one the insect that stings?'

Blinking myself conscious I noticed he was talking about the mosquitoes that were buzzing around our heads, so I headed back onto the path pulling him behind me and found the bench where he'd been waiting when I arrived. As I brushed the sand off my feet I tried to think of the best way to get around his question about my age. He sat beside me and watched with a look of intrigue as I eased my feet into my shoes, my gloss red toenails poking through at the top. It was the intimacy of that moment that confirmed what I already knew. I definitely wasn't going to risk losing him with a mere number.

It was also at that moment that I saw the resemblance Dirk had to my father and I got a kind of weird feeling. I think it was the prominent chin, the dark hair. No question about the hands, they were strong. I wondered why I would be attracted to someone who reminded me of my father and I knew there was an answer that eluded me. It would be lying somewhere in Julia's *Introduction to Psychology* text books. I decided not to look them up. It was time I practiced restraint in analyzing every situation in which I found myself. I would let nature takes its course.

Like beer in front of a German the question about my age disappeared quickly when I suggested it was time for a drink. Dirk agreed with a nod of his head, a nod that wasn't sent in any direction but one that stayed with him. It was a nod I came to be very familiar with. It was a nod that was proud, definite, obliging. More of a pledge than a nod. On that pledge we crossed the road.

The Belvedere Hotel (referred to as The Bel by locals) sits almost opposite the jetty at Woody Point. We found a bar table in the middle of the room and I slid onto a stool beside Dirk. In a corner to our right there was a singer groaning his impersonation of a Bob Dylan song from the sixties.

I was comprehending parts of Dirk's speech but it was more a meeting of minds, something akin to intuition that kept us attuned. I smiled and focused on his lips, a bit of lip-reading never goes astray in a crowded room. But that didn't work. The pronunciation was German even though the words were presumably English. So I did what anyone would do when you don't understand a word being said to you. I faked it. That didn't work either. It was like trying to fake Michael Jackson's Moonwalk, it was complicated and at least once I put my foot in my mouth.

'Everyone . . . before that,' he finished.

I nodded, not certain what he said. 'A cat?' I asked.

It was a serendipitous moment. His face lit up and softened. 'Nor, nor', he said. He touched his fingertips to his forehead but the ends of his mouth were turned up in a smile.

'Not cat, I say we were close before that. Now I tell you about Germany,' he continued. 'I was born behind the Wall. You know the Wall?'

'The Berlin Wall?'

'Ya.' He breathed out heavily on the sound of the word and his hands hugged the beer glass as if to celebrate the moment of being understood.

I let out a sigh of relief. It felt as if space helmets had been removed and we were now talking instead of beaming thoughts to each other. We didn't have to be afraid of floating off into space anymore. He could relax his grip on the beer glass. We were no longer in micro gravity. Floating across the board-walk was a thing of the past.

'When the Wall came down everyone went their own way,' he said.

'The Wall destroyed families when it went up. And it also destroyed them went it was taken down?'

I had to admit to myself that I didn't know much about the divide between East and West Germany prior to the nineties. I was surprised.

He nodded. A pledge to his word.

'We leave after that. Everyone travel because before, we cannot. First Europe then other places. Always work. Then we are coming to Australia for holiday. We are still in the ship and I think (the pledge nod when he said this) this is the place I want to come, to live here.'

'You decided so quickly?'

'Ya,' he insisted. 'Why not?'

I was hoping it was a rhetorical question. 'And your wife?'

'She agrees. I come first.'

'That's brave.'

He raised his eyebrows and lowered his head.

He was no longer looking at me or Bob Dylan. He was studying the beer as if he might see something in there that would help him get through whatever he was about to confide to me. I examined the beer momentarily as well. There was nothing in there that helped me come to any conclusions but then I'd never been a big beer drinker. I returned my gaze to focus on his face. That was easier to read. There was sadness there, loneliness too. He told me openly that he wasn't accustomed to talking about himself or his feelings. And I intuited that he'd made a silent pledge to trust me.

'And your wife arrived a few weeks after you?'

'Nor, she does not arrive.'

'Do you mean she left you here? In a strange country? Alone?'

He nodded at every question. This was a pledge to truth, he wasn't lying. He glanced in the direction of Dylan who was still moaning his song about times changing. I imagined from what Dirk was telling me how the conversation between he and his wife would have gone when he phoned her in Germany.

What are you doing? In German with a touch of anxiety of course.

I do not want to live in Australia. Also in German. Fast, angry, breathless German.

We can talk about this. He tried to stay calm but inside he was grief-stricken. He felt as if he was dying.

We have nothing to talk about. I am not going to live in Australia.

We had an agreement. You cannot leave me. By this time he was panicked and when she hung up he was crushed. He never heard from her again.

I will never forget the look of desolation on Dirk's face, the abandonment written there in lines painted with grief and how empathy swelled within my chest and a compelling need to pledge my loyalty arose and spattered from my lips all over him like blood and how Dylan's song playing in the background seemed to escalate with every passing moment until it climaxed and became a part of our conversation. 'Things change Dirk. But whatever happens I will be your friend,' I promised in a rush of emotion. 'I will be here for you as long as you need me to be.'

My heart was bleeding. Sadness is a deep emotion and while I'm convinced that the notion of love at first sight is ridiculous, I'd fallen on second sight without so much as being aware. Metamorphosis had taken place. Dirk had moved right through from stranger to potential to definite.

Some of the relationship books I read during counseling after my divorce defined falling in love as an attraction to the image of the childhood caregiver, that at a subconscious level we want to heal our childhood wounds. When my daughter Julia was thirteen she reckoned falling in love was all about your star sign. *Pisces are softies,* she told me with utmost conviction. *Vulnerable to love and emotion,* she annotated. I'd thought about that notion of being vulnerable because of the star sign under which I'd been born and chewed it over for a while but didn't find it relevant for me. I wasn't thirteen.

My friend Josephine liked to say that falling in love is equivalent to the saying, you're only as old as the man you feel, that falling in love is only as big as what you feel. Personally I always thought that falling in love was about being a sucker. Maybe that's the basis of Julia's assessment and what she was really trying to say. *We Pisces are suckers. Period.*

Dirk looked at me with the roundest eyes I'd ever seen. 'You are a wonderful woman.' He took my hands into his. If I got to hold those hands forever I'd be willing to learn to lip-read. 'Coom oon.' He gave me a gentle nudge. 'This music is too much.'

I followed him outside, all the while thinking about vulnerability and falling in love. It was a bit like the sound of the German letter *O*. It was entirely irresistible.

'We can do this again?'

I blinked back to the moment. 'Yes.' I glowed.

And now I had a reason to fall in love. Dirk needed me. Desperately. And that only added to my feelings of guilt about my deceit. If I believed in Karma I might have gone home that night aware that a lie told will be a lie returned. But I didn't. I went home feeling like a teenager who'd fallen in love with Harry after a One Direction concert.

Chapter 3

SUPPOSEDLY one sign that shows the man you're dating likes you is if he introduces you to his friends. I'd read that in several of my relationship books. It's a generally lived-by rule of thumb for a lot of single women.

'Not if his friends are Nazis,' Josephine mused.

We were talking in her lounge room. I'd been through an intricacy of objections from Josephine about Dirk since Josephine's return from Europe, all of them citing how different European men are to Australian men and how sexist and controlling some of them can be. None of her arguments made sense except according to the rules and theories by which she lived.

'It's true that it is a sign that he might be serious if he introduces you to his friends, but Maria,' she objected, 'the German didn't introduce you. He introduced them.'

While that was partly true it sounded more like a point of law to me than a way to know if a man was interested. I regretted telling Josephine anything about meeting Dirk's friends. I was absolutely keeping quiet about the drinking issue.

I hadn't mentioned anything to Dirk about his drinking either although it had worried me all night at the party with his friends and later when I was meant to be sleeping. It wasn't something I easily knew how to address. When we arrived back at his house he hugged me into the bedroom, leaned his body toward mine and eased me back onto the bed. While the drinking was something that was burning in my mind, at the time other things were more pressing. An hour later and we were asleep.

Three hours later Dirk was up with a can of beer in his hand and I went back to worrying. I felt reluctant to say anything because I may have been wrong. Maybe what I was seeing was normal as he told me. (I am German. Germans like the beer). So I stayed silent.

'So he drove to that party without saying where you were going?' Josephine was now cross-examining me.

'Kind of,' I replied not wanting to disclose the immense embarrassment I'd felt when I entered the home of a married couple to see a group of people set up on the back balcony having dinner, all eyes on me.

'Where on earth did you think you were driving to on a Saturday night?'

'I thought we were going for a meal at the local Asian restaurant. As it turned out it was an Australia Day party with his European friends.'

Josephine rolled her eyes. 'An Australia Day party with no Australians? You have to be kidding me Maria.'

'I was there, not that anyone knew I was Australian. They kind of went on and on about how unbelievable it was that no one was Australian.' I sighed. 'I didn't want to disappoint them.'

'And you had no idea you were going to meet his friends?'

I was wringing my hands in my lap by now. I felt as if I was on a stand in front of a jury. If I told Josephine that he'd stopped to buy a cask of wine and some beer and that

I thought it was for the two of us when we got home, she'd increase my prison sentence.

'What were these friends like? These Nazi people that you met?'

'They weren't Nazi Josie, they were German and there were Austrians and a few Russians.'

'And they spoke English of course.' She plonked her mug onto the coffee table in front of her with certitude that they didn't.

'A few of them did,' I replied sheepishly.

'And they knew that you were going to be there?'

I nodded slowly biting my bottom lip.

Josephine flew from the couch as if there had been a bomb alert in the courtroom. 'I can't believe you Maria, you're being so gullible. He was getting them to inspect you, not the other way around.' She made her way towards the kitchen. Her words were like little hand grenades being tossed over her shoulder. 'That's not a sign he likes you, that's a sign he likes them. You're just some kind of possession.'

My friendship with Josephine seemed to be spiraling into some kind of sparring match. It was going downhill fast and I felt helpless to save it. She was my best friend. She was meant to be accepting and nurturing toward me, not tearing at me with the realities of life like a magistrate in a court of law. I was beginning to feel swamped by her rules and judgments. They resembled the same type of thing I was facing at home with Julia who had taken to measuring me under her mature-woman microscope and what she'd read on the internet about dating-after-fifty.

I felt as if everything was turning sour around me, that, no matter what I did, I wasn't living up to anyone's expectations. Was I meant to be turning into someone like Barbara Walters regardless of the fact that she was almost thirty years my senior? And the type of woman I could never even aspire to imitate. I was thinking that when I got old I'd be more the Betty White type: funny, cute and sexy with the exception being that I'd have no money in the bank. The trouble was that most people were already thinking of me as old and I hadn't yet reached sixty. My Helen Mirren era was on the horizon for sure, but she was still more than ten years in front of me. Why did age matter so suddenly?

Josephine, her small thin body wrapped in a yellow dress and black tights, returned from the kitchen with hot coffee for both of us. She placed the mugs onto the coffee table.

'Would you like cake?'

'No,' I answered with a smile. 'I'll keep the figure I've got thanks.'

'You're doing well,' Josephine said as she disappeared into the large folds of the couch tucking her legs under her and pulling a cushion across her lap. Just to ensure she was barely visible, I thought.

I remembered watching the Oprah show when Oprah turned fifty. She joked about how everyone said *you look great,* and then added, *for fifty.* The *for fifty-five* phrase was now spinning in my head and I couldn't help but add it to Josephine's summation. *You're doing well. For fifty-five.*

'What color are you using on your hair these days?' Josephine asked, bringing my thoughts back. 'It looks different.'

'What kind of different?' I blew across the top of my coffee. I wasn't sure if this was an addendum to the *for fifty-five* annotation. It looks great *but different*. Maybe I was becoming paranoid. 'I'm still using dark blonde,' I told her.

Josephine leaned forward to pick up her mug. 'I was thinking it matches your fair skin. It definitely makes you look younger.'

'Why do I have to look younger? What's wrong with looking my age?'

Josephine raised her eyebrows. 'Forget your hair. Where's this thing with the German going?' Court was back in session.

'I don't know where it's going, I love Dirk and we get on well, I want it to last.'

'You still think you have a chance to make it last with him?' Josephine appeared smug. 'Even after he made a fool of you in front of his friends?'

'He didn't make a fool of me.'

'You weren't embarrassed that he hadn't let you know you were going to meet them?'

'Not really,' I fibbed.

'He's obviously a control freak, I can't believe you don't see that. Imagine if an Aussie guy did that. Took you to a party without saying, firstly,' she counted one finger, 'where you were going and most importantly,' she counted three more fingers, 'that you were going to meet his friends for the first time. You'd be livid, you'd say he was a yobbo. The German does it and it's okay?'

'You've become so caustic Josie, what's wrong with you? We used to be able to talk, I could confide in you and know you'd support me, now it's like talking to my ex-husband. Nothing I say or do is right.'

'I don't think I've changed Maria, I think you're being blinded by a man who may want something more from you than a bit of free loving.'

'And what is that supposed to mean?'

'Has he ever asked you for money?' Josephine's demeanor had changed. Instead of the little magistrate hiding behind the bench of cushions, she sat up and emerged as if she was a Supreme-Court judge.

I straightened in my chair. 'Of course not, whatever would make you say that?

'We've both seen these things happen, we work in criminal law Maria. Please don't tell me that you haven't thought of it?'

'Josie that's insulting and it's lame.' I tried to think of words but I was lost for them. 'To think that of Dirk is . . .' I stopped. 'You don't even know him and you come up with all this nonsense.'

'If he asked you for money you'd tell me though Maria. Right?'

'He's not going to ask me for money. Josie you haven't thought about the type of men you date?'

'Of course I have. I met a guy online the other night,' she chortled, returning to her usual flippancy. 'He came over and we had sex. It was a O.N.S. The men I meet only want that.'

'A what?'

'I'm a one-night-stand girl Maria. That's how it works for me. And anyway he wasn't German, he was a true blue, a dinky-di Aussie.'

My blood went to boiling point in record time. I returned the coffee mug to the kitchen, came back into the lounge room where Josephine had once again retreated into the cushions. I collected my bag from the armchair.

'Josie you shock me at times.' I pulled my phone out of my bag. 'I've got to go. Julia expects me to look at apartments with her this afternoon. I'll see you at work on Monday.'

The friendship began to slip from there on. It was a gradual decline until we became simply work colleagues.

When I got home Julia was in tears in front of the lounge room mirror.

'What is it, darling?' I took hold of her shoulders and turned her to face me. 'Are you okay?'

I'm fine,' she retorted. 'Don't baby me.'

I didn't think I was. I sat on the edge of the coffee table and tried to be as un-motherly as I could be.

Her beautiful blue eyes looked at me through pools of tears. Her hair which fell loosely around her face was all fluffed up, fresh and clean from what looked like a recent shampoo. It was no longer blonde, it was now a mousey shade of brown.

'They ruined it,' she whimpered. 'Look.' She whisked a piece of hair from the side of her head onto her face. It wasn't more than a few strands but it was green. I wasn't sure if it was the color that was wrong or the length.

'What were they meant to do?' I inquired safely.

'They were meant to highlight it, not make it green.' She rolled her eyes in a similar way to how Josephine did, only she was more animated and her eyes widened so that the look she gave me spoke so loudly I thought I'd go deaf. She turned around to look in the mirror.

'But it's such a little bit,' I offered meekly. 'I think your hair is beautiful.'

'You would say that, you're my mother.'

'I'm not saying that because I'm your mother,' I argued. 'I'd say that if I were your aunt or even if I was . . .' My mind rummaged for support. 'Bella Swan.'

My daughter swung around from the mirror. 'You wouldn't know who Bella Swan is.' She bolted toward the front door.

I got up from the side of the coffee table.

'That's unfair Julia,' I called after her. 'We saw *Twilight Breaking Dawn* together. All those vampires and . . .' But she was gone before I could rub the dent from the edge of the table out of my buttocks.

I wondered, given what Josephine had been saying to me, just what were mothers and daughters and friends meant to say to each other? Weren't we there to support each other, share hankies and compact powder to dab on our noses when the going got tough? I didn't know anymore. I was beginning to wonder if I'd taken up my roles properly. Maybe I was transforming into a vampire like poor Bella. It seemed that no one loved me or understood me anymore. And no one accepted my love. That thought made me feel empty and sad.

Things at work weren't any better. Josephine and I were descending into a werewolf era. I had been enjoying having Josephine back in the office after her European trip before our friendship began to disintegrate. She was normally a light in my world, someone I could relate to and debrief with over a Subway lunch. Now everything was falling apart.

I was the team's legal support assistant. Part of my job was to be a smoke screen for clients but the increasingly simmering workplace atmosphere was almost providing its own smoke. Josephine worked in the team adjacent to mine. Both of us were in sections that handled criminal law matters.

Chloe-rose was one of two junior lawyers in my team. With her up-turned nose and large round eyes that looked out through a forest of thick eyelashes that held much more than a trace of mascara, Chloe-rose was one of those people you got to work with only once in your life. If you were that unlucky. At twenty-five she was a qualified lawyer and basked in the esteem that came with it. Our team's other junior lawyer was David. He kept to himself pretty much and he was easy to work with.

I wasn't as happy with my new supervisor's attitude toward me. Ursula was a good lawyer but a bad manager. And I couldn't shake the idea that she was somehow plotting against me. I'd pushed the feelings aside mostly and got on with doing my work. In her late thirties, I thought Ursula should have at least some professionalism in the way in which she dealt with staff. Sadly it turned out she didn't.

'Did you ever see the movie Matilda?' Josephine asked me one morning not long after I was transferred into the team.

I swung around in my chair. 'Wasn't that the movie with the wicked teacher?'

Josephine pointed her tiny index finger at me. 'When my sister visited with my niece and nephew I watched that movie a thousand times,' she told me. 'I'll be watching you,' she mimicked, her eyes narrowed, her finger jabbing the air in my direction.

I imitated with her. 'I'll be watching you.'

We laughed and pointed at each other. Josephine animated her eyebrows and sent a backwards nod in Ursula's direction.

It didn't take me long to realize that Ursula was far worse than I first thought.

Chloe-rose and Ursula made a formidable team. I should have been more wary. They liked to dismiss me easily, criticized my responses in work matters and in small talk, made unusual remarks about the clothes I wore, tossed off my social opinions, and told me that I was too sensitive. Anyone would have thought that we were competing in the Miss Australia quest and I was from Mars. I just didn't fit in. Maybe they saw the Pisces in me. Maybe they recognized that I was a sucker. Whatever it was, they didn't seem to like me. I felt intimidated by their behavior and found myself trying to placate them on a daily basis. The only relief I got was on Thursday afternoons when Ursula clocked off at one thirty.

No one ever knew why she went early that day every week. It was just an accepted fact. But it made me happy. And if Chloe-rose happened to be in court or a meeting while Ursula was gone, I actually got to relax.

The first time I became suspicious that Ursula was working against me was the day she called me into a conference room to plan a series of meetings that would take place over the following month.

'Maria,' she said from across the table. She pointed to a chair opposite her.

I sat down and folded my hands in my lap.

'I want to do an analysis of your role.'

I nodded. This seemed fair to me and when she assured me that it had no bearing at all on my work performance measures, I was more than happy to assist in any way I could.

'I'm going to monitor the work-load for a time.'

'Sure,' I answered.

'I will expect you to keep a record of all of your tasks and do up a weekly report.'

'Okay.'

'So we will set our meetings up for every Monday at eight-thirty and we will meet in this conference room. I will go over everything you've recorded for the previous week. You will need to name the task, date and time as well as the amount of time each individual task took you to complete. Your report should have all of this as well as a written summary of exactly what was entailed in the job and how you went about completing it.'

I went back to my desk, armed with sheets of paper covered with rows and columns where I was to write in details of every piece of work I completed.

By the third meeting I was pretty much over keeping the exacting record of my work and asked if we had gathered enough information.

'I can see that the role is too demanding for you,' Ursula answered. 'We will have to see what we can do about it.'

'Ursula, the only thing that is demanding is the ongoing record-keeping of tasks that you're getting me to do. The work isn't a problem.'

'Maria,' she said as she straightened in her chair. 'I will be relieving you of some of the work. I've noticed you are falling behind on some deadlines. I'm not sure if you're up to the demands.'

My mouth fell open and stayed in that position for a moment.

'Yesterday I had three files to be delivered to the court registry,' I said. 'I had to gather signatures, make phone calls to barristers to organize collection of documents and then photocopy and collate them. When I completed that, it took me most of the afternoon to write down every little job involved in doing it. Ursula, can't you see that getting me to do this is soaking up valuable time?'

Ursula stood up. She looked at me with a scowl. 'Some people just can't cope.' She gathered some papers together and slipped them into a file. 'I don't like your methodology, I think there are better ways of doing things.'

I felt like a porcupine on a buffalo's back. I was completely out of place, everything was prickly and, unlike Ursula, I couldn't nitpick.

'Try it for another week Maria,' she said as she picked the file up from the table. She walked toward the door with it tucked under her arm. 'And where on earth did you get that skirt? It doesn't suit you.'

She walked down the corridor. 'I'm off to court,' she called for everyone to hear. 'See you all later.'

That's the day my work began to whittle away in front of my eyes. Trying Ursula's insane record-keeping for another week didn't make any difference. At first it was Josephine coming to my desk asking if I had anything she could do. I gladly handed her files thinking that her team might be in a slump. But when I overheard Ursula having whispered telephone conversations in her office and my name being referred to, I began to suspect more.

That's when things took an unpleasant turn. When I walked into our booked conference room one morning when Ursula was late for our meeting, I found her diary open and my name written in it in red ink. *Maria was three minutes late. Maria was away sick. Maria couldn't finish the transcribing in time. Maria's not up to the job.* There were notes with no date references scrawled across the two open pages. And they were all about me.

In every area of my life, whatever I tried didn't seem to have any effect on the relationships I valued. I felt as if I was being forced into becoming the woman everyone wanted me to be: old, unreliable and frumpy. At work I greeted the lawyers every morning and offered to come in early or stay late when there were urgent matters. I was friendly and helpful towards colleagues. On a personal level I checked for new wrinkles and stray hairs, made sure my eyebrows were waxed and colored, kept up my gym routine as much as I could but as far as my workplace, friends and family were concerned I wasn't good enough. So for the next few months I tried to take a low-key approach both at work and at home.

I'd pretty much covered my worries in depth with Dirk in our time together and I felt he understood. That gave me a sense of belonging and a feeling of calm. He was protective in his response, urging me to concentrate on doing any work that was given to me and not to worry about what others thought. I felt he was becoming a defender of my truth and I came to the conclusion that Dirk was my only true friend and companion and the only one who loved me.

Chapter 4

IT was becoming apparent that I was reading the wrong relationship books. None of them addressed how to manage a friend who was a nymphomaniac and hated Germans, a daughter who thought the correct route for a mature-age woman was over-fifties accommodation followed by a nursing home all before you turned sixty, or a manager who didn't like you. Even though Dr. Phil was smiling at me on the front cover of his *Love Smart* book I felt alone in a huge ocean of self-pity and last year's *Better Homes and Gardens* magazines. I was beginning to understand that if I wanted to feel loved and have awesome self-confidence I had to get out there and do something. But what was I meant to do?

My relationship with Dirk answered that question. I began to spend several nights a week over at his place, if for no other reason than to pretend that I was still a normal woman and not someone with the sexual desires of a biro lid. He was becoming more and more important to me. And there was no pretending when it came to our chemistry. He made excitement run through my veins like dye in a coronary angiography. The only blockages were Josephine and Julia and of course the bad vibes at work.

The first time I visited Dirk's home in Wavell Heights, I was struck by its cleanliness and austerity, the bare walls, floors without rugs, dark brown sofas bordering the lounge room. The only decoration in the entire house was on his nightstand, a black and white picture of his parents in a frame. *The photo was taken a few weeks after the Wall was built*, he told me the first time I examined it. He proceeded to explain the story of his parents, of the night they were woken by loud voices, of how they hid behind closed curtains peering around the edges as fence posts were hammered into the ground outside their window and of his life growing up under Communist rule. They were times so far removed that the very idea of that being his life history seemed so remote as to be incomprehensible to me. It didn't seem to be part of the Dirk I knew and loved. It gave me a sense of foreboding.

Had I been attentive, I would have listened to my inner voice and realized that it was calling me to look elsewhere. But I didn't. I had enough doom and gloom in my life which was being transmitted via body language and formally written emails from my colleague Josephine, bouts of bullying from Ursula and through clashes with Julia.

Dirk usually worked on Saturday mornings so I was spending Friday nights at home. I made a promise to myself that I would spend time with Julia as long as she was around.

That meant tiptoeing around and fitting in with her plans and moving-out dramas. Julia and Jamie had inspected and rejected so many rental properties that I began to wonder if they might have been having second thoughts about moving. It was either that or they were becoming clandestine real estate professionals. That they hadn't made any formal arrangements to move gave me some hope that Julia might get further into her psychology studies and postpone moving or at least announce that she'd made a fortune buying and selling real estate. Jamie was a few years older than my daughter and was beginning to show the hallmarks of a young man with intelligence and a sound ability to make plans. But he still wasn't earning an income. It didn't matter how well he was doing in his studies, in my book until he finished his IT degree he was still a geek with a hopeful future but a poor present.

When will you arrive? Dirk's message pinged my phone late Friday night.

I will be there in the afternoon.

Come over early I am not working tomorrow.

I'm not sure.

It's your decision. I accept whatever you do.

And what I did was to forget my plans to be with Julia. I got ready early the next morning to drive to Dirk's place.

'But I thought your message last week meant that you were going to be with me this morning at an inspection,' Julia yawned as she stumbled from her bedroom at eight o'clock looking as if she wasn't awake.

'It did,' I replied. 'But as you didn't respond I got the idea that you were going with Jamie. I'm happy to change my plans.'

'No,' she huffed. 'Forget it, it was probably a bad idea anyway, you wouldn't have liked it.'

'I don't have to like it sweetheart,' I soothed with a smile. 'The rental is not for me.'

She looked at me as if she was about to take me by the arm and help me to the bathroom.

'I was going to take you to inspect a retirement village.'

'A what?' The inside of my mouth became dry at that point. If I had wanted to cry I don't think my body would have produced any moisture. All of my bodily fluids had gone straight to my heart to assist it to keep pumping. It pumped so fast that I thought it might escape my chest. Instead I felt my arms become rigid and my hands clench into little fists. A voice boomed in the distance somewhere and it took a moment for me to realize that it was mine. I'd thrown it so far that it had hit the dividing fence beyond the open sliding door and was coming right back at me. The neighbors were probably onto the police right now to report me. Julia was cowering on the couch. Either that or she'd settled there to sulk.

'You don't have to swear,' she blurted. 'It's not the end of the world, we all have to get old.'

My words squeezed through my clenched teeth like putty through a scraper. 'I am not old.' I took a deep breath, counted to ten as I exhaled, decided the best way to continue was to defuse the situation and deal with the issue later. 'I am happy to accompany you to other inspections,' I announced formally. 'Shall we go?'

'Don't worry. I'll be fine on my own.'

'Good.'

I left the room.

'I can't rely on you for anything,' I heard her say.

She made me feel as if I'd left her standing alone at the doors to a one-day bargain-basement sale. No amount of my backtracking was going to get her to stand back. She would buy without me and she knew I didn't care. I was the worst mother in the world because I never kept my promises. Even ones I hadn't actually made. And apparently I was the oldest mother in the world too. I rushed out the door in my own huff, stomping on the feelings of guilt as if they were the toes of nasty shoppers at the sale.

Outside, the air was saturated with foreboding. The little whirlwinds of a pending storm rushed around my ankles and blew leaves into the air. It was one of those storms which come from the south west and it would bring the kind of rain that keeps on falling until you think that there will be no end to it even though you're intelligent enough to know that's not true. It matched my mood: dark, doleful and ready to burst.

When had life become so unpredictable? I felt that I'd failed in every area. Maybe it was because I wasn't good at reading crystal balls. If I could just get a grasp on what might lie ahead I could be ready and waiting. But life didn't work like that for me. The University of Life handed out degrees or diplomas to most people but not me. For me it had only work emails and SMS messages from my daughter.

I flew by intuition and it was becoming obvious that I might have been flying in the wrong direction for most of my life.

When I arrived at Dirk's place I was surprised to see him waiting for me under an umbrella at the back gate of the two-frontage block. As I went to get out of the car he put his hand up, signaling for me to stay put. I opened my car window a finger width and called to him through the rain.

'What is it?'

'Wait there, wait there,' he called. (The nod.)

He ran the fifteen yards to where his Toyota Hatchback was parked beside the back door. He closed the umbrella, gestured to me again with the wave of a hand and a nod meaning for me to stay where I was. (I could tell that this was a pledge nod). He jumped into his car and started the engine.

I opened my window a little further and blinking back rain called to him hopelessly. 'What are you doing?'

Without answering he turned his car around in the yard and drove to where I was parked coming to a stop close to my driver's door.

He pushed his passenger door open. 'Coom oon Aussie Girl, get in.'

'What about my bag?'

'We get that later, because.' He jabbed the air a couple of times with his finger pointing to the rain. 'Coom oon.'

I squirmed from my car to his, slammed both car doors shut and pushed wet hair from my face as he drove to the back door of his house. That's when my laughter broke forth and I felt my entire body relax. Dirk's usually restrained chuckle was actually audible and I found myself giggling at the sound of it. That's another thing that attracted me to Dirk, his ability to intrigue and delight me. He treated me as if I was Princess Kate and he was William even though it probably wouldn't be too long before Camilla and Charles would be a better description of each of us. We hurried out of the car with Dirk holding the umbrella above me until I'd jumped over a puddle and landed inside, through the open back-door.

The smell of sausage and sizzling bacon greeted my stomach juices with gusto as I stepped into the kitchen. There was enough food in the frying pan to feed the entire German army and for a moment I wondered if the European friends might be joining us for breakfast. If so there would be no Australians present, I chuckled inwardly. The toaster spewed its contents into the air and I made a dive to catch it before it hit the floor. Dirk went straight to the fridge, took out sausage pieces and laid them on the back door step for a stray cat which hung around his house. He washed his hands at the sink and switched the stove off.

After placing all the food on our plates he carried our breakfast to the front balcony. I followed him with mugs of coffee and the cat followed me. We all ended up together at Dirk's little balcony table beside the railing on which Dirk had tied an Australian flag, a sign of his commitment to his new country.

'You do know that only Bogans put flags on their balcony railings don't you?' I commented as I placed the mugs on the table.

Dirk's eyes were shaded by dark bushy eyebrows which became furrowed as he peered into my face, evidence that he was troubled by my words. It's a look I came to know well, a look that suggested fear, uncertainty, a willingness to undo something he'd done if that was necessary, if what he had done had gone against the order of how things should be.

'What is this? Bogan?'

'Bogans are people who put flags on their balcony railings.' I resisted the urge to giggle.

He examined my face for clues as to the authenticity and seriousness of my claim. I recalled a joke he'd told me about a man who walked over to a group of people and introduced himself by saying *you must be German* and when they asked him how he knew he taunted *because none of you are smiling.*

'A Bogan is someone who is socially clueless,' I teased. 'Someone who doesn't know what is the fashionable thing to do.'

He got that I was kidding around, the brows straightened, the blue eyes twinkled and he did smile. Inspiration, that feeling of wanting to love him, rose up in me.

He stood behind me, pressed and rolled his fingertips into my shoulders. 'Stay till Monday Aussie Girl?' he whispered before going back to the kitchen.

'Good plan, I will,' I agreed.

When he returned a couple of minutes later he put a hot croissant in front of me. And for the stray cat he dropped sausage pieces onto the balcony step. She sniffed the food but a ripple of rejection ran down her glossy black coat. She rubbed her slender body against Dirk's legs.

'She is here only because she loves you, mein Deutscher Mann,' I said.

Dirk acknowledged my German comment with a haphazard kind of nod and when the cat jumped up onto the vacant chair beside the one he'd slid into, he stroked her head and smiled at me.

'What's your plan for the next weekend? Come you to my place?'

Dirk had never been to my house. Whenever I mentioned it, he had a reason why he couldn't come over. First, he had to work on Saturdays so it made more sense to be at his house Friday nights. Second came his laundry on Saturday afternoons. If I asked him to drive over after he finished washing the clothes he usually quipped that he wanted to ride his bike. It exasperated me and I usually ended up letting the idea drop.

I decided to give it another go. 'We could go to my place next weekend.'

'There is more room at my place,' he answered. 'And when you are home you have to do with your daughter.'

I took a sip of my coffee as he continued.

'If you can Maria, come to my place. I must speak to my parents on the Skype in the afternoon and also after work I will have one beer too much for the breath control police.'

I sat in stunned silence. He was right of course. It was far better to be at his house. It was quiet, it was private but most of all it allowed him to indulge in heavy drinking. I chewed on some bacon rind and didn't say anything further.

Dirk went straight to a new topic. 'What's with the girl?' he asked as he munched on a piece of toast.

I knew he was talking about Chloe-rose at work. I'd whined to him on the phone on Friday at morning tea break when I was debriefing with a coffee and a Panadol.

'It's the same,' I replied, allowing my thoughts to forget his previous comment about drinking. 'But I blame Ursula. She's been getting Chloe-rose to give her work to Josephine instead of me.'

Dirk's face became grave. 'Maria you must keep your job because. You must.' He often broke his sentence in that way. You must do something because. It was one of his idiosyncrasies that I loved.

'You cannot complaint about this one.'

'About Chloe-rose?'

'This one you can complaint,' he conceded. 'The manager you cannot because. You must keep your job. I know how to do this one, I am German, no one does the work like a German. I will always beat the work mate, you must beat the girl.'

It appeared that Dirk couldn't understand that it wasn't a matter of being better than Chloe-rose or for that matter being better than Josephine. He didn't seem to get it that no matter how much or how hard I worked, what mattered at my workplace was whom you knew and whether or not they liked you. Still, he cared and defended me and that did matter. The cat pounced to the floor and disappeared under the table. She rubbed against my leg as if to say *he's just a man, a German one at that*. But no, that was Josephine's voice that had crossed my mind. I gently pushed the cat away with my foot. I didn't need any reminders of the cattiness that had emerged between me and my best friend.

Josephine wasn't speaking to me now and she seemed to be accepting my work with eagerness. If she had to give me a file she left it on my desk while I was out to lunch and if she had a message for me she sent it via email. That Chloe-rose was now passing all her work onto Josephine made me feel that she had sensed the icy interactions between us. As a result I felt inferior and I tried to make up for it by running after the lawyers, doing all sorts of errands which would ultimately save them time in their work. At the same time I had resigned to accepting that no matter what I did, Ursula and Chloe-rose would never like me.

Dirk and I finished our breakfast in silence. As we scrapped the little that remained on our dishes into the plastic liner of his bin he spoke to me without eye contact.

'Is it okay for you, I want visit my friends.'

My mouth dropped open. 'Wait up. I thought I'm here so we can spend time together.'

'It will be only for one hour,' he replied. 'I must pick up my spare bicycle tire they fix for me, what do you think?'

'I suppose I can get some more sleep.'

'Goot.' He nodded. 'When I get back we will talk. Do not wash the dish, they are for me to do. But you must be sure you do not leave the light or power point switched on.'

I shrugged with an apologetic smile.

By the time I got my coffee mug from the balcony Dirk was in the Toyota gingerly maneuvering out of the driveway beside my Hyundai. I closed the door behind him, scampered to the kitchen window and watched him drive down the road. I did a double check on lights and power points and took my coffee with me into the bedroom. I placed the mug on the nightstand beside the picture of Dirk's parents and plumped up the pillows. Grabbing the picture, I flopped with it onto the bed to take another look and imagine what it must have been like living behind that bloody Berlin Wall. Before I knew it, I'd dozed into a restful sleep.

My peace was short lived. I was woken by my phone and when I answered Julia was on the other end.

'Where are you?'

'Julia, must you start every conversation with that question?' I bit my tongue immediately after saying it and added, 'I'm sorry darling but it's becoming a habit.'

'Jamie's broken down again'.

I pressed the base of my hand to my forehead and exhaled deeply, held in the swear words I desperately wanted to utter and allowed silence to fill the air momentarily.

'Did you hear me?'

'Towie, remember?' I had been unaware that my teeth were clenched.

'He can't this time. We're going to look at an apartment together and we have to be there by . . .'

'Stop right there Julia.' I held my hand out in front of me as if she was in the room. 'There will be other inspection times.' I returned my hand to my forehead. 'And Jamie has a mother who he actually lives with and probably a father for that matter. You, nor I, are responsible for helping him out of his breakdowns. He is the one who is so keen to find a rental and if you continue to be there for him at every turn and agree with everything he wants, pretty soon he's going to take you for granted.'

There was silence for what seemed like an hour but could only have been a few seconds. When Julia spoke it was like the breeze after the storm that I could feel floating through the kitchen window.

'I've never thought of that before, Mum. I didn't think about how much I've been running after him. If he says jump, I jump, you are so right.'

'Good. Right.' Even I was flabbergasted at my wisdom. 'Okay then.'

'There is one other thing'.

I felt my jaw clench. 'And what might that be?'

'Dominic came over to see you.'

I took a deep breath as a whirlwind of thoughts raced across my mind. I couldn't think why Dominic of all the men I'd casually dated over the past few years would be back in touch with me. I pushed the thoughts aside for the sake of clarity.

'Okay darling,' I answered. 'I will see you Monday.'

'Yep,' Julia replied. 'Thanks mum.' And for the first time in months I felt that she had relaxed. She sounded like the Julia she used to be.

I went to the kitchen and yanked the window closed with a thud. All I had to do now was to inject some of my home-grown wisdom into my own affairs. And I knew exactly where to start. I had to stop being the victim and become more assertive at work. And there was one person who could help me do that.

Chapter 5

CHLOE-ROSE stood at the photocopier looking as if the pale walls behind her had been designed as a backdrop. They paled farther into the background behind her tall slim silhouette.

With her silver Prada patent leather shoes, black pencil skirt and the purple figure-hugging, ruffled-at-the-front blouse vying for attention, I approached with the awkwardness of a teenage boy about to ask for his first date. The stark opposite of Ursula who wore the trademark black like most of the lawyers, Chloe-rose had a flair for color. Her freshness and clarity compared to Ursula was the difference between a brittle one-year-old bottle of correction fluid and a fresh Bic white-out tape.

So as not to seem out of place in my efforts to confide in her I began tidying the papers lying on the sorting table. There were three photocopiers and the other two were empty so I fed the letter I needed to copy and turned in Chloe-rose's direction.

I wasn't accustomed to socializing with the lawyers on this floor. They weren't as friendly as some I'd worked with on other floors over the years. Most were like aliens with big heads. A few didn't mind mingling with humans. They took part in a kind of camaraderie ritual in the mornings before starting work, exchanging recipes, pregnancy tips, anecdotes for childhood illnesses and what the best age was to commence potty training. And that was just the male lawyers. Of course none of this was of any use to the junior lawyers in their work but it served as a rite of passage for them, an entrance into the bizarre world of senior lawyers. For the administrative staff it served to level out the playing field. Of course unless I could get them to like me, none of my offerings would be taken as sacred. My chocolate-raspberry cookie recipe and the cookies themselves would continue to sit on the morning tea tray forever forsaken, rejected as unacceptable. But I had the distinct impression that it wasn't about the cookies. From the moment I arrived on the floor everyone had ignored me. My life at work had become hell.

As I was about to make small talk Chloe-rose tossed her strawberry locks so they fell about her shoulders like a large bouquet of roses. She left the room without noticing me.

No doubt she was heading to court. Her first stop would be the ladies' room where she would twist her hair into a tight but thick ball on top of her head and secure it with invisible clips. Next she would fill the small carry suitcase with the required files and documents, straighten her skirt, lift her suit jacket onto her small frame and slide into it effortlessly. Finally with the pirouette of a ballerina she would head out the door and make her way to the court precinct pulling the suitcase behind her. The clients loved her precise manners and impeccable timeliness even if it was true that a lot of them were prisoners in the holding cells below the courts. She may not have had the political correctness or social wisdom needed to work in a team environment but she knew how to argue a case.

Chloe-rose could work many cases without having to request extensions of time to file court documents or unnecessary adjournments. Chloe-rose with her shimmering new law degree and popularity with management and clients was just what Ursula needed to help her shine her way up the ladder. Ursula was unscrupulous. If she wanted something she wanted Chloe-rose to get it for her regardless of whom Chloe-rose had to intimidate, cajole or seduce to get it. And Ursula wanted to be Director of the section. Nothing and no one was going to stop her from doing that.

Being new in the team, transferred from the first floor six months earlier, I felt that I was going to be in the probationary period indefinitely unless Ursula began to accept me and recognize my input. There was an undercurrent running against me and it was beginning to affect my ability to work. Without Josephine to turn to I was desperate to bring back some kind of balance in my workplace so I could function. I longed to be accepted.

I can't remember how I got Chloe-rose to agree to have lunch with me but before I knew it she was back from court and we were sitting at a chunky table in the Japanese restaurant around the corner from our office building. There was a storm brewing outside. A lull was in the air, the stillness threatening to shatter at any moment. It contrasted with Chloe-rose's mood. She cheerily placed her Marc by Marc Jacobs bag on the table in front of her, completely ignoring the pending downpour and glanced at her smart phone.

'We have to get that appeal matter filed in court today. Maria, have you collated the copies?'

'I have,' I replied. 'I had it completed yesterday afternoon. I'll go to the registry and file this afternoon if you're finished with it.'

'That's excellent Maria, how perfect of you,' she condescended.

I smiled as I let my eyes travel across the plates of Chicken Teriyaki the waiter was placing in front of us. Food has a way of leveling us. Or is that death? Either way we were leveled by the smell of the food and Chloe-rose hit the ground first.

'What exactly did you want to see me about Maria?' She placed a napkin on her lap. 'I'm sure there must be something on your mind.' Her rosebud lips turned up at the corners in a smile.

'I thought you might be able to give me a few tips on how I can make things work better for you and especially for Ursula,' I confided as I readied my chopsticks.

'What do you mean by work better? It's working just fine isn't it?'

I wasn't getting my point across. I adjusted my chopsticks.

'Most of the work is being passed to Josephine in the other team.'

'Oh that.' She was poised in front of wobbly chopsticks holding a piece of limp chicken. She took it into her mouth being careful not to damage her lipstick.

'I'm left twiddling my thumbs some days.'

'Oh Ursula's fine with you,' Chloe-rose responded, flicking her empty hand in the air. 'I don't think she has a bother in the world.'

She'd obviously missed what I was trying to get at.

'I think . . .' I began.

'It's probably the age difference,' Chloe-rose said. 'You know how it is.'

'No, I don't know how it is, what exactly do you mean?'

She looked at me with eyes that now appeared as innocent as a wolf at a lamb picnic. 'I think when you came into the team Ursula expected that her admin assistant would be a little younger than you are. I'm okay with it. And David. Well who knows with David?' She let out a giggle and took another swipe at the chicken. 'Ursula works best with someone younger.'

I will never forget the feeling of horror that descended on me as that social lariat tightened around my neck. The blurring vision that started the migraine pounding in my head was only a fraction of what I was to feel as I began to comprehend that I had just been cornered in a stage of my life where age was not only beginning to define how others treated me but how work was delegated. It would cause a destructive dark cloud of fear to surround me as I anticipated that I might be dragged along unwillingly to a lonely retirement and a slow death. I finished my lunch quietly, soaking up Chloe-rose's saccharine smile for dessert. I went back to the office feeling crushed.

A whirlwind of rushed emails between Ursula and me led to hushed discussions among the lawyers in the days that followed until I finally found myself sitting opposite

Ursula in her office. Her desk was littered with a million framed photos of her three goggled nieces in paddle pools. They had little yellow and pink swim floaties hanging on their arms and looked out at me with the innocence of cherubs. As I thought of how much they must love their Aunt Ursula, I began to wonder if there was something I had missed in my judgment of the woman. Still it was she who had been making things difficult for me, not the other way around.

Things were so bad that work was now coming to me in dribbles of filing with the odd telephone message to follow up on. If work was any more boring I would have begun to think I was working for the accountants in the finance section. Ursula was being so mean she made Judge Judy look like the Easter Bunny. I couldn't let sparkling paddle pools and sun-filled splashes with nieces deceive me.

'Maria, thanks for meeting with me today,' Ursula communicated with a pronounced effort to be friendly. 'I've read over your email outlining your concerns and I've come up with a new system that might work for us.'

She had piqued my interest. I let my eyes drop from the pink arm floaties and focused them on Ursula's long face. It wasn't without its good features I had to admit. Certainly the dimple on her chin made her appear approachable and I recognized where her nieces might have inherited their expressions of bossiness.

'What have you got in mind?' I asked.

'I'm putting Josephine in charge of Chloe-rose's work, and my work. You will help David.'

'But Josephine is . . .' I didn't get another word out. Ursula had stood up and was leaning heavily on the desk gripping the edge of it as if it might take flight if she let go. Her beady brown eyes were narrowed and her black fringe of curls stuck to her forehead like pubic hairs to a toilet bowl. If I could have flushed her away I would have used the full rinse button and hoped there was Harpic in the water.

'Maria you have made an accusation to me in your email that I do not take kindly to. I do not, I repeat, do not give Josephine work because I think you're too old, or for that matter because I don't like you.' She cleared her throat and sat down. 'I simply do not know where you got that idea from.'

And I wasn't going to tell her.

I wouldn't have had to go higher if Ursula had been fair. But she didn't like my accusations of discrimination. It wasn't about fairness, it was about her wanting me to go away. I didn't word any complaint with *bullying* in it until it was obvious that Ursula was not going to back down with regards to how she was treating me. She was so entrenched in her ways that the idea of my suggesting that she was giving my work to the other team because she didn't like me or my age made her livid. Her anger was mainly noticeable when I walked into her room. The only difference between Ursula and a blood-sucking bat was that Ursula was scarier. The well-known joke about the only difference between a lawyer and a liar being the pronunciation of the word certainly didn't apply to all lawyers, but it did apply to Ursula. Rather than adopt a team approach Ursula soldiered on with her one-eyed goal of making me look ridiculous and unable to meet work requirements. And the results of the time-keeping which I painstakingly completed over weeks eventually disappeared with old manila folders into the shredder.

Then she began to patronize me. She forgot her comments about my capabilities and my appearance.

I began to notice that instead of ignoring me everyone was now going out of their way to be nice to me. Lawyers who had never given me the time of day began greeting me in the mornings. They nibbled the cookies I left on the kitchen bench and I was included in their small talk about specials on baby food. Senior management began to know me by name. That's when I knew things were getting really bad.

But nothing changed by way of the work situation. Ursula gave me little or no work. David felt so intimidated by it all that he didn't dare leave his junior lawyer work on my desk but trotted off to Josephine on the pretext that I looked busy. I *was* busy. I'd taken up twiddling my thumbs to a deadline.

Before I knew what was happening I found myself typing up an email to Felix, the senior manager, asking for practices to be investigated. Of course in keeping with protocol it was senior management who subsequently took my complaint back to Ursula which only added fuel to her inner fire. By that time I had my own issues of anger to deal with and I was left with no other option but to go to Joseph, the Chief Executive Officer, but not before Ursula had made a barrage of discreetly timed pokes and jabs at any work I did manage to do.

It's a headache-inducing exercise to point out bullying and unfair practices when you work in a government organization. It's like having bad breath. Everyone scurries for cover. And that's exactly what happened. Everyone who one day had suddenly become my best friend now couldn't remember my name. When the monthly bake-off came around for checking off what we'd bring in, my name wasn't on the list. It made me begin to wonder if the only good thing about the lawyers I worked with was that they made the telemarketers who called in, seem genuine.

Joseph's reaction probably had more to do with the report Ursula made as a response to my complaint rather than any accusation I made about her. Otherwise, I think he would have ignored me until I went away. When you're at the top you've had practice at waiting for people to go away. And they usually do in time. That's what long service leave, stress leave and retirement are for. CEO's have to protect themselves and upper management from mutiny so they have conversations with Human Resources via briefing notes and HR have fake conversations with less-valued employees like myself. Before you know it someone has left or disappeared and everyone walks around saying, 'who knew?'

It was a month to the day of my first complaint when Joseph turned up at a colleague's farewell afternoon tea. He was wearing one of those business shirts that's somewhere between smart and casual, checked, sky-blue, similar to the color of his eyes. It was Dress-down Friday, which I considered an oxymoron. Apart from Chloe-rose, the Public Servants I worked with dressed down every working day. Joseph sidled up to me with Ursula's manager, Felix. They positioned themselves at my side. That's when I began to wonder what they were up to.

Felix adjusted his pants at waist level, tucking in a huge stomach. He panted a heavy hello. At the time I didn't take too much notice of the fact that he made a point of emphasizing my full name before shuffling his heavy body away and leaving the CEO beside me. Joseph didn't talk to anyone else but me, small talk like nice cake, lovely scones, that kind of thing. He'd never spoken to me, or laid eyes on me before. I might be slow but I got it eventually. He wanted to check out the mature-age woman who had made the complaint. After that day, as long as I worked at South State Legal, I never saw him again, except for when I handed him my response to Ursula's scathing report a couple of weeks later. I never heard from him either except through the briefing notes to HR. I didn't talk to human resources anymore. I just responded to their emails.

Dirk stood back gritting his teeth throughout the entire debacle weighing the evidence as if he were on a jury. Every now and then he would try to dissuade me from proceeding with any complaint against Ursula. 'Maria you cannot complaint about the manager,' he coaxed.

I tried to explain to him that I'd been discreet but that Ursula had blown it up through false accusations about me and that the Chief Executive Officer had become involved. In the end Dirk never quite understood that it was Ursula's betrayal that hurt more than anything. He was more concerned for my work stability, worried that I would not be able to get another job if I lost that one. I'm not sure if it was because of my breaking a strict way of doing things that he had taken a pledge to, but he soon withdrew and I began to feel alone. And. Wrong.

On the afternoon I received HR's email with Ursula's report, there was a shortage of paper towels in the ladies' bathroom. They were in the bin with my tears and mascara on them. Crying was the first thing I did. The report Ursula wrote was biased, untruthful, derogatory and worded in such a way as to protect herself from my accusations. If she'd gone any further anyone would have been excused for thinking I should be charged with disorderly conduct or public nuisance for having pissed in the one and only front foyer pot plant. It wasn't a bad idea but I talked myself out of it.

The second thing I did after I got the report was to type up my response. I also typed up a five-page complaint to the Crime and Misconduct Commission. I thought it wouldn't be a bad idea to let them in on a little look-see into the affairs going on within a government organization. I handed the report to Joseph immediately by side-tracking his watch-dog secretary and slipping into his office on the fifth floor late in the afternoon. He took it from my hand and nodded.

As soon as I returned to my cubby hole, I packed things I'd decorated my desk with for years. Each item highlighted a particular note in my career as a legal assistant. My mug and one-cup tea pot were stuffed into my bag along with a fluffy-ended pen, a coaster from a printing company, a vase and a pen printed with the name of a firm of lawyers. Not that I knew then that Ursula and

Felix were already planning my transfer. I didn't. Intuition had clicked in and I felt certain that I wouldn't be given a chance to defend myself against Ursula's report. I tossed the complaint I'd written to the Crime and Misconduct Commission into the rubbish bin on my way out. I didn't need any more emotional challenges in my life.

As I was leaving, Josephine got in the lift at the second floor. Our eyes met briefly and for a moment I expected that she might offer sympathy. Instead she pressed the *close* button and as the doors shut, she moved to one side. I looked at her dumbfounded. She must have seen the tears in my eyes because when the doors opened again she stood back for me.

'How are things going Maria?' I heard her say.

I sensed from her attitude that she didn't know about Ursula's report. I understood the politics of the situation. After she found out about it, and if I actually got to keep my job, Josephine would have to choose sides and decide whether she'd be in a position to fix our friendship.

'I'm fine,' I lied and briskly made my exit on the ground floor leaving her standing at the lift.

I was like a mouse escaping its cage. I felt terror of what might lie ahead but it was mixed with the exhilaration of being free.

Chloe-rose was out the front sucking on a cigarette when I got there. She flicked hair from her face and did a backwards nod for me to approach her at the same time tottering toward me in her stilettos.

'I'm sorry for how it has turned out,' she said. She puffed a cloud of smoke towards her right shoulder. 'I had no idea how badly affected you were Maria. I should have seen it coming with Ursula, she'd been plotting ways to undermine your work for months but I didn't see it. I was blind and I should have been more perceptive. I'm so sorry.'

I was stunned. Not for one moment did I think that this girl had any more than a glimmer of empathy in her and I thought all of that was used up on her clients. I was about to tell her that I didn't need sympathy, that she should feel sorry for herself for having to continue to work under the regime when Ursula appeared behind her on her way back from court. Ursula was all smiles as she greeted us. I was aware that she would not yet know that HR had already emailed me a copy of her report.

Chloe-rose spun around when she heard her voice. 'How did you go? Was it a win?'

'Yes we won the case,' Ursula replied juggling large folders of case material.

I was about to depart when Ursula called me. 'Maria I've sent a report to human resources.'

I did a half turn to look at her.

'I think you will want to see me about it on Monday.'

'No need,' I answered. 'I've read it.' And before I knew what was tumbling out of my mouth I added, 'You can stick it up a dead bear's butt.'

Chapter 6

WELL I took care of that, I thought to myself as I sat in the train. I ripped my I.D. pass from where it was nestled in my lap attached to my jeans' pocket, wrapped it up and tossed it into my bag. Good thing it was Friday. That gave me about forty-eight hours to come up with a magic formula which would contain the right ingredients to keep my job, take time off and manage my sanity. I caught a reflection of someone in the window and thought what a tired and anxious woman she looked. It was me. I didn't need a holiday. I needed a good dose of Charlie Sheen. And what Charlie Sheen had. Or better still what about some time with the nerds on Big Bang Theory? Half a day with Sheldon Cooper and I'd know that I was actually sane.

I tried to think of when this all started. When did I suddenly become old and unwanted? When did everyone around me begin to see me in a way that belied my true self? When did I turn into a victim of bullying?

Before I was transferred into Ursula's team I loved going to work. At the same time a year earlier I was doing Pilates classes and pumping iron at the gym sometimes up to three or four nights a week. I was happy. I was radiant. How come in a period of six months I'd lost interest in my fitness regime and was now lucky if I made it to the gym one night a week and was actually able to take the stairs instead of the elevator? How come I was turning into the irritable, bitter person everyone seemed to think that someone my age should be? Or wasn't I coping with what life had dealt me? I didn't have the answers but I was guessing they lay deep within my psyche somewhere. I just didn't have the money to pay someone to dig them out. I would have to self-analyze.

'You what?' was Julia's animated response when I told her how my day had been. 'You have got to be kidding me?'

'It slipped out,' I explained as I kicked my shoes into the middle of the lounge room and flopped onto the couch.

'So you like told her to stick it?' My daughter's blue eyes were the size of Wedgwood plates. 'Mother you are so obviously senile.'

'I suppose I am if truth be told,' I mused. 'But if that were true I would have said much more than that and it would have begun with the letter F.'

'It may sound incredibly dumb but what are you going to do now?' Julia's voice sounded as if she was the mother instead of the other way around.

'Disappear into my bedroom, throw myself into a heap on my bed and bawl my eyes out.'

Julia's boyfriend Jamie, was lurking somewhere in the kitchen. I gathered my shoes and swinging them on two fingers I called. 'Hi Jamie.' I went to my room before he could answer.

My escape didn't last long. Before I knew it there was a loud knocking and when I opened the door Josephine was standing there looking like a big puppy that had lost its Kong. She threw herself into my bedroom and set up shop at the end of my bed opening her bag and pulling out a long brown envelope.

I sighed. 'I've given the stuff up,' I said sarcastically. And then slamming my door closed I continued, 'what are you doing here Josephine?'

'Maria I've been an idiot. I've been the worst friend you could ever have, I've been . . .'

'Hang on tell me something I don't know.' I slumped onto the end of the bed beside her.

Josephine smiled. 'You don't know how sorry I am. When I saw those tears in your eyes this afternoon, well I wanted to reach out but you seemed to be intent on ignoring me.'

'I've been otherwise occupied.'

'Everyone knows about the complaints you made. You look so stressed, so ragged, so . . .'

'Okay, stop with the compliments.'

'Read this.' Josephine handed me a letter.

I sat beside her at the edge of the bed and began to read.

'What is this?'

Josephine beamed. 'My resignation Maria. I didn't want to do it until you had the outcome of your complaint. What I didn't know until Chloe-rose told me this afternoon was that you've been shafted. I had no idea what Ursula was up to, all I know is that I have to get out of there. She threatened my job if I didn't do your work. She basically made it impossible for me to talk to you.'

'Do you have a new job?'

'No Maria, we have a new job.'

'And that means?'

'Now that Chloe-rose has experience, she's going to work for her father. He's a partner at Crime Legal which, as you are well aware Maria, is only one of the most well-known criminal law firms in Brisbane.' Josephine's voice was rising an octave with each word she uttered. 'Chloe-rose told me she can get both of us a job there Maria.' She bounced to her feet and jumped up and down in front of me like a child at a birthday party. 'Chloe-rose will need legal support and she wants you.' She clasped her hands in front of her chest and squealed the rest out. 'And someone is leaving so I'm getting that role.'

Not wanting to be too much of a triumphalist I waved my hand into a stop signal. 'Wait here.'

I walked gallantly downstairs to the kitchen, grabbed the bottle of red that I was saving for a rainy day, pulled two wine glasses from the cupboard, expelled a squeal of excitement which I could no longer keep inside as I walked through the lounge room which resulted in a flurry of jerky movements from the couch where Julia and Jamie were obviously making out, raced back up the stairs to the bedroom, slammed the door behind me with my foot and leaned against it.

'Unbelievable,' I yelled. My feet felt as if they were about to lift off the ground. 'I can't believe it. Oh Josie, take these things before I drop it all.'

Josephine rescued the bottle and glasses from the end of my waving arms as I went toward her, put them on the nightstand, disappeared for a minute and returned with a corkscrew.

'You have to use one of these wretched things to open this bottle,' she explained.

And like a pro she screwed it in and popped the top.

'Nothing like a good screw.' She had a smile that stretched across her face.

She filled a glass, handed it to me, poured one for herself.

'Here's to that bitch burning in hell forever.' She raised her glass to mine.

'Forever.' I toasted.

'And our new jobs,' she added, taking a gulp of wine and plonking herself onto the edge of the bed. 'And to BFFs.'

I raised my glass in the air. 'Best Friends Forever.'

'Right,' Josephine declared. 'Now that we've got that all sorted.' She reflected for a brief moment. 'How's things with the German?'

I shrugged as I sat beside her. 'A little pinched with all that I've been going through at work and he's going to Germany for a while, otherwise good. But that reminds me.' I tapped her on the arm. 'I had a message on my phone from Dominic.'

Josephine swung around to face me. 'Johnny Dominic Depp? I knew he would come back to you. Gorgeous Dom. So when are you seeing him?'

'I haven't replied to him, my mind has been spinning.'

'But you will surely. He's the sexiest man alive, after the real Johnny Depp, and he wants you Maria.' She shook my arm. 'That's got to give your hormones a little work out.'

I laughed. 'My hormones aren't gym junkies but I guess I could stretch them a little.'

'Don't stretch, reach out, call him. Where's your phone?' She stood up and scanned the room.

'What about Dirk?'

'It's Flyday, the German flees on Flydays.' Josephine pulled my phone from my bag.

'I'll call him later Josie, I don't know what to say.'

Josephine settled on the floor and leaned against the bed, wine glass in hand. She drew her legs up and caught them by her folded arms. From where I sat on the bed I was looking at her left profile. Her pale skin glowed with cheeks of pink. She was lovely. She was like a sister to me.

'I've missed you Josie.' I put my hand on her shoulder. 'It's not all your fault. I've been distracted by the conflict going on at work and it's upset me that you've been so against Dirk. But I never stopped to think that he has been gobbling up so much of my time.'

Josephine looked up at me and smiled. 'That's men for you, can't live with them and you shouldn't live with them.' She laughed. 'Maria I think you should see Dom. I think the German is not good for you. You guys aren't exclusive are you?'

'Exclusive? Like shoes or handbags you mean? Oh exclusive,' I taunted playfully. 'Like in not seeing anyone else? We've never talked about it.'

'Good, that means you can see Dom,' Josephine chortled. 'Nothing like a bit of hot sex for your vision.'

'My vision?'

'Maria, it's true that we lose a clear picture of things as we age but I think you need to get prescription glasses.'

She had folded her own glasses onto the nightstand and moved to lean against it. She was peering at me with her big green eyes.

'You haven't seen it yet but the German looks like a bulldog.'

It was true that I was love-sick but love-blind? I'd never given it a thought. I laughed heartily.

'Bulldogs are beautiful and docile and friendly. I love them.'

'They are ugly and willful,' she replied. 'Why did you stop seeing Dom?'

'I can't remember, it might have had something to do with not keeping up with his sex drive or something trivial like that,' I joked.

'Well hone up those muscles and collect a hormone script from the doctor,' Josephine quipped. 'You don't have time to waste on relationships that go nowhere.'

'What makes you think that my relationship with Dirk is going nowhere?'

'Didn't you say he's German? If it was going somewhere he would have told you by now, Germans are direct, straight to the point, they make plans, you should know that.'

The realization made me laugh. How many times had Dirk told me something to my face that another man wouldn't dare say. *I don't like that dress. Don't wear those shorts, you don't look good in them. I don't like the way you make the coffee. Why do you hang towels on the line like that, that's not right.* Josephine was right. He hardly stopped telling me how things were and what I should do.

Why then hadn't he told me where our relationship was heading?

'Okay you're right, I'll call Dominic tomorrow. He's another example of an IT geek. Mind you, he's younger too, he's only forty-bloody-nine. He probably only wants to say hello.'

'Ha ha and you must be the world's only living brain donor,' Josephine joked. 'Hello Maria,' she mimicked in a deep voice. 'I just came by because I don't have a hard-on.' Josephine laughed and sipped more wine. 'Your lights are on Maria, but nobody's home right now. Yes, he's a bit younger than you are but he's not German. He's a dinky-di Aussie.'

'Don't be so crass,' I chided. 'Nationality doesn't count. And anyway, if Dominic only wants sex why would I bother?'

'Why wouldn't you?'

We clinked glasses and laughed.

'So what makes you think that's not all the German wants?'

'Actually he doesn't want sex much at all,' I confided.

'What are you telling me woman?' Josephine got onto her knees from where she was sitting on the floor and leaned toward me with wide eyes. 'Do you mean the sizzle has gone out of his sausage? That I was right about him being as cold as a polar bear's behind?'

'Whoa.' I spat wine as I laughed.

'Sounds to me like you need to call hot Dom tonight Maria. I didn't know you were suffering so badly.'

'Hang on.' I put my hand out in front of me, got up and put the wine glass on the table behind Josephine.

'That's enough about my sex life, what about you? I don't see men lining up in your driveway.'

'I'm still on the dating site,' she confirmed as she sat back on her haunches. 'No one special, a few bonks. Met a guy the other night I might see again but, you know me, I'm not into having a relationship around my neck. The freshness of a new man is like a good deodorant. They last for forty-eight hours, they respond to action and if he's a good one, he will have zero percent alcohol.' Josephine laughed.

There was a light tapping sound and we both turned our heads toward the door.

'Is this a private party or can I join in?' Julia's sweet voice asked from the other side.

I rushed to the door. 'Of course darling.' I swung the door open. Julia shuffled in letting the door make a soft clip sound behind her. I gestured for her to sit down. 'Pull up a bed, I hope you brought your own glass. Has Jamie gone?'

Julia nodded as she sat cross-legged beside Josephine. 'I heard you guys laughing. I haven't heard laughter in this house for months.'

I hadn't done any guilt tripping in more than a day but that statement jolted me back to my senses. What was I thinking? It's funny how grown up you can be when your young adult daughter is present.

'That's so sad to hear you say that sweetheart.'

'Oh lighten up Maria,' Josephine intercepted. She leaned across and wrapped her arms around my daughter. 'Julia's as guilty of breaking the laughter circle as we are.' She shook Julia playfully. 'You and your moving out plans, you're only doing it because Jamie wants you to. You should be grounded until you come to your senses or at least until you have a job.'

Julia's cheeks spread their pinkness to her entire face.

'Come on girls,' Josephine continued. 'Let's be real here. We have to soldier on with smiles and comradeship, this is life, it doesn't get much better than this. Go get yourself a glass Jules and have a spot of red.'

By the time Julia was back with the wine glass Josephine had grabbed my phone, found Dominic's message and was threatening to press the little green button. I was stretched out across the bed wrestling her for the phone when Julia came through the door.

'Jules here catch,' Josephine called as she threw the phone to my daughter.

Julia caught it as if she was a pro baseballer.

'Quick press Dominic's number and call him,' Josephine instructed while she held me down.

I was giggling uncontrollably but managed to conjure up a mother's grunt which usually went with the command *don't you dare*. Just like Pavlov's dogs, association kicked in and Julia stopped in her tracks. There has to be some benefits to motherhood.

I pulled hair from my mouth, pushed it from my face, slapped Josephine on the backside and got to my feet.

'There will be no more shenanigans with my phone,' I announced red-faced and sweaty.

Julia's smile dropped.

'Don't listen to her Jules,' Josephine called in an imposing voice. 'She might be your mother, but she's my best friend. Now give it to me, give it to me.'

Josephine caught the phone like a basketball player and threw it back to Julia who by now had withdrawn her need for me to guilt-trip. Taking a breath, Julia tossed the phone back to Josephine who hit the dial button. I held my face in my hands to suppress my laughter but Julia's giggling was like a school girl in class.

'Hello Dominic? How are you this evening?' Josephine sounded like a telemarketer.

I cringed as I heard her say my name and almost fell into a coma when she announced that I'd asked her to call on my behalf to organize a time to get together, that I was working long hours and didn't want to leave it any longer to contact him. When she disappeared into the bathroom and closed the door, my heart beat heavily in my chest and when she emerged and dropped the phone into my bag and sat silently at the end of the bed I was preparing for humiliation.

'Well?'

'I reckon he'd have a smile on his face like a snake in a chook pen by now,' she boasted. 'Next up is what to do with your hair.'

'What's wrong with my hair?'

'There's nothing wrong with it that a fresh color and a few inches off won't fix,' she answered. 'But as they say, the secret to a bad hair day is to leave your shirt buttons undone.' She laughed. 'Just get in that shower and shampoo it, you've got an hour and a half before Dom arrives.'

'Josie, no, you didn't?'

'He knows you're available too, if you know what I mean.' She animated her eyebrows. 'And after your shower? That Red Door perfume you bought five years ago? Use it.'

'What about Dirk?' Julia's wide eyes peered at Josephine.

'Ah ya? Apologize me?' Josephine's face remained dead-pan. 'What's a Dirk? Oh you mean the German? Well we all knew he'd last for about as long as a snowflake in summer didn't we.'

At which time each of us had the same thought and fell onto the bed laughing.

Chapter 7

THE party soon came to a sudden halt. For me anyway. Over the next month my life resembled an extremely slow funeral parade. I took a sickie on the following Monday and received an email from Human Resources later in the day letting me know that my position was being re-developed. Whatever that meant. They told me they would transfer me into Accounts. I let them do all the paperwork while I stayed on sick leave but I never went back. It would have been like going to work in Siberia. I didn't need any more cold fronts.

That same week I saw Dirk off to Germany to visit his sick mother and get his divorce. That's when I found myself feeling lost and without purpose. My emotions were the equivalent of an adolescent's highs and lows. I feared what Josephine had hinted at. I might be going through menopause. But when I asked the doctor for patches he thought I wanted to give up smoking and it wasn't until I began to feel heavy headed and nauseous that I went back to see him and got things cleared up. By that time my emotions were like those of a two-year old let loose in a Baskin-Robins shop. I knew what I wanted one minute and not the next. When I got what I wanted I gorged myself and threw up.

I knew that for Dirk's sake I had to become clear about our relationship. He knew I was seeing Dominic and turned a blind German eye justifying it with a stern nod because of his own marital status but he spoke to me as if I was a wild daughter who would have to settle down sooner or later.

Josephine moved into her new job, the position that already existed at Crime Legal, the private law firm where Chloe-rose's father worked. She told me that a legal secretary for Chloe-rose was yet to be approved in the budget and with the economic downfall it was likely that Chloe-rose would have to push her own wheelbarrow back and forth to court. For me, life was a whirlwind of downhill adventure. One of the advantages of maturity is being able to cope with downhill adventure. At least that statement made me laugh when it popped into my mind. It wasn't my experience. Pretense, now that's what I was good at.

Not getting the job Chloe-rose had hoped for me meant that I was left searching job vacancies and ironing clothes for job interviews which I hadn't yet scored. Most of my time was spent agonizing over cover letters and my CV, with Josephine sending links to pages of information on tips about how to summarize why I was the best person for the job and Dirk emailing to remind me that I had to be the best, like a German. Trouble was, I didn't know why I was the best person for any job. Or if I was. The only thing that got me through that month was Dominic. He lit up a light in my life that burned without flickering. Having him chase after me filled me with exhilaration and desire but I had to waste all of that exuberance and put it into job applications.

The second time I went out with Dominic my despondency disappeared. I took Josephine along with her date Andrew and a wilder night could not have been had by a fox in a hen house. As was usual for Josephine she had met Andrew twenty-four hours earlier in the hotel where she was staying for three nights to attend induction training in Brisbane's central business district.

At the entry to Anzac Square in Brisbane there is a statue of the Boer War Soldier on Horseback. I could see that horseman and the clock tower behind it through the window of the lifts when I came down to the foyer of the hotel after Josephine's accident. It was fifteen minutes past midnight. The four of us had untangled ourselves from the double bed in Josephine's room – where we'd returned after our dinner date to drink wine and discuss the pros and cons of group sex – to go for an out-of-hours swim in the hotel pool. Half an hour later Josephine slipped onto her backside as she was getting out of the spa.

As I came out of the lift I saw the ambulance through the glass doors. At the same moment Josephine was wheeled out of the opposite lift on a stretcher and was moved into the foyer. She looked pretty chirpy considering she'd sprained an ankle and had been cautioned by hotel staff that further stays would be banned if breaking of hotel rules was ever repeated. As she was being strapped into the back of the ambulance, Dominic and I took a few pics on our phones and she took snaps of us together laughing and pulling faces at her. I climbed in to sit beside her. Dominic and Andrew waited for a cab.

It was five hours and several x-rays later by the time we got back to the hotel. We'd finished building a pillow mountain on which Josephine could rest her sprained ankle when Andrew suggested that Maccas was probably open and we should get some breakfast. It was a unanimous decision by Josephine and me that the two men should wander the city until they found golden arches. We would keep the bed warm. A couple of hours later the four of us were in the bed discussing every sprained or broken bone each of us had sustained throughout our lives and drinking the remains of cold coffee. When I noticed Andrew's hands beginning to move underneath the blankets I decided it was time to put an end to the good-bedfellows situation. I extricated myself and caught a cab home. I could have almost bought the cab instead, the trip was so expensive.

I was tired but I still had enough energy to take Josephine's call a few hours later.

'The man is a sex machine,' she panted before I could say hello.

'I do hope you're talking about Andrew.'

She laughed. 'Him too.'

'Josie?'

'Joking, joking, Deppie left right after you, I'm surprised you haven't heard from him.'

'My guess is that Dominic is at work, it's Wednesday Josie. I've got a bloody job interview today. Don't you have to work?'

'Sprained ankle remember?'

'Oh yes, take care. Some of us have lives to go on with.' I ended the call wondering when I had become so bitter as to think that a sprained ankle was just Josephine's luck.

I was about to take comfort in a Cherry Ripe chocolate bar when Dominic called to tell me what a great night he'd had. I was happy for him and happier still that I didn't remember it all.

'Tell me Dominic,' I said. 'Did we do anything I need to regret? Should I be afraid to open my door to visitors?'

His laughter didn't reveal much but I was left with the distinct feeling that he was up for more.

My job interview was at three so I had time to rest, prepare, iron and worry. In that order, I told myself. I set my alarm and headed to bed. After Dominic's call I felt a sense of satisfaction, a kind of rejuvenation of my senses regardless of the fact that I was dead tired. I slept soundly for an hour and when I awoke I made coffee and settled at the computer to read up on the interview tips the recruitment agency had emailed me. The position was for a secretary at a private firm of lawyers that had government funding for criminal matters. It was right up my alley. I printed off the forms so I could take them with me to the couch and eat the chocolate bar at the same time.

Adaptability: what strategies do you use to manage change? A night out drinking, four in the bed and a visit to the hospital, I wrote. *Goals: what are your career aspirations?* Strengths: *How do you use them? What are you doing to address weaknesses?* My discordant equilibrium took a reality check. I exhaled a long breath of carbon dioxide and wished I had a gas oven in which to rest my head.

Interview number two was a fizzle as well. It didn't eventuate. A young woman rang to thank me for my application and asked if I was aware that the position was for a receptionist in a brothel. I thanked her for the information, hung up and put another red cross on my list.

I moved onto the third and fourth interviews with grace and confidence. I was poised, well presented, on the ball with answering questions. I was like an acrobatic clown. I could simultaneously think on my feet and hit the ground running. If anyone had asked me to walk a tightrope I would have jumped at the chance and done it while transcribing the *Australian Guide to Legal Citation*.

And I'd had a haircut. Instead of ironed straight, collar-length hair, I now sported a pixie cut and had returned to my natural brown and added blonde highlights. It announced professionalism and it put a stop to Josephine's hinting about my hair.

I was regularly informed post interview that I came across well and while I wasn't actually successful in getting any job, I was shortlisted. Several times. That's when I began to better understand what the word *shortlisted* actually meant for me and it was this: *you have great experience and skills, you come across wonderfully in an interview but we wanted someone younger.* I also became excruciatingly aware that it also meant if you don't get the job you don't get the money. I was psyching up to my savings and superannuation funds dropping to zero.

That's when Josephine came up with a brilliant way to make money. I should sell things on eBay.

'What things?' My sense of curiosity had been sharpened.

'I don't know, can't you knit or something? Maybe you could make candles or puppets?' Josephine was overflowing with innovative ideas.

We were sitting in a coffee shop near her workplace. Dominic, his Johnny Depp mouth grinning from ear to ear, put his tablet in front of me and showed me pictures of someone making a comforter.

'This lady sells on eBay,' he said.

I looked at each of them aghast. 'You guys think my career is washed up don't you.' Tears spilled from my eyes. 'You think I'm never going to get a job. You think I'm too old.'

As they sat there looking blindsided by my outburst my heart overflowed with envy at the thought that both of them being gainfully employed actually had somewhere to go after lunch and eventually a deposit of money would turn up in their bank accounts. The only solution I could come up with was not to discuss my job hunting with either of them again.

At home it was much the same.

'Why don't you just retire?' Julia asked innocently one evening when I was dabbing the blisters on the back of my heels with anti-septic ointment.

The *just* part of that question really irked me. I didn't see myself at retirement age. Maybe I was missing some important life-stage signs but I knew I still had it in me to work for another twenty years. More if I wanted to. I wasn't going to be relegated to a stereotypical position in life because others saw me in a certain age group. And financially no one seemed to understand that I didn't have a million dollars in super. I was a female Baby Boomer. I didn't have super except for what I'd stuffed away after my divorce. It was enough to stock up on underwear if they were Target brand but otherwise I would be panty-less for the rest of my life if I had to live off of it. That was another idea Josephine thought of: selling lingerie.

Josephine hypothesized that if I could get Dirk to buy women's undergarments in Europe and bring them home for me I might be able to identify a niche market. I pursed my lips for almost a minute on that one. It wasn't a half-bad idea. She went on to say that I could use my daughter as a model and set up my own website, which of course Dominic could easily build. My pursed lips twisted to the right on that suggestion and I took her back a step so that Julia was out of the picture. Every picture.

Josephine decided that if I wasn't interested in lingerie then at least I should give raising puppies a go. For the next three weeks she researched dog breeding. I was meant to be making a business plan. Josephine got in touch with a local breeder friend and agreed to look after a litter of three Labrador pups which had been weaned but not yet homed. They were adorable but couldn't figure out the difference between grass and my polished timber floors. My lounge room began to resemble a kindergarten playroom. Rugs, bowls and toys were everywhere. As least this began to put Julia's skills to good use. She made a psychological assessment that Josephine was trying to make up for some issue within herself. Maybe Josephine was denied pets as a child. Maybe she had a secret desire to become a dog trainer. Or possibly and most likely, she felt guilty about having a well-paid job when I didn't. That rang true for me.

I was proud of my Julia. Not only had her interest in her studies begun to grow but she was becoming more understanding of my situation, even though she still saw me through her mature-age blinkers. I took pride in knowing that my only child might one day be the Dr. Phil of her generation, a female Dr. Phyl that is. And I'd begun to notice that Julia and Jamie were on a calmer path together. Jamie was in his final year of IT and though I thought at first it would hardly be possible, he was becoming more geekish every day. And that resembled Dominic.

The puppy-raising idea might have taken off if Josephine hadn't persuaded Dominic to go back to the lingerie idea. He turned up one evening with a few items that Josephine had ordered online. That's when I started to evaluate how important Dominic was to me. When I refused to model a see-through black bra he happily settled for a re-run of *Two and a Half Men* instead and went home early, but it was time for me to reflect on the relationship that was developing between us. And more importantly, between Dominic and Josephine.

The two of them seemed to be working together to order things online. Dominic was either over at Josephine's place giving her tips on website development or she was at his apartment making online orders on his computer. Not that I cared. I didn't. I had little more interest in Dominic than the garter skirt that I received in the mail from Josephine's online order. For me his resemblance to Johnny Depp was waning and I had begun to notice that, from where I was standing, after the packaging was taken away, he had little by way of personality or pizzazz. I began to feel embarrassed that I'd even been mildly attracted to him and that led to me getting back in touch with the growing sense of failure within myself.

I was beginning to feel that maybe I really was washed up. Maybe I was a fifty-five-year-old Peta Pan who'd never grown up, who'd never been loved. In my efforts to avoid conforming, I now thought I'd missed the boat altogether. Other women my age were beginning to get comfortable about using senior's discounts, an idea which positively made me shudder. Others were buying recreational vehicles that they could travel in, while those who could afford it were retiring and taking it easy with their lovely husbands. I felt as if old age was standing on my doorstep and if it had its way it would chauffeur me off and tuck me up neatly behind manicured gardens in a retirement village.

As Julia and Jamie began to spend more time at Jamie's place I was alone most of the time. I felt deserted in some ways and very selfish in that feeling. Maybe it was time for me to sell up and downsize. That's another thing that normal mature women were meant to do.

Dirk would be home in a couple of weeks and I was searching for ways to create a future with him. Maybe I should give up the idea of buying a place altogether and share his rental house. Thoughts went over and over in my mind but in the end I knew that I didn't feel any more inspired than when I'd sat down to open the next box of panties that had arrived for Josephine's intended lingerie business. That's when I called Dominic and asked him to come over and collect everything including the Labrador pups and take them to Josephine. I slipped a little note onto one of the packages letting her know that the thing I'd had with Dominic was over and that the garter business just wasn't going to can-can off.

Josephine had another solution for making an income. Instead of living off my super or setting up a new business why didn't I buy an existing one? I admitted it wasn't a bad idea. But what business? That question was almost answered when I met Craig.

I was at the library looking for anything I could get my hands on about small business. Craig was in the same row and made a comment about the *Running a Food Business for Dummies* book I was holding and it went from there. If Dominic (used to) resemble Johnny Depp, Craig was the perfect image of Jamie Oliver and he was a sandwich artist to boot. I'd never known a sandwich artist before. I wondered if there were Sandwich Artist degrees.

After that whenever I was in the fresh vegetables section of my local supermarket I thought I saw Craig's face on the Jamie Oliver posters advertising his recipes, all of which could be made in fifteen minutes. I figured that if he could make good in fifteen minutes he was the perfect man for my busy job-searching-come-business lifestyle.

'Fifteen minutes?' Josephine was horrified. 'If it was all over that quickly with my man I'd have to get another.'

'We are talking about food Josie, not sex,' I pointed out.

She laughed. 'If he told you he could satisfy you in fifteen minutes you can bet he wasn't talking about food.'

'Josie you have a one-track mind,' I scolded. 'We were talking about a sandwich business. Craig is selling his, but forget that, I can't see myself mashing boiled eggs and mayonnaise onto bread for a crust, it's not me.'

Josephine laughed heartily but I felt jaded.

'Josie don't you ever think that life is passing you by while you hop from one bed to the other with any man you meet?'

'No.'

'Well I do and I'm not even hopping. I'm tired and I'm stressed and I've had enough of floundering. I want to finish the rest of my life having done something I can be proud of.'

'You can be proud,' Josephine encouraged. 'You've achieved heaps, what about Julia? You've done a great job as a single parent. And your lovely house. You've got it all paid off haven't you?'

'Mmm.' I was thinking more about my intimate life but had resigned a long time ago not to discuss that with Josephine. 'I've been bullied. And I've lost my job.' Before I knew it tears had begun to stream down my cheeks. 'And I miss Dirk terribly.'

'So it's really over with Dom?'

'Feel free.'

'What's he like in bed?'

'Josie sometimes I can't believe you.' I pushed tears from my face with my fingertip. 'I never went there with Dominic.'

'What?'

'I know, hard to believe but it's true. I think Dominic is incompetent.'

'You might mean impotent.' Josephine's laugh sobered me but when I laughed hysterically I sounded like a mad woman and I had to face it, I was terribly out of balance.

'Josie be kind to Dominic, he's a nice man, and he's looking for love and commitment. I'll talk later, I'm off to pick Dirk up from the airport this afternoon.'

After I hung up I sobbed quietly on my bed for a while. I'd almost forgotten the deep commitment I'd felt towards Dirk, the immense love which passed between the two of us and how desperately he needed me. I felt a great wave of sadness go over me as I recalled the grief he was going through when I first got to know him. He had merely stuffed that emotion away after that night. It was probably still inside of him simmering away like a saucepan of mulled wine in winter time. Nothing could make me want to forget him and in fact I felt a little guilty that I'd let my emails to him drop.

But I'd given him the time he needed to sort his life out. He would be ready now. And I was going to make it work with him if it was the last thing I ever did. He was the only man I could imagine living my life with. The only man I could commit to.

Chapter 8

ONE of the problems with self-deception is that it makes you feel uncomfortable at a deep level. You can argue it away with labels such as *stress* or *anxiety* but the down side of denial is that a myriad of events which could help you with the healing process pass you by. You don't see them because you think you have no need to see them. And you ignore the signs that you're walking a fine line. In this way you fail to recognize the red flags and the alarm bells going off all around you. You know that you can get away with the odd fib or the denial of the real truth with others but inside of yourself there's a feeling of being crumpled. If you let it go on long enough you can get used to the non-ironed effect but the reality is that the look eventually becomes crushed rather than crumpled and you end up with no choice but to pull out the ironing board. I knew I had some ironing to do.

First, I had to get back to some serious job search. With most of my energy being directed to business ideas I'd dropped my daily browsing of Seek and Careerone. Josephine was still hopeful that the position at Chloe-rose's firm would materialize seeing as the practice was doing well. I had allowed that positivity to contribute to my lack of effort in the application and interview section of my life. The thought of laboring through vacancies and addressing key competencies left me with sweaty palms. I abandoned the thought and returned to my mood of denial which was far more relaxing.

I hadn't yet grieved the loss of my job or the betrayal I felt. The sadness was there most of the time hiding behind bitterness and insane efforts to keep busy but I didn't want to go there. It manifested in sudden mood swings, annoyance into acceptance, miserly to generous. The generosity continuum was the most worrying. I threw twenty dollar notes at buskers and handed out fifties to homeless people. That some of those homeless people were really just local teenagers skipping school spoke tons about my ability to recognize how unbalanced I was. But I just couldn't allow myself to think about the hurt and fear that was living inside of me. When I went there I had to think about the bullying and the reasons for my job loss and unemployment and that took me to only one thing, my age was against me. I was too old. Everyone said so. I believed it must be true.

I hopped onto the computer and did a quick search of job vacancies, updated my online resume and logged off all within ten minutes. That got rid of those thoughts. For the moment. But there was something else left to do. That thing was called sorting out my relationship with my daughter.

Julia had been staying at Jamie's for two weeks straight. I had no idea when she was coming home, if she was coming home, whether or not she was moving out, or whether or not for that matter, she was still alive. I got the feeling she was. I'd had the occasional message on my phone asking if there were any online packages delivered for her or if I could make a small bank deposit into her account.

There was no denying that my relationship with my daughter had begun to slide. I kept telling myself that she was a grown woman but that only served to send shivers of guilt up my spine over the thought of what I hadn't yet taught her. Had I told her everything she needed to know? Did I warn her about things like how to attend to a sick crocodile or a beached whale? What about walking alone at night or staying clear of flood waters? I thought not. But all of it was just a great big flood of guilt and I was swimming in it. What I really wanted was to relate well with my daughter but it seemed she had set up too many walls for me to do that. I sent her a message to come over for a movie with me on Friday night. The weather was becoming cool. We could snuggle under a blanket, drink hot chocolate and eat pizza. I was pleasantly surprised when she agreed.

One more important thing I had to do was to sort things with Dominic. I called him and organized to meet for coffee around the corner from where he worked at his morning break. I knew I wasn't being generous with my time but I was still living on the notion that he would understand and in fact, would already be there with what was happening with us. I hadn't allowed for Dominic's integrity. As it turned out I'd forgotten that he really did accept me for who I am.

Dirk's flight was due at four so I had several hours after letting Dominic down in which I could compose myself and return to some kind of normality. I'd put off saying anything to Dominic about not seeing him any more by assuring myself that he had already guessed how I felt and that he would be so happy to find Josephine take up a romantic interest in him that he'd quickly forget all about me. But given that Josephine had asked how he performed in bed some weeks after I'd indicated that it was over for the two of us, I got the feeling that Josephine must have been only slightly interested in Dominic otherwise she would have made the move by then. Or maybe Dominic wasn't interested in Josephine? And Josephine was busy at work. I didn't know what was happening, I had hardly seen her or Dominic since the puppy puddles had disappeared and the garter lingerie efforts had snapped. I had to face Dominic myself.

Dominic had his tablet on the table in front of him when I arrived as well as two coffees and a buy-nine-and-get-the-tenth-free card checked off only twice. His greeting was lost in the chatter of the morning coffee crowd and I had to guess that it was *hey* as he pushed his chair out and did a half stand. I *hey'd* back as I tossed my bag onto the table, brushed my lips to his cheek and sat down opposite him. He turned the screen for me to check out the website he was on. The *Family Law* website. I blinked and nodded. That's when it dawned on me. I knew absolutely nothing about Dominic.

'How's work?' I asked ignoring the opportunity to inquire about his knowledge of law.

Almost his entire upper body nodded *good* and strands of brown hair fell across his eyes and momentarily covered his brown-rimmed glasses. I hadn't seen those glasses before. His cupid-bow lips, framed by the smallest tufts of mustache, upturned into a smile that held my undivided attention. Is this what Josephine had been talking about? How could I have been so blind? He was gorgeous.

'I've missed you Maria. Is everything okay?'

I allowed my gaze to travel his face, the chiseled jaw and cheekbones, the soft brown eyes that were like dark chocolate and I found myself in awe at what I'd failed to see.

'Maria?'

I picked up the coffee. 'Thanks for getting this.' I took a sip. 'I'm okay, just a bit lost. As you know I've given up on business ideas, I don't think I thanked you for your help.'

'You did.' He smiled and touched my hand.

'And looking for work has made me tired, I think I've given up on that as well.'

'Have you given up on me?'

I bit my lip discreetly, took in the sight and touch of his hand on mine. I hadn't felt this kind of warmth from Dominic before. My fling with him had been some kind of a joke in my mind, a stupid flirtatious affair that Josephine had orchestrated and that I had tagged along with. Guilt began to fill my mind. I had never considered Dominic's feelings. He was a mystery to me. And now that he was in front of me and I was seeing him for the first time, the mystery was unraveling before my eyes in a more beautiful and tempting way than I could ever have imagined. I was intrigued. I was gob smacked. I was powerless to know what to do.

Maybe I didn't know what I wanted after all. Maybe I didn't know anything. My immediate past was a blur, the termination of employment, the hurt that Ursula had left me with, my uncertainty about Dirk. And my future looked as bleak as the clouds outside the coffee shop window. My life had taken on the blue rinse of mature women who had given up.

'I'm not sure what you and I were about Dominic,' I told him. 'I don't even know what I'm about. Who am I? I don't know anymore.'

He smiled. 'Let me see, you're a beautiful woman with big blue eyes that implore me to love you.'

I put my coffee mug on the table, dropped my head and studied my hands in my lap. 'They're mostly hazel but thank you,' I whispered. I looked him in the eyes. 'Dominic I thought everything in life was fine until everyone started to treat me differently.'

'I know,' he soothed. 'I'm not far behind you, in age I mean.'

'Yes you are Dominic you're not fifty yet, I'm six years ahead of you.'

'Six years is nothing Maria.'

I was delirious with surprise. I had never, not even on our four-in-the-bed-and-the-little-one-said-night imagined Dominic to be so deliciously understanding and sensual. I found myself wondering where on earth my feelings could have been all that time. Now they were rushing to my nerve endings like acupuncture needles. They were about to gush forth in a frenzy of frothy emotions at the very thought of having someone like Dominic love me.

I stood up. I couldn't let him witness my tears, my absolute despair with how life was treating me. I'd acted like a tower of strength in front of Dominic all along, now here I was leaking unhappiness all over the place. He deserved someone who had it all together. Not me. Not Josephine. He deserved a goddess.

'My age was enough to lose me my job,' I blurted as I picked up my bag and shoved it under my arm. 'Dominic you are one of the most wonderful people I've ever known.' I dropped my eyes.

His face was filled with tenderness and I couldn't look at it another moment or we would have had a flood of tears all over the table.

'I've got to rush now. I have to get Dirk from the airport this afternoon.'

Dominic stood up and took my hand into his. 'Maria don't let what happened to you at work dictate the rest of your life. If you let it get you down it will destroy you.'

He wasn't going to drop the truth of the situation. I'd done more ironing out with him than a Chinese dry-cleaner could have done.

I scanned the coffee shop for anyone listening. 'It's already destroyed me,' I whispered.

I kissed him on the cheek, went out the door and strode toward the train station. How could he know that his affection was beginning to tear me in two. What about Dirk?

I was on the platform when I saw him, his caramel trench coat and the leather man bag he carried stood him out from the crowd of morning shoppers. He high-five waved as he strode toward me.

'Dominic, what are you doing?' I called.

He sat beside me yanking the bag from his shoulder. 'Thought I'd come along for the fun. I've got time clocked up so I called in and here I am.'

'But your platform is on the other side.'

'No I'm on the same line as you are but what I meant is that I'll come to pick up Dirk with you.' He looked at the time board for our train's arrival. He looked back at me and smiled. 'If you don't mind of course.'

I laughed. 'You're incorrigible. You remember who Dirk is right?'

'Of course, you've talked about him enough. I'd like to meet him.'

'Dirk will be expecting me to stay the night with him.' I blushed as I lowered my eyes from his gaze.

He looked at me with a straight face. 'That won't stop us having a coffee somewhere first will it?'

I laughed loudly. Dominic's audacity was refreshing even if it was out of place.

'Will you be able to get home okay?'

'Getting a cab won't be a problem.'

'Right, good, okay.' I nodded resolutely. 'First we go to my place to get my car. I will have to pack a few things and put some washing on before we leave.'

Dominic nodded. 'No worries.'

If you've ever seen a man tinged with the glow of happiness you will know what Dominic looked like in that train. Nothing could have subtracted from his demeanor, not hail, not wind, not rain. But I did wonder if Dirk might. I began to weigh my situation. I thought my mind had brilliant clarity but now things had begun to look confusing. I loved Dirk. And I'd been honest with

Dominic. I felt no guilt about that. So what made Dominic think he had any chance with my affections? Was it because of Josephine's derision of Dirk? Did he want to see for himself what kind of man I was involved with? Thoughts flipped in and out of my mind as we rode in silence. And all the while there was a huge connection between us. It was as if we were spinning our own little cocoon. I'd soon pop out with butterfly wings and Dominic and I would flutter off into the sunset. I said nothing until we got to my place.

And that's when it all changed. I turned into a maître d' and began to rattle off instructions as if he was my house boy.

'Dominic you wait here while I get the washing machine started and pack a few things. Feel free to help yourself to a coffee. Oh and Dirk doesn't know how old I am. I'd like to keep it that way.'

It was all straightforward as far as I was concerned. What could be simpler?

Dominic nodded with a smile as wide as his face and I began to wonder if he was just a little conceited. Either that or he knew something I didn't.

'How old does he think you are?'

Had this man changed or had I developed a new awareness of him? I paused at the entrance to the laundry. What made me think that Dominic wouldn't ask anything?

'I don't know what he thinks,' I replied as I began to toss towels into the front loader. 'Well no actually I think he thinks I'm his age.' I felt blood rush to my face so I hid it by digging into the laundry basket.

'Which is?'

Good grief the man never gave up. 'Forty-two,' I replied with my head inside the machine.

'I heard you say forty-two, right?'

I stood up, slammed the machine door shut, and measured the washing powder.

'That's right and if my boss thought I was forty-two I would still have a job. Oh how that makes my blood boil.' I let out a small grunt and turned the setting knob to a light cycle.

'I get that but about Dirk. You plan on telling him the truth when?'

Questions never felt heavier. My shoulders felt as if they were now carrying an entire load of wet towels.

'When it is time,' I stated decisively. I marched to the door. 'Dirk loves me but is it really your business Dominic?'

'What makes a time right Maria?'

He wasn't wavering. But did I have to answer all of his questions? I was feeling more off balance than the washing machine. I pressed the pause button and reset it to a heavy load.

'The right time is when it becomes too heavy to continue to rotate,' I mocked smugly. I closed the laundry door and leaned against it with my arms folded. I exhaled deeply. 'When he can accept it,' I finally announced.

'So there has to be a right time when someone who already says he loves you, can accept you as you are?'

I stood open-mouthed for a moment before bounding up the stairs to my bedroom, the question reverberating in my mind.

A time for someone who loves me to accept me as I am? The words traveled from my left brain where they sounded all very logical, to my right brain where they mixed with emotions and sent me into a fast spin. Where did Dominic think he was coming from intruding on my morning as if he were a telemarketer? Who placed a halo over his head? I picked up my overnight case, tossed in a few things, stomped my way down the stairs.

'Dominic I don't know. Do you get that? I do not know. Life isn't that cut and dried, not for me anyway. And I just do not wish to talk about it.' His eyes were turning into dark chocolate cooking melts, narrowing so they were small but still yummy. He deserved an answer. 'I just guess there is a time for everything,' I relented. 'Isn't that how it goes? A time for every purpose under heaven?'

He wasn't going to drop it that easily. 'And what is your purpose Maria?'

'My purpose? Oh Dominic, what are you talking about?' I gave my head a little shake as if I might wake up from a dream. I dropped my overnight case to the floor.

'Just wondering.' His raised his palms in front of his chest in soft surrender. 'Don't we all have a purpose?'

'Um, sure, of course we do and right now my purpose is to stop you from asking me these annoying questions.'

'Have you found your purpose in life Maria?' His face had taken on the aura of an ethereal being. I had to bring him back to reality. My reality.

'Dominic why are you asking me all this stuff? I have no idea what my bloody purpose is. I don't care what it is. It probably passed me by thirty years ago, knocked on the door when I wasn't home. I'm probably meant to be on a trekking expedition in Nepal or maybe I should be running a Buddhist institute in Moreton Bay. What's your purpose mister spiritual guru? No, wait, you've been called to take me to purgatory so I can suffer for all my wrongs, right?

Dominic laughed.

Oh how wonderful it was to have a man's laughter echo in the empty corners of my lounge room. My whole body softened at the sound of it. It was like the invigorating calm of a hot shower. If I could have bottled it I would have. I'd place it on my kitchen bench for the times I forgot that happiness still existed and open it when the nights were cold and lonely.

'Maria, I just mean . . .' He smiled. 'Don't you think you're setting things up for failure by lying to Dirk?'

'Oh we're back to Dirk? You haven't got a purpose either have you? How did I see that coming?'

Dominic got up from the couch where he'd been pontificating to me from behind a coffee mug. I kicked my overnight bag out of the way and strode to the kitchen.

'I've thought about purpose,' he said as he followed me. 'I think there has to be more to life than what I've found so far.'

I lifted the kettle onto the stove element. 'And what have you found so far Dominic?'

'What you've found Maria, the endless struggle to get to the top while others pull you down. A world filled with people stomping on less fortunate people. The absence of a higher purpose.' He stood in front of me.

I edged away a little. 'But you're successful in your job, you make a good income.' I popped a tea bag into a mug and poured boiling water onto it. 'And you're a very good friend.'

He dropped his gaze and I'm sure I saw a touch of child-like embarrassment.

'If you were any better a friend I could hire you out. I could start a business called Real-life Friends or Friends R Us.' I giggled as I dunked my tea bag up and down in the water. 'Dominic I'm not lying to Dirk, I just haven't blurted out my truth yet. Telling him my age might drive him away. I have to give him time to know me and love me first. You understand that don't you?'

Dominic gave me a look that typified an angel. It was soft yet firm. Understanding yet compelling. It was as if he'd been sent with a divine message and he was going to give me that message no matter what. I felt the pause before he answered me. That pause was like a living entity between us. It throbbed with the likeness of an approaching epiphany.

'Maria,' he purred. 'To know you is to love you.'

Oh where was a Kleenex when you needed one? I felt as if I was going to faint in the warm glow of his goodness.

'But Dirk can't know you unless you are open and honest with him, like you've been with me.'

I maneuvered around him with my mug of tea completely ignoring the fact that the teabag was turning the water into a black gully of tannin. My only defense was to take him back to the beginning.

'Tell me your purpose Dominic.' I slid along the couch.

He sat beside me. 'To make the world a better place,' he answered without giving it a second thought. 'And a part of that is to be here for you.'

I lifted my phone from the coffee table. 'Oh look at the time.'

I dabbed my fingertip to the corner of my eye and had to admit to myself that Dominic was one hell of a man.

As we drove to the airport I couldn't help but think of Dominic's words. Had he really said *to know you is to love you*? No one had ever said that to me before. I didn't even know if it was true. Or if it could be true. But as we got closer to our destination, my destination, my mind began to leave Dominic's presence and all his questions and suggestions behind and instead it filled with imaginings of what it was going to be like to be back in Dirk's arms.

To hear that accent again, to have it flow over me like cream over a hot scone. To have him tell me not to do something this way or the other like a policeman on duty, to laugh and joke with him, to have him touch me and the sheer delight of his kiss on my neck. I'd forgotten Dominic was in the car with me by the time I pulled into the car park at the airport and when he spoke I jumped.

'Would you rather I not be with you?' he asked sweetly.

'No of course not,' I answered, secretly wishing I could be more truthful and that I had not agreed to his being there in the first place. 'Dirk will love to meet you.'

The flight arrived on time but as usual it took an eternity for the passengers to come through Customs. When Dirk finally appeared my heart leaped into my throat and I felt all the old feelings stir within me until I was filled with adoration and empathy, love and tenderness, excitement and lust. He looked all Europeaned-up with his steel-blue shirt under an inky blue jacket over dress pants. His dark hair was cut very short so that I could see a cute little cow-lick at his hair line.

He saw me and I've never seen him look at me the way he did. His head was cocked to one side so that he was looking at me as if he were summing me up with a come-hither kind of expression on his face. He approached me with the walk of a man who was confident and sure of himself. I approached him carefully, aware that any kind of intimacy might embarrass his German privacy.

'Hallor,' was all that passed his lips but he couldn't prevent his smile or the happiness in his eyes from shining through.

I had to hold back from throwing myself into his arms, ripping his shirt off and seducing him on the spot. It felt as if I was trying to prevent myself from breathing and when I spoke it came out as a whisper. 'Welcome back.'

He had not yet seen that Dominic was with me so it was with much discomfort that I pulled Dirk to me and whispered, 'I have a friend with me. Dominic.'

Dirk's brows furrowed and he gave me a look that asked many of the questions I was asking myself. What did Dominic mean to me? Why was he here? Were we involved? What was I thinking? But as we walked to where Dominic was standing hardly more than a yard behind us, Dirk leaned forward and offered his hand. Dominic took it with eagerness.

Looking at the two of them gave me a feeling of perplexity. Was I not in control of what I was doing anymore? Why had I agreed to having my boyfriend meet my, well, boyfriend?

It was like one of those movies where you meet yourself in some distant time zone. That's what it felt like for me, that this self of mine who loved Dirk was meeting the other part of me that was fascinated with Dominic. If only we could put them both into a big vat and see if we could turn out a Dirkonic. Now that would be interesting.

'How about a coffee?' Dominic suggested.

'Ya,' Dirk replied wearily.

I knew there wouldn't be much to talk about, a few questions about the flight and some superficial banter but Dominic would be summing everything up.

I reluctantly agreed to put myself through more mental anguish in the knowledge that right after coffee Dominic would get into a chauffeured car with a little glowing sign on the top of it and be taken home.

Chapter 9

MY own ride to Dirk's place was like a personalized episode of *Millionaire Hot Seat* with me trying to answer a series of multiple-choice questions so as not to worry Dirk too much about my ongoing unemployment status or my friendship with Dominic.

'He is not a lover?'

'Definitely not.' I held my head high.

He accepted with a nod. 'How is the job finding?'

This was the million dollar question of course. Option A. Good but no job. Option B. Not so good but still looking. C. I'm never going to get a job, I'm too old. All of the options set me up for a tirade of why I have to be the best, like a German. So I couldn't answer except to ask him a question. What would you do if you were a fifty-five year old woman and no employer wanted you? But if I asked that question we were back to my dilemma of not having yet exposed that I was fifty-five. There was no other option but D.

'Job search is over.' I turned my head in his direction. 'Josephine says that Chloe-rose is getting that role set up. I should be able to move into it soon.' I felt terrible but how could I tell Dirk how worried I was? I was at my wits' end but he wouldn't be able to understand that. I fixed my eyes straight ahead.

'What does this mean? If there is no start date you cannot say you have this one.' Apparently he wasn't going to accept option D.

'You don't know how difficult it is Dirk,' I moaned. I rubbed my forehead and took a big breath. I'd made a mistake by making that remark and I quickly set out to fix it. 'Tell me about your trip, I can't wait to hear all about it.'

'It was not so bad,' he said, still trying to get his repertoire around the Australian expression *not too bad*. 'My mother, she is not so goot.'

'Oh I'm sorry to hear that, will she be okay?'

'Ya, I think so.'

The rest of the drive was silent except for the occasional instructions on when to put my indicator on or when to go a bit slower. There were a couple of comments about how I should have cleaned my car out more thoroughly and how surprised he was that I would not only drive barefooted but would also leave a spare pair of shoes on the back floor. Until we drove into his driveway. That's when I sensed jubilation inside of Dirk, a hidden excitement that he had not yet divulged. He almost bounced out of the car.

'It is goot to be here Maria, coom oon.' He held his arms out to me.

He had lost the German formality. He was back in his new homeland, the quintessential Aussie again, as much as he could possibly be. As I eased into his embrace, smelled his skin, kissed his neck, I felt nothing but the familiarity of his being, his essence, his remarkable distinct self. He held me as if there would be no tomorrow and I held him as if I wanted today to be eternal. I wanted to be with him forever.

'Let us go in, we get the bags later,' he whispered into my ear as he held my face firmly to his and breathed in my aroma. His hand caught mine as we walked up the backyard only dropping it to search for the house keys which he had pulled out of his bag at the airport and dropped into his jacket pocket. 'Where is the cat? I do not see this one.'

'The cat is a stray, maybe she lives at many places.'

The words had hardly left my mouth when the sweet sound of love purred and called us. I had a sudden memory of when I was a child and our cat brought a grasshopper to our doorstep and called us. We were the grasshoppers. She wasn't only welcoming us home, she was bringing us home.

'It is she,' Dirk bleated in his own cry of love. 'Coom, we get some food for the stray.' And before I could answer he had disappeared inside and was scavenging through an empty refrigerator. 'I am frong, there is nothink,' he called.

I laughed. 'It's not frong Dirk, it's wrong.'

'Frong is frong?' His brows were furrowed.

'Yes frong is wrong, wrong is right.'

'Maybe I get the longing life milk to put for her.'

'Dirk you make me laugh with your words.' Excitement had taken over and I was like a child at a Wiggles show. Everything he said made me laugh with glee.

He shook his head like a toy puppy dog. 'This is funny for you? Try the German, you can make me laugh,' he joked.

He took a carton of store-brand milk from the cupboard, pulled the tab and poured milk into a saucer. As he rushed through the back door he bumped into me with such a jolt that the milk made a fountain between us, splashed across our faces and came down on the front of our clothes.

'Sorry, apologize me,' he begged. And examining my face with a shy grin he repeated, 'I am sorry Aussie girl, coom oon, we clean up.' His hand went to my breast and he kissed my mouth with such intensity that I thought the milk might turn into cream and melt all over me.

'Wait,' I murmured as I pushed him away. 'Let's not rush, there's so much for us to talk about.'

'We talk later.' His other hand climbed under my shirt.

I squeezed around him and bounded into the cold kitchen which had lacked the vibrancy of our chatter and play for weeks. As I washed my hands and dabbed my shirt with a cloth I yipped with excitement.

'You need a shower after the trip and some food and you are probably dead tired.' I was rambling like a schoolgirl after a sex talk, a mixture of excitement and apprehension running wildly in my veins. If I'd stopped to think about it I would have recognized that my conversation with Dominic had left a measure of uncertainty within me and especially an air of tentative curiosity about Dirk and how he truly felt about me and where he intended our relationship to go. But I couldn't get a clear thought to go through my silly head.

Dirk took the saucer to the sink, re-filled it with milk and put it outside. He came back into the kitchen and pulled off his jacket.

'Okay, we can wait. I will have the shower and a beer. Maria you can find some dinner in the pantry? Maybe some sardines.'

I heard him chuckle as he went to the bathroom.

As mesmerized as I was by the idea of sardines, I suggested that I should go to Dynasty and get Chinese take-out.

'Goot idea,' he called before I heard the shower start.

I dabbed my shirt a bit more and fixed my lipstick in the reflection of my phone screen. As I went through the back door I flicked the laundry light off. In an instant of joviality I bounded back into the kitchen and wrote a note for him in German. *The light is off.* I stuck it on the fridge where he would see it when he came out of the bathroom. That would make him chuckle and as I imagined that, it made me chuckle.

By the time I arrived back Dirk had finished a couple of beers and had been dozing on the couch in front of the television. I'd left the backdoor unlocked for that very reason but when I walked into the lounge room with a plastic bag filled with containers he pulled himself out of sleep as quickly as if he was a child who had been caught napping on a stay-up-late night.

'Aussie girl,' he announced as I placed the containers on the dining table. 'While I am remembering this one. On the next Saturday we go to the restaurant with my friends.'

I recalled that this had been arranged before he left. It was the monthly get-together of the friend clan and this time I was invited. Usually it was on a Friday night either at someone's place or at the German Club straight after work. I hadn't seen the friends since the Australia Day party. I couldn't remember their names or what they looked like. I nodded and left the room to get plates and chopsticks. I returned with an extra spoon with which to dish out the food.

'After the party last time I talk to my friend Klaus,' Dirk continued as I began to distribute the beef and black bean sauce.

'And?' I spooned fried rice onto each of our plates and plonked myself onto the couch beside him. I passed him a plate.

'My friends think you are nice person.' He took the chopsticks I handed to him and tried to manipulate them to work.

'Cool.'

'But.'

'But vot?' My mouth was half full of rice.

Dirk was beginning to look like a zombie, a five o'clock shadow was turning into eight o'clock stubble and jet lag was setting in. I wondered if I should drive home after we finished our meals and leave him to sleep for a week.

'Maria,' he slurred. 'You have not told me your age, one of my friends asked me this one.'

I shoved myself down one end of the couch and pulled my legs under me.

'What business is it of your friends?' I could feel my face getting hot and it wasn't from the steam of the Chinese food.

'It is not for their business, it is for my business,' he answered.

Dominic's gentle reassurance crossed my mind, *to know you is to love you, Maria*. There was one thing about me that Dirk didn't know. Why was I so afraid to tell him?

'You haven't been concerned about this before Dirk.' I was stalling for time. My heart had begun to thump rapidly inside my chest. I cleared my throat. 'Why is it important now?'

I began to wonder if Dominic had whispered something or maybe he had slipped Dirk a note under the table in the coffee shop. The thought was ridiculous but it helped quiet my mind from wanting to rush from the room and drive home leaving Dirk to eat his meal alone.

'Maria it seems like you must be same like me but you have made the jokes sometimes that makes me thinks you are older.'

'And if I am? Older? Is it a problem?'

'Maybe it is, because.'

'Because what?' I felt like a bird trapped in a cage. Someone was getting up close and personal peering at me through the bars. They were bound to see the scaly mite on the ridge of my nose.

'Maria, what is the age?'

I felt a tingle of anger, a rush of dread, a cacophony of noises in my mind all shouting and declaring that this was not something I had to reveal, while simultaneously Dominic's voice came in right over the top of it all encouraging me to be truthful in my purpose. Even though every fiber of my being proclaimed that it was definitely not the right time to consider revealing the truth about my age to Dirk, purpose took over and before I knew what I was doing I plodded my way back to the kitchen for my bag, pulled my license from my purse, returned to Dirk and slammed it face down on the couch beside him. All the ironing out had now been done. All that had to happen was to see if I had used enough spray starch and had the setting adjusted correctly.

At almost the same moment that Dirk went to pick up the piece of plastic and turn it up to read my date of birth he off-balanced his plate and black bean sauce splashed down onto the floor. Getting my second wind and without much thought except for self-preservation, I quickly grabbed the license and popped it into my back pocket.

I resettled onto the couch while Dirk went to get a dish cloth. I could string this out a little longer if I tried. I smiled sweetly at Dirk when he returned to clean up the sauce. 'Dirk, my age is something we can discuss at another time.' I smoothed my hand across the top of his head as he knelt beside the couch with the cleaning cloth. 'You are jet-lagged tonight and I think we should concentrate on getting you fed and into bed.'

Dirk made a German-sounding grunt as he got to his feet. 'There is a problem with the age Maria, I know this one.' He walked down the hallway to the kitchen. 'You are older I think,' he called.

I got the distinct feeling that this was not going to be easy but by the time he returned I was a little more ready to relent.

'Okay, I am older than you are,' I confessed with dignity as he walked into the room. 'It's only by a few years though,' I quickly added. And there it was. I'd done it again. How could I ever take it back? If I had that bottle of Dominic's laughter I would have pulled it out of my bag and soothed myself into thinking that everything was fine. 'I am still me,' I said. 'I am still Maria, I am the same person Dirk.'

'Ooo.' It was a soft sound, the sound that usually made me gush with delight.

'It used to be coom oon,' I mimicked as he sat beside me. 'Now it's ooo?'

Dirk's lips had become that thin line he got when he was feeling proud, but this wasn't pride. This was dismay. He barely opened them to speak. 'This is not how it should be Maria. The man is always older than the woman in Germany, in all the places.'

I edged my way back to one end of the couch while he made himself comfortable at the other end.

'I can't believe you're saying this Dirk. I can't believe that I'm not more important to you than that notion. You are kidding me, right? You're being a Bogan?'

He smiled momentarily but he couldn't help the furrowed brow taking over. 'Maria let us not think about this one now.' He picked up the chopsticks and maneuvered them to the beef strips, poking and prying as if he was trying to find support for his beliefs.

'Can I help you with that?' I laughed as I picked up the food and offered it to him. 'So you think an age gap between us is not acceptable?'

'I don't know,' he replied sheepishly as he took the food into his mouth and began to chew. 'What do you think?'

'It hasn't stopped us so far.'

We didn't say any more. Sometimes words are not necessary. We both knew what each other was thinking. What we didn't say was more than what we could have said. I didn't want to admit it and I vigorously denied it to myself, but if I had looked closely I would have seen the writing was on the wall. Written in German of course. But to my mind it was all double Dutch.

By the time I got back from taking our used plates to the kitchen Dirk was in a deep sleep. I tossed a couple of blankets on him, sat quietly at his side for a moment. What I had to accept was that, although it had been there all the time, the age gap was now a gaping black hole in our relationship. And I was falling into it at the speed of light.

Dirk slept in. It was eight o'clock in the morning before I saw him with a beer in his hand. He made himself comfortable at the foot of the bed while guzzling from the can. I had been up early and had coffee while standing at the kitchen window. I watched the early morning bicycle trekkers, their bodies wrapped in red cycling jackets, their heads protected by backward-pointed helmets. They looked like little splashes of color against the gray background as they sped by.

Sometimes I felt as if I was pointed in the wrong direction. Sometimes I felt that no matter how I tried to go forward something was pointing me backwards. I was always looking back wondering why things weren't the same anymore. I'm not sure how long I stood there sipping my sachet cappuccino reflecting on my backwards slide. I do know that I gave thought to a million other things as well. Topmost in my mind was Dirk.

No matter how I looked at it, my relationship with Dirk was like hot salty popcorn. It had a backdrop of mystique and intrigue, romance and action. I could have taken him to any movie and felt right at home. And it was the most calming, inspiring relationship I had ever known. It was as if we'd come together as ice-skaters, did a tap-toe jump and before I knew it we were pair-skating in perfect synchronization. It was magnificent. It was sheer delight discovering my way with Dirk. I came to the conclusion that I would not let my own fears trip us up. I was making the age issue bigger than it should be.

If Dominic was right about anything, it was that I had to be accepted for who I was. And regardless of Dirk's initial reaction, he did accept me. He loved me and was the most attentive man I'd ever known. Dominic had his own reasons in trying to sabotage my relationship with Dirk and I couldn't let that happen. Dirk supported me and although he had found it difficult to comprehend the issues that had arisen in my job, he had rallied for me. He had expected me to be the best and believed that I could be.

After my coffee, I had returned to bed where Dirk lay sleeping having shifted from the lounge room during the night. I was tired, restless and cold. Dirk's body was hot so I had snuggled myself into it and nestled my head onto his chest. Before I knew it I'd dozed off. Next thing I knew he had disentangled himself from my clutches and acquired a cold beer which he was holding against my thigh.

'Goot morning Aussie girl, you slept well?'

'Get that cold tinny off my leg. You should not be drinking at this time of the day.'

Dirk's face lit up. 'You do not like this one?' He rubbed my leg warm, reached over and kissed my cheek. He sighed. 'It is goot to be back.' He pulled himself to the other side of the bed and leaned against the wall.

'Tell me everything,' I urged. 'Did you get the divorce stuff sorted? What happened?'

He dropped his eyes to the beer in his hand. 'My wife, she is not available for me.'

'Oh.' My voice echoed disappointment. 'What will you do?'

'It is okay, I can get a divorce without her, you know this one. But I wanted to be sure.'

'Of course.' I lowered my gaze. 'You love her.'

'Nor, it is not love. Love is not somethink I think of. But we are together a long time, since we are fourteen. And after that nineteen years marry-ed. I want the twenty anniversary, this is important for me.'

I pushed myself up on my elbows. 'The anniversary is important? Dirk there has to be more to life than order and the way things should be.' I released my elbows and hit my forehead with dramatic flair allowing my head to fall back onto the pillow.

'I am German.' He did the nod.

'Yes, but Dirk.'

'But it is over,' he admitted. 'I will not see she again.'

I saw a tear escape the side of his eye and my heart mourned with him. I loved this man so much that I would have done anything to convince his wife to come back to him. I just wanted his happiness however that might come about. I envied the loyalty he had for her. I felt that any woman who received that kind of loyalty was blessed with gold from heaven. It was something I'd never had and I couldn't understand why a woman would let it go. They'd grown up together. They were set free together, discovered the world together. I felt Dirk's grief. And I felt sure that his loyalty was as much to the life they had shared behind the Berlin wall as it was to meeting the marker of a twentieth wedding anniversary.

'Tell me about your mother,' I whispered.

'Soon it will be she's birthday.'

'Her.'

'Her birthday. She will be seventy-five.'

'That's not so old.'

'This is very old. In Germany everyone die younger, in Australia people live longer. Tomorrow it is Saturday, you can talk with me on the Skype to my parents.' He chuckled. 'Of course they do not speak English and you do not speak German so it will be short conversation.' He tackled me on the bed, us both laughing.

'Nein.' I growled playfully. 'Ich spreche Deutsche.'

Dirk chuckled. 'You do not speak German.' He edged his way across the bed and went to his wardrobe. 'I want ride my bicycle now before the morning is too late.' He slid into black bike shorts.

'Every time we start a conversation you want to do something else.'

He pulled a jersey over his head, leaned over and planted a kiss on my mouth. 'It will be a short time.'

I sat up and pulled the blanket around me. 'I have a movie night with Julia tonight and Josephine asked me to dinner tomorrow. I won't see you until Sunday.'

'I must ride the bicycle today, I am not fit, I have been sitting on a plane for long time.'

My phone had been ringing out for a couple of minutes. Dirk went to the kitchen and came back with it stretched out in front of him. He handed me the phone, pointed to his helmet and back-nodded toward the door.

I did a thumbs up with a sigh.

'Josephine?' I answered. 'What's up?'

'Maria, Dominic has done it.'

'What has he done?'

'He got you a job. He just called me from work. He's been on the phone about it this morning. He was a bit shy about ringing you when you are with the German.' She laughed. 'Meet us for lunch.'

'As it happens I can, but what if I'd made plans?' With Dirk's aloof departure and Josephine expecting me to run at the drop of a hat I was beginning to feel that anything I wanted just didn't matter.

'Oh please Maria, I know you do nothing more than either sit at home or at the German's place. That reminds me, Dominic was full of you when he called. And he's met the German I believe. Mmm, interesting, two on the run, you devil.'

'It's not like that Josie,' I objected but she was speaking over me.

'Johnny Dominic Depp.' She squealed down the phone. 'Didn't I tell you he's the best?' 'I'm working at the Redcliffe office today, be here at twelve.'

My entire body screamed with the uncertainty of what Dominic could have landed for me but I groaned and said, 'okay.'

I rushed to the back door but Dirk had gone. I gathered my things, sent Dirk a message and headed home in the weak winter sun. Could it be possible that Dominic was right about identifying your purpose? If so, surely mine had to be not to waste any more time. I had to get out of my own jet lag. But what job could he have landed for me?

Chapter 10

JULIA was keying a message on her phone when I got home. She was on the couch wrapped in her bright yellow throw with her feet tucked under her. Her hair was in a low ponytail which was partly hidden under the wrap. I was struck by the resemblance she bore to her father. It was the ridge of her nose or maybe it was the way she twitched her mouth. I was there too in the pale skin of our Irish ancestors.

It had been a long time since I'd looked at her with the eyes that saw her in that moment as she sat completely oblivious to my presence in the room. There was an aura of child-like beauty and peacefulness about her. It was like watching an angel taking rest from play. I used to watch that angel every night when she was a child after I tucked her into bed.

There were text books lying all around her looking as if they were waiting patiently for the moment when she would snap them up and begin reading. Her laptop was perched precariously at the corner edge of the coffee table.

'Hello darling, I'm home.'

'Hey,' she answered without looking up.

'How's everything?'

'Okay.' She still hadn't looked at me.

'Okay, that's good.' I turned to go to the kitchen.

'We found a place.'

I turned back. Her eyes were locked on the screen of her phone.

'Jamie got approval just now.' She jumped out of the yellow glow and did a little dance around the couch.

'Julia, where is it?'

'It's in Brighton,' she shrilled as she flopped back to the couch and picked up the laptop. She tapped on the keys. 'Come here, you can see it on real estate dot com. It's a two-bedroom apartment, fully furnished, three hundred and thirty dollars a week.'

'Julia? A week? How? I mean seriously, how can you and Jamie afford that?' I stood behind the couch and looked over her shoulder at the picture of the little apartment that was actually one half of a house which had been tastefully renovated.

'Jamie is working full time as of last week, Dominic got him a job at his work. He can complete his degree part time. And me?' She swung around to look at me. 'I got a job at Aldi supermarket. I start next week. And I'm going to study part time as well.' She let the laptop fall softly to the couch. She got to her feet and squealed as she jumped up and down on the spot.

I was astonished. 'Dominic? How did all of this come about?'

Had I completely underestimated my daughter? And Josephine? And Dominic? Obviously.

'Lots of conversations,' she replied. 'Josie got Dominic sorted and Jamie had to prove he could do the work. Jamie and I had lots of disagreements about it at first but finally we agreed how to do it all and voila.' Julia was dialing on her phone. She looked up at me and put her finger to her lips.

As she began the conversation with Jamie I went into the kitchen riding on her excited voice until I came to the back door which I slid open. I stepped outside and closed it behind me. A juvenile butcherbird was perched on the railing of my veranda practicing its call. We exchanged a reciprocal *I'm here in peace* look and it remained where it was, apparently glad of the company. There would be a parent bird nearby I guessed, watching its young take on its social role, learning how to fit in, how to get along in the world. It was growing up.

I wiped at a tear dripping down the side of my face. How could I cope with Julia leaving home? I missed her just for the two weeks she had been away. How could I live without her? Would this be the last time we ever lived together? As I broke down into a sobbing mess the bird took flight across the backyard. I followed it with blurred vision. How I wished with all my heart that I had Julia's father by my side. It wouldn't do me any good but it was the way things should be. Julia was leaving. Did you hear that bird? Julia. Leaving home.

Julia found me outside twenty minutes later pulling tiny weeds from the row of potted geraniums along the retaining wall. I had dabbed my eyes dry with my sleeve and found my gardening sunglasses so she didn't witness red and puffy eyes. She skipped up behind me and put her arm around my shoulders. How lovely it felt to have her warmth beside me.

'You don't mind if I take a rain check on our movie night do you Mum? I've got to go meet Jamie and get some paperwork signed. After that we're going to the apartment right away.' She let out a little squeal. 'We will get to keep the keys. We might sleep there tonight in our sleeping bags.' She clapped her hands together like a two-year old.

I stopped the clapping and held her hands in mine. 'I don't mind at all sweetheart.' I kissed her cheek and embraced her small frame. 'I just want you to be happy and I want you to know I accept your decision to move out. I love you Julia.' We walked to the door together and she scooted off as if she'd just won Gold Lotto, leaving the couch covered with the yellow throw. It looked like a giant broken egg yolk.

I had to accept that I was now an empty-nester. Oh how I hated that label. As if I was some kind of hen or old chook or butcherbird mother. My nest was empty. I walked into my lounge room and looked around. Indeed it was a nest. I'd preened it and plucked it and collected all kinds of little tidbits for it and now it was going to be empty. The reason for all my preening and collecting was going to be gone. What purpose would I have any more to continue to live here? Of course Julia would be back to pack and get all her things but in my mind it was already a done deal. She was gone. The baby bird had flown and mama bird was left alone to peck the leftovers on the back veranda.

I called Dirk and let out most of my feelings to him about it, but he was matter of fact. Julia was an adult. At that age he'd been an adult for six years. Fourteen was the age of consent in Germany when he grew up. I knew that and it wasn't what I wanted to hear from him. I wanted someone to stop her. Stop her. She couldn't leave. She just couldn't. It wasn't that I was afraid to be alone. It was that I loved her with all my heart and I would miss her with my entire being. Dirk was more interested in the fact that I was being offered a job. It wasn't good that I was feeling depressed. I should pull myself together and focus only on getting the job, he told me. I reluctantly agreed and promised him I would be at his place Sunday morning.

It was five to twelve when I pulled up outside Josephine's work place. I'd spent the entire morning feeling sorry for myself after Julia left. Every step I took seemed to ring with the silence of her impending permanent absence and every beat of my heart sounded a descending note.

Dominic's car was parked on the street. My down-trodden heart did a little flutter when I saw it. What was it fluttering about for goodness sake? I was not interested in Dominic. Apart from his beautiful features which he probably inherited from one of his parents and which he added to through his superb taste in dress, his loving, empathic and sensitive attitude towards others and his ability to be the most real person I'd ever encountered, what was there to admire? I sighed. Nothing else attractive about Dominic at all, I chided inwardly and let out a bigger sigh. Surely Dirk had all of those attributes? And more.

Before I could get the key out of the ignition I saw Dominic heading up the path towards me. I let out another sigh, only this time it was laced with lust. *Oh get over it,* I whispered to myself but as he strode toward the car and waved his hand in a high five then lay it across his heart, I felt myself tremble. Was it possible that he'd become more attractive since yesterday at the airport?

'It's a bit cold out,' I heard him say as he opened my door.

I eyed the black jacket, and the blue scarf he had around his neck. I pulled my own scarf more securely as I got out. Josephine was behind him and before I could say anything they had piled into my car with Dominic in the back seat.

'Maria get back in,' Josephine instructed. 'Drive. Down by the bay to Margate will do nicely thank you. That's where Harold is meeting us for lunch.'

'And Harold is?' I started the engine.

'Chloe-rose's dad, he's working at Redcliffe office, your new boss.' Josephine laughed. 'Or at least he will be if you impress him.'

'You said Dominic got me a job.' I looked at Dominic in the rear vision mirror. He gave me one of his magical smiles.

'He did.' Josephine swung around to Dominic. 'Didn't you tell her you've been helping Harold set up his new data base Dom?' She eased back into the seat. 'Don't worry, all you have to do is smile, act intelligent and answer his questions.'

'I can act intelligent,' I chortled as I drove off. 'Look at me, I'm with Bonny and Clyde, what isn't intelligent about that?'

'Maria you are the most intelligent person I know,' Dominic commented.

'Same,' Josephine agreed.

I laughed. 'But you're both liars.'

Dominic sighed. 'That hurt.'

'I was joking Dominic.' I screwed up my face and glanced at him in the rear-vision mirror. He winked at me. Wasn't he being just a little too try-hard?

'Dominic was joking as well,' Josephine said.

'No he wasn't, he thinks I meant it. Dominic has some kind of belief that I should be perfect.' I redirected my glance to the back seat. 'I'm not perfect Dominic,' I called, my eyes darting from the road to the rear-vision mirror and back. 'I do really bad things sometimes. And I'm old.'

'Oh Maria don't start with the old thing again,' Josephine snapped. 'Give it a rest.'

'I don't think I'm in the mood to meet my future employer Josie. Ring Harold and tell him I got run over by a bus.'

'You'll do no such thing,' Dominic chided but it was too late, Josephine was dialing.

'Okay', she dramatized. 'See if I care.'

'Girls, girls,' Dominic begged. 'Josephine give me that phone. Maria drive us to Margate please.' He reached his hand across the back of my seat to my shoulder. 'Maria is something wrong? I've never seen you like this before.'

'What could be wrong? Except for the fact that you helped my daughter's boyfriend get a job and now she's moving out.'

'Julia's going to be okay, don't be upset.' A quick glance in the rear-vision mirror confirmed he was being sincere. Just the same I ignored him and turned up the air conditioner.

As we drove, all that could be heard was the sound of hot air streaming through the air vents. It was stifling but it was easier than the hot air of tension between us all. As I pulled into a car park beside the beach where Dominic indicated for me to stop, we all exhaled at the same time.

'Maria, I'm at your side right through this,' Dominic said.

Josephine nodded in agreement as she swung around and slapped Dominic's knee. 'Isn't he fantastic?'

I didn't need Dominic to bolster my ego if that's what Josephine was thinking. 'You don't have to be by my side Dominic.'

But the two of them were out of the car and had already begun to cross the road. I was talking to myself.

Harold was sitting at an outdoor table directly across from the bay. The first thing I noticed about him was the sheen on his bald head. The second thing was the occasional little tufts of fuzz up there shining in the midday sun. But what really stood out about Harold was the inverted smile. It looked like the unhappy smiley face I used on my phone to let Julia know when I'd had a bad day. He stood up as we approached and pushed a couple of chairs out from the table.

Dominic introduced me with his arm lightly touching my waist. 'Harold, this is Maria. Maria, Harold.'

'I've heard a lot about you Maria.' Harold bowed slightly as we shook hands. 'First from Chloe-rose.' He looked at Dominic. 'But I have to say that the glowing report Dominic gave me finally pulled me in.' He looked back at me. 'We do have more work on and Dominic's been helping us with the data base for a couple of weeks.' He slapped Dominic on the back before beaming a smile in Josephine's direction. 'And of course Josephine is one of our prized legal secretaries.'

Harold and I dragged our chairs across the pavement to the table. Dominic and Josephine went to order and little old me was left to do the talking.

I smiled. 'I'm very appreciative of your time Harold.'

'No problem. What will you have?' Harold got to his feet.

'I've got it,' Dominic called as he returned to the table.

Harold patted him on the back and re-settled in the chair. I got the feeling that Dominic had ingratiated himself almost to the extent of being like an adopted nephew. It seemed there was nothing Dominic could do that didn't impress Harold. By the time we had finished our meals Harold had complimented him at least a hundred times.

'Maria I'm going to be on leave for a few weeks,' Harold told me. 'Why don't you come by the office on my return or sooner if you like. I'm sure Josephine won't mind showing you the ropes.' He smiled at Josephine before looking back at me. 'Bring your resume and we'll introduce you to Loretta. She's our HR team in Redcliffe.' Harold chuckled with a little snort. 'You can work out a suitable start date about a month from now, in our Redcliffe office of course.' He pushed his chair back and got to his feet. 'Did I mention it's only part-time?'

I stood up and we shook hands. 'Part-time is perfect.' Our handshake was friendlier this time. 'Thank you Harold.' I gave him my broadest smile.

We watched him cross the road and stroll along the path beside the beach.

As I dropped back into my seat Josephine let out a squeal. 'You did it kiddo.' She slapped my back. 'All thanks to our beautiful Dominic.'

I turned to Dominic. 'Thank you.'

'Maria I didn't do anything, you sold yourself, your background and skills are brilliant. All I did was remind him of your existence. It was Josephine who supplied your CV.'

Josephine's voice lilted through the sea air. 'Oh Dominic you're so modest, Maria owes you big time.'

I let out a small self-conscious laugh.

'It's true,' Josephine added. 'Chloe-rose and I have been trying to get you a look-in for the entire time we've been working for Harold. Nothing.' She tapped Dominic's knee. 'Until this sun god came along.'

Dominic pushed out from the table. 'More coffee?'

'Why not?' Josephine checked her phone. 'There's still time.' She looked from Dominic to me and back. 'Or would you guys prefer to be alone?'

Dominic left to get the coffee without answering. I followed him with my gaze until I thought he was out of earshot.

'Josie I wish you wouldn't keep pushing Dominic toward me.'

'I'm not pushing him, he loves you to bits and he's so wonderful.'

'He doesn't love me.' I heard a tut of disapproval escape my lips.

Josephine held her hand to her forehead and exhaled. 'He does and you are a very lucky woman to have his attention. I couldn't get him to look at me if I did a head stand on the table stark naked.'

'You make it sound like he's some kind of Greek god. He's not a Greek god.' I laughed loudly. 'He's a geek god.'

Dominic returned to the table as my words were being uttered. 'Sounds like I should go, I don't want to be where I'm not wanted.'

'No Dom,' Josephine soothed. 'It's not like that. Maria doesn't know what she wants.'

'How can you say I don't know what I want? How can you two keep making decisions for me? I'm so embarrassed. You said we were having lunch but you've brought me to a job interview. I'm in jeans for goodness sakes, does no one care about consulting me?' I fumed.

'You look great,' Josephine said and turning to Dominic she reiterated. 'You're wonderful Dom, Maria should be grateful.'

'I'm sure she is but I'll leave you girls to it and catch you later, I've got to get back to work.' He strode up the road without another word.

'Look what you've done Maria.' Josephine smacked my hand where it lay on the table. 'You've upset him.'

'I didn't upset him, he's a big boy, let him go sulk if he wants to.'

'Maria, I just don't know what's wrong with you. The man is a hero. He got you that job and you are nothing but an ungrateful little twerp.'

'Josie it's not that I'm ungrateful, it's just that Dominic seems to be pushing himself into my life. He even got Jamie a job.'

'That's because he's such a wonderful man. A wonderful man who happens to be in love with you.'

'You don't listen to me do you Josie? You never listen.'

'What do you want me to listen to Maria? More of your moaning and complaining? Life has just thrown you the most beautiful man in the world and you're still hanging out for a stupid German.'

'Dirk is not stupid. He's a loving man and I happen to love him in return and it's not about hanging out. Why doesn't anyone care what I want?'

Josephine gathered her bag. 'Got to get back to work. I'll walk, it's not far. Oh and cancel that dinner tomorrow, we just caught up, no need for any more catching.'

'Okay by me,' I replied.

But she still hadn't heard me and that made me feel as if my world was beginning to unravel. Helping me get a job was one thing but respecting me and accepting me for who I was and how I felt, was quite another.

Chapter 11

IF I'd given more thought to it I would have been conscious of the fact that Dominic deserved more than a mild thank-you from me. I wasn't trying to act like a spoiled brat. It was just that at a deep level I felt something was wrong. Something was not quite right. Something, by golly, was amiss. It stood out like a surfer on the two-inch waves of Moreton Bay. But why was no one else seeing it?

The thought of Dominic being so considerate and empathetic intrigued me. Didn't he have any faults? But maybe it wasn't Dominic. Maybe it was Josephine trying to control my every move. Or maybe it was my own defensive attitude. Whatever I had intuited at that lunch meeting was small in comparison to the despair I was beginning to feel about Josephine and Dominic and the way they were trying to manipulate my life. Until I could get them to understand that I didn't need them to help me out at every step, I was going to keep coming across as ungrateful.

I decided to find out a bit more about Dominic the Wonderful. I would go to see him after dinner. I messaged to let him know I'd be there about eight and to SMS his address to me. But first I wanted to talk to Josephine.

Josephine was surprised to see me. She gave me a look that said more than hello. It was *hello what do you want?*

'Hey,' I chirped. 'Whatcha up to?'

She threw her head back and placed her hand on her almost non-existent hip. 'Who wants to know?'

I did a mock surveillance behind me and turned back to her smiling. 'I think it's only me asking'.

'What makes you think I'd want to see you?' Her hand was still on her hip but her head had tilted to one side.

'You're a friend aren't you? Shouldn't friends come with benefits? I need the benefit of a friend to talk to.'

'And what benefits do you bring with you?' She dropped the hand from the hip and put both hands on the door to open it a little.

'I make really good coffee.'

'Get your ass inside.' She swung the door wide.

I followed her into the lounge room. 'I'm here to say sorry. It's not that I don't appreciate all the effort you and Dominic have made. I do. Very much.'

'Good to hear it,' she replied. She started toward the kitchen. 'Coffee? Tea? Or . . .'

'Me?' We both laughed at the ritual we had created at our morning tea breaks at work.

'Certainly not you,' I sneered good-naturedly. 'Tea thanks and remove the tea bag after three dunks, I've had enough tannin for the week.' I was at her heels.

'What's that supposed to mean?'

'Oh me and Dominic having tea. Josie, he said some pretty heavy things, he was talking about having purpose and he said that to know me is to love me.'

'And your point is?'

'I don't know where he's coming from Josie, it baffles me, it scares me, it makes me want to run.'

'It should make you want to get laid woman, what is wrong with you?'

'You see, that's the point, I don't know what's wrong with me, if there is anything wrong with me that is.'

'Oh there is,' she quipped as she dropped the tea bag into the bin. She put some milk into my tea and pushed the mug across the bench to me.

'Thanks,' I said. 'Josie ever since I lost my job, well ever since I turned fifty to be honest, my world has somehow seemed to become grayer.'

'You color don't you?' Josephine quizzed as she eyed the roots of my hair.

'Ha ha, be serious. Everything is tainted by an aura of either rejection or a help-me-out kind of attitude, I don't know what's real anymore.'

'Oh nothing's real, you can count on that.'

'It's like people are expecting me to lose my independence, like I can't make decisions for myself.'

She laughed. 'You can make decisions, they're just bad ones.'

'Josie I'll be fifty-six in a few months' time and then sixty is on the horizon. It's as if life is coming at me like a bull to a red flag. And it's angry.'

We'd been talking across the kitchen bench and Josephine's kitchen bench was only about a yard long. The entire kitchen was only a couple of yards square but it was homely. Josephine had decorated it with the style that she loved. Coziness. Warmth. And color. We collected our mugs of tea and carried them to the lounge room. Josephine placed her mug on the coffee table and threw herself into her cushions on the couch. I followed suit and sat in an armchair.

'I don't know what to say,' she announced. 'If what you say is true, it's a bit too scary. Am I adding to your world's grayness?'

'I'm sure you're not meaning to.'

'Good come-back, so I am?'

'I don't know Josie, life isn't like it used to be.'

'I grant you that but maybe it's not meant to be.'

'We used to travel along like there was no tomorrow. Well now there really is no tomorrow or very little of it.' Josephine raised her eyebrows.

'I mean do you realize that I have thirty years left if I'm lucky? I used to have fifty years, sixty years.'

'Thirty years is a long time old girl, oh sorry.' Josephine pushed under her glasses and clipped the ridge of her nose with her finger and thumb. 'Sorry about that slip of the tongue.' She readjusted her glasses and looked at me intently.

'I am old Josie. And thirty years left of what? People treating me as if I'm a child? Like I'm no longer useful? Or wanted?'

'Look I know I joke about it but you're not old, not even close,' she answered. 'Come on, brighten up, you've just got a new job. You know how it goes, don't worry, be happy.'

I looked down at my empty hands. 'I can't get a spark of excitement up about Dominic landing me that job. I'm grateful. I'm relieved about the income.' I looked at her.

'But it's not my life, it's not who I am. I'm not sure I want to work in a legal office again after everything I went through.'

'You sound like a teenager who doesn't know what she wants to be when she grows up.'

I nodded. 'Exactly.'

Josephine laughed tentatively. 'Oh Maria, what can you do?'

My phone sounded at that question.

Josephine pointed in the direction of the phone as she pulled herself up. 'Get it, nature's calling me anyway.'

When Josephine returned I'd finished my tea and was leafing through her Violin Music booklet.

'Anything happening?' she asked.

'It was Dominic.' I sighed. 'He can't see me tonight, he's busy.'

Josephine let out a raucous laugh. 'You were going to see him?'

'I wanted to drop by and thank him.'

'And he's too busy for you? Now that is something.'

'No it's not, I didn't give him much notice, it's nothing.'

Josephine continued to laugh. 'Dominic too busy for Maria, can't you see, you silly girl?'

'See what?'

'He's playing hard to get. Oh Maria, you are so naive and he knows it.'

'How is he doing that? I don't understand.'

'If he's not available your interest might increase.' She was laughing raucously.

'He's probably got a luscious date,' I said.

'See, there it is.' Josephine's laugh was mixed with a snorting sound.

'Don't be ridiculous. I'm sure Dominic has many women in his life.'

'There you go.' She guffawed. 'I bet you have never given that a thought before.'

'Josephine stop it.' I fumbled with the music booklet and stacked the sheet music back onto the coffee table. 'I really don't know what Dominic does with his life.'

Josephine was red in the face laughing. By the time I'd returned after taking my mug to the kitchen I was sure she'd have another nature call to attend to. She was pissing herself laughing.

Sunday morning was like any other day except for one thing. My conversation with Josephine the previous night had left me wondering why I didn't see things the way she did. But the fact was that she was probably more interested in my getting together with Dominic than I was. Or so I'd thought before I started thinking about his life. Her comments had opened up a plethora of fantasies about him. At the same time I was excited to be going to Dirk's place and looking forward to delving more into his experiences and especially his plans. I wanted to be a part of them. He was the man for me. I decided to leave for Dirk's early. There was no reason not to as Julia had not returned.

When I got to Dirk's place he was in riding gear maneuvering his bicycle from the laundry. He strapped his helmet on as I walked across the grass toward him.

'Goot morning Aussie girl.' His smile was as welcoming as a sunrise on a frosty morning. He put his arms around my waist as I stood in front of him, kissed me and gently tapped the helmet to my forehead.

'Hello, looks like I'm on cue to have some quiet time.'

He did a little bounce of his head from side to side. 'You do not mind this one?'

I smiled. 'No, go ahead with your ride.'

'You can help yourself to anythink.' He pointed in the direction of the house. 'There is bread for toast.' He grinned as he swung one leg over the seat. 'But I do not have the Vegemite.' He chuckled. 'I will not be for a long time.' He pushed forward and gave me a small wave.

I closed the door behind him, went into the cold kitchen and watched through the window as he rode down the road. It was too early to ring Julia so I resigned to doing it later. I made coffee and took it with me into the bedroom where the morning sun was desperately trying to force its warmth through the gap between the curtains.

I placed the mug beside the solitary photo on the nightstand, dropped my bag and jacket onto the bed and pulled the curtains wide open. I positioned myself at the bed's end where the rays were the strongest, pulled a pillow to me and a blanket around me.

Instantaneously my gaze was drawn to the picture of Dirk's parents and I found myself studying the young couple who were sitting on the beach, their backs to the photographer. They were in their early twenties when the Berlin Wall went up, Dirk told me the first time I picked up the photo. There was a poem his mother used to tell him as a child. Translated it was something like *behind the wall is a spark of light*. I hugged him and made my own rhyme *hold it fast, hold it tight*.

I quieted my mind and allowed it to wander, pushed aside all thoughts of Dirk and Josephine and Dominic telling me how I should be living my life. I couldn't remember the last time I allowed myself to be calm and my mind to be free. And that's when I saw it. It moved towards me as a fine mist might across a plain. But it wasn't mist. It was light. I wasn't afraid or concerned. I was settled in the peace it was bringing to me. I was in awe as the mist of light enveloped me. I felt love, I saw my inner beauty. Tears ran down my face as I recognized my worth. Then as quickly and mysteriously as it appeared, it was gone and I dozed in a light and peaceful sleep.

An hour later, feeling fully refreshed I was about to make my second coffee. I had decided to delay ringing Julia. I had a rare sense of personal freedom, a sense of exquisite peace and beauty and I wanted to rest in that as long as I could. As I took a mug from the cupboard I noticed through the kitchen window that the cat was making her way to the back door. I swung the door open to see her perform her usual display of affection for Dirk.

'Wie gehts Aussie Girl?' Dirk greeted, his eyes deep pools of blue in a red and hot face dripping with perspiration.

'Wait.' I hushed him and went outside. 'You're asking me how things are going, right?'

He leaned the bicycle up against the house and kissed my forehead solemnly. He followed me inside, took a knob of sausage from the fridge, commenced to cut off small pieces. 'Your German is goot, where did you learn this?'

'Wait, let me think of the answer first. Ich. Gut. Mein Deutscher Mann.' I was beaming with pride as I poured coffee into the mug. 'I'm more than a pretty face,' I scolded jokingly. 'Not to mention I have browsed *Reverso* more than once and memorized a few things.'

Dirk smiled and placed the sausage pieces at the back door, brought the bicycle to the laundry and headed to the bathroom. He was back within minutes, water dripping down his face as he briskly rubbed his hair with a towel. He swung the towel around my waist and pulled me to him. It felt so good to laugh with him. Kissing me gently he then withdrew the towel and took a beer from the fridge.

I sat at the kitchen table. 'Isn't it too early for beer, Deutscher Mann?'

'Do not think too deeply about this Aussie Girl,' he replied as he sat opposite me. 'You are worried about this again?'

'Just observing.'

'You cannot worry about this one.' He spoke as if he hadn't heard me. 'I am German.'

'I know.' I tried not to sound sarcastic. 'And Germans like the beer.' I smiled.

A hint of anxiety had settled on his face. 'There are some thinks you do not understand about the German.'

'Like what?'

He stood at the sink and looked through the window, his back to me. He observed a car drive past before dropping his gaze. It was an unusual pose for Dirk and it made me feel uneasy. He turned to face me.

'There is somethink I have not told you.'

My hunch was correct. There were things on his mind. I studied his face for signs of what he was about to reveal, waited silently for him to continue.

'Yesterday.'

I sat very still. 'Yes?'

He returned to sit at the end of the table. 'I was on the Skype with my father.'

I folded my hands in my lap. 'Of course, your commitment with your parents every Saturday afternoon at precisely two o'clock.'

'It was bad news for me.' Tears welled in his eyes. 'My mother, I told you she is sick.' He wiped his eyes with the back of his hand, fumbled around in his pocket.

I sprang from my chair and in one bound I was kneeling in front of him, peering into his face, my heart reaching out to the grief I saw there. I rested my hands on his knees as he wiped his eyes and rubbed his nose with a handkerchief.

'She is dead,' he mumbled. His vacant stare focused straight ahead. I got to my feet and stood at his side. As I encircled him with my arms he continued as if I wasn't there. 'She is died after I leave.' He used the handkerchief to muffle the guttural sounds of his sobbing. 'I did not know she would die.'

All I could think of was the young woman in the photograph, the woman on the wrong side of the wall. 'I am so sorry,' I finally whispered as I sat down. 'Why didn't you call me?' I reached my hand across the table. He patted it briefly and sat up straight in his chair. I withdrew my hand.

'It is okay,' he declared stoically as he tucked his emotions back inside of his chest. 'I can accept this one.' He got to his feet, cleared his nose one last time and returned the handkerchief to his shorts' pocket. He sat back down.

Overwhelmed by his show of emotion and stunned by how quickly he had stashed it away, I excused myself and went to the bathroom where I gathered my thoughts and tried to settle my feelings. Dirk couldn't possibly know how I'd admired his mother in the photo. He couldn't know how deeply I felt for his loss and I couldn't begin to think how to express that to him. I felt disengaged, as if I had become an intruder. I felt as if I'd walked into the middle of his mother's funeral service. No one knew me.

He was still at the table when I returned.

He looked at me with a vacant stare. 'You are different than me Maria.'

'Pardon?'

The intent written on his face struck me with such force that I would have laughed at his ensuing words had I not known how serious he was.

'Maria the vacuum cleaner, you leave this one out of the cupboard. The light Maria, you leave it on all the times. All the thinks, we are different.' He stood up and got another beer out of the fridge. 'When I am with you it is okay.' He sat back down. 'But when I am not with you I think all the times, we are different. You are Australian, I am German.' He stopped for a moment before continuing. 'Before my separation everythink was perfect, I had a perfect marriage.'

'A perfect marriage?' I scoffed. 'That's ridiculous, the idea of a perfect marriage ending is simply ludicrous.'

'Ludicrous? What is this?' He gave me that perplexed look and I felt the usual rush of tenderness.

'I mean it's simply not believable that a perfect marriage would end.'

'It was perfect,' he insisted forcefully. 'We lived in separate place when I work away but when we are together in one place, everythink we do is organized. She does the cooking, I do the yard. If it is cold she knows I will have the heating perfect, I know she will have a meal for me, it is a perfect marriage.'

'You've been separated for three years, how is that perfect?'

He continued his monologue as if he hadn't heard the question. 'Everythink must be in order for me, everythink must be perfect.' He looked at me sternly. 'Maria I cannot see for us a future, you are older.'

'Dirk what do you mean?' I was sure I hadn't heard him correctly.

'I think of this all the times. I cannot jump about my shadow, we have no future.' It was like we'd discussed this topic many times before but if we had, I certainly hadn't been there.

'What are you talking about?'

'For we.'

'Us?'

'Ya, us, we cannot be together. You are old, you are different than me Maria, we have no future, we are different.'

His utilitarian words produced an echoing effect in my mind. They sounded like a roll call in a German prison but there was only one name he was calling and it was mine. And what was following my name was the list of wrongdoings I had committed. But he could have stopped at the word *old*. That word had struck me most painfully. He had plunged it into my heart and he could never withdraw it. It had crushed me more than anything he could have said. I would never forgive him. He continued to speak as if I wasn't there or maybe he wasn't talking about me. Maybe he was talking about someone else, someone whom he didn't love, someone whom he didn't call the color of his life, the best friend of his life. But it was my name on his lips.

I was shrouded by a feeling of detachment. His words fired across my mind. They felt like blood trickling down my forehead. It was as if I was lined up in front of a firing squad but the wall behind me was fast becoming a wall between us and I would soon be imprisoned on the other side of it. The reality of that was like the beat of a large drum inside of my head. The atmosphere was surreal, as if I wasn't present or I was witnessing someone else go through the spectacle. The thought of the mist of light which had come upon me and the peace it had left me with were gone and I had forgotten the excitement I'd had at wanting to tell Dirk about it. I could only hear his words and think of what they meant for me. For us.

He launched himself from the chair and marched to the window. He stood with his back to me, his posture rigid and still, not at all like the man in whom I'd seen so much gentleness. He turned to face me and it was there, I was sure I could see a flicker of it, the love he had for me but it was fading fast and as he spoke, it was as if he'd never known me.

I looked down at my hands in my lap. 'But we have been so close,' was all I could manage to stutter.

'It is true.' The tone of his voice sounded as if he'd uncovered a hidden truth that was nonetheless obsolete. 'We are very close, I have not had this before in my life, I am not close like this to anyone.' He did his usual pledge nod. 'But I cannot jump about my shadow.'

I bolted from the table and stomped into the bedroom. I tossed my things into my bag: my toothbrush and make-up bag that had fallen out, my jacket lying on the end of the bed, my mobile showing a missed call from Julia. I picked up the long empty coffee mug and returned with it to the kitchen.

'If that's how you feel then fine,' I spat as I dropped the bag and kicked it across the floor to the door. I washed the mug vigorously knowing that he would inspect the results for perfection. 'I'll be leaving now.' I sounded like a termagant even to myself. I gathered the bag and threw it over my shoulder.

He swung to face me from where he had gone to stand at the back door. His face had the surprised look of a child caught stealing from a cookie jar. 'Nor you cannot leave, I want not hurt you, I love you.' He came to me and took me into his arms. 'Maybe I make a mistake, let us talk.'

As the true meaning of *keeping your options open* hit me, I winced at the impact of his self-centered insight. I grasped for some respite from the confusion of his pointless backtracking. My mind was reeling from his pendulous emotions. I knew he'd been drinking but that was commonplace. It could not be blamed for instigating what he was doing. I was confused and torn and the headache pounding at my temples compelled me to want to take my exit.

'I said I'm leaving,' I shouted. Tears were stinging my eyes but I wouldn't release them, not in front of him.

I calmed myself. 'I'm sorry to hear about your mother and I'm sorry that you feel this way about us.' I looked at the floor. 'I didn't know any of this.'

I walked around him toward the still-open back door where I'd left my sneakers in keeping with Dirk's no-shoes-inside-policy. I plunged my right foot into my shoe and easing my foot in with my toes I stuffed my index finger between my heel and the back of the shoe and pulled it on with the laces still tied. As I did the same with my left foot I was sobered by the thought that not untying my shoelaces was probably one of the things on the we-are-different list. My chest tightened and I felt heat spread across my face and down my neck. I flicked hair from my forehead as I righted myself, took a deep breath and exhaled with an audible sigh. I held my hand to my brow. My anger had begun to subside but it had been replaced by a trace of hideous darkness.

I took one last mental picture of the colorless kitchen, eyed the note I had written in German and left under the energy-rating sticker on the fridge.

'Let's not do this,' Dirk said. Tears were streaming down his face. He came to me, stroked my head and combed my hair through his fingers. 'I want not do this, we must talk, I make mistake.'

'No,' I barked and swung away from him.

The cat scrambled into the shrubs as I stepped outside. The world was a reflection in a carnival mirror. I swayed under the light weight of my bag as I stumbled toward the car trying to see through blurred vision. Inside my bag the phone was ringing as if it was the last song playing at the end of a sad movie. I ignored it. My thoughts were scattered, my emotions overwhelmed. I couldn't help but wonder how I had managed to write that note on the fridge in German. Nothing came to my mind at that moment that triggered a memory of those foreign words. It was ridiculous to be considering it. All I could think of were the jokes and laughter and how leaving a light on by mistake messed with Dirk's head. Now I realized it was a part of what had destroyed us and the laughter had been folly. I was a fool. I felt like an adolescent who had made an inappropriate comment at her grandmother's funeral. But it was me who was the age of a grandmother, me whose life cycle was entering winter. Why had I thought I could find love at this late stage of my life? Why had I been so immature? So stupid?

I tried to recall why I had come to love Dirk, tried to think of all the reasons I'd used to explain it to Josephine at different times. But to explain why I loved Dirk was to try to explain inspiration. It was to try to explain what conduction is, how light, sound, emotions are transmitted. I hadn't begun to understand it until Dominic talked about purpose.

As I took the last step toward the car I noticed that Dirk was behind me. He reached for me and spoke with the German accent I had grown to love.

'I feel me sad, please Maria we must talk some more, it is my fault.'

It wasn't a comprehensive statement but there was some truth in it.

His face was the color of the stainless steel kitchen sink I had just washed my mug in. His eyes were set in dark circles. 'Maybe I make mistake,' he repeated.

'It's no one's fault,' I lied as I felt my anger return. 'Give me time to think. I will contact you.'

'Whatever you take for decision I will accept.' He stood straight, as if he was a leader at a G-20 Summit.

I threw my bag into my car, got in, slammed the door and gripped the steering wheel until my knuckles were white. Releasing a puff of breath I started up the engine, shoved the gear stick from park to reverse, swung myself around in the driver's seat and backed out of the driveway. I was conscious of Dirk standing on the footpath as I accelerated and drove off but I didn't glance back. Even though there was so much I wanted to say, I don't think I could have found words to describe my pain.

Tears streamed down my face to such an extent that I had to pull over two blocks away to wipe them and blow my nose. As I rummaged through my things for a Kleenex my phone rang again. I looked at the screen. It was Dominic. That's when feelings of guilt and irresponsibility rose up to strangle me, the thought that here was someone who cared for me as much as I cared for Dirk. But I think what scared me the most was the anger I felt towards myself. Mixed in with it were confusion, shock, and desperate, desperate sadness. I found a dead tissue in my bag and pressed the answer key dabbing at my face with traces of old blotted lipstick in the process.

'Maria?

'Hi Dom. Inic,' I croaked. I cleared my throat.

'Maria are you okay?'

'Yep.'

'You are not, where are you?'

'I'm driving home.'

'No, don't drive. Tell me where you are.'

I ended the call after giving a description of my whereabouts. I couldn't read the street signs for a few minutes but finally was able to get it out. When I put the phone down I broke into a sobbing mess. I was doing it again. Packing heartache into my already wounded world. Would it ever stop?

Chapter 12

HE stood at my car door looking down at me through the closed window as if I was a child asleep on its mother's knee. But I wasn't asleep. I had lowered the back of my seat and was curled up in the fetal position in a trance of sadness and never wanting to come out of it. The morning sun was performing a warming ritual over my body. If there was a god of poor decisions I would be the perfect human sacrifice.

As I became aware of Dominic's tender smile and understanding eyes peering at me, my tears started up again and I began to sob into the inch-square of Kleenex that was left in my hand. Dominic pointed to the door handle. I yanked myself up and released the lock button.

'Maria.' He pulled the door open. He put his arms around me. 'What happened? Are you hurt?'

I shook my head as I stretched the flimsy scrap of tissue in front of me. Dominic left the door ajar and dashed to his car returning with a small pack of Kleenex. He handed me the packet and crouched beside me.

'Has something happened to Julia?'

I shook my head as I pulled the tab off the Kleenex packet.

'Jamie?'

I shook my head and pulled a tissue free.

'Then what is it?'

I blew my nose and dropped my head. 'Get in Dominic,' I whispered.

Dominic came around to the passenger door and got in as I returned my seat to its rightful position.

'Maria, I hate to see you like this.'

'Yes I must look a fright,' I teased half-heartedly.

'You know what I mean.'

I nodded and blew my nose again. 'What can I say?'

'You don't have to say anything, it's Dirk isn't it?'

I swung around in my seat to face him nodding in quick succession. 'Yes,' I blurted like a seven-year old just caught out for not doing her homework. 'Dominic I'm a fool.'

'A fool with a big heart if you are a fool at all, which I think not.' He brought my head to his shoulder. 'Come on, he's not worth crying over.'

'Yes he is,' I objected defiantly. 'He is still someone I love, no matter how much he's hurt me.'

Dominic smoothed my hair with his hand and lifted my face to his. 'Are you going to be okay driving? I'll follow till you're home, okay?'

I nodded. 'But I need to be alone after that.'

He smiled with a knowing look.

After all my efforts to convince Josephine that Dirk was the man for me, the thought of facing her with the truth of what he'd done left chills running down my spine. If real-life drama was what Josephine was looking for, I could serve it up as a smorgasbord. Just choose which variety of drama you would like. Workplace bullying? Here, have some salt to rub into the wounds. Unemployment? Peanut butter sandwiches are a specialty. What about being ditched by a boyfriend? A bit of relish with that? Ageism? Good old yoghurt has calcium for the bones dear. No, Josephine could wait. What I really worried about was how I was going to convince Dominic that I would survive. Alone.

He saw me home safely but for the next week his messages pinged my phone every few hours. I let his phone calls go unanswered. I was into the second week when I began to think that if I didn't invite him around soon I might end up with the police knocking at the door checking to see if I was okay.

But I had to be able to pull myself out of bed first. Not that I was in bed. The couch had become both my day time and night time base. It was waking before midday that was the real challenge and it was the end of the second week before I could do it. That was the same week that Julia and Jamie turned up with one of Dominic's friends driving a ute to move Julia's belongings, which consisted of a nightstand, comforters, sheets and pillows, suitcases of clothes, DVDs and books and her favorite yellow throw. Her childhood toys lay scattered and rejected in her room after she left, having been extricated from the wardrobe and abandoned. Shoes and bags had taken priority.

I plonked myself down with Julia's old toys and we cried together. The warmth of the bedroom had disappeared with Julia and the toys and I were left cuddling into each other for body heat. It wasn't until I opened my eyes staring into the face of a Barbie doll that I snapped myself out of self-pity and began to tidy up and make plans for my own immediate future. Like getting some decent sleep and eating more than toasted crumpets and drinking beverages other than instant coffee.

How I felt about Dirk hadn't changed. I understood exactly where he was coming from regardless of the fact that he'd been so unbelievably blunt and hurtful. I knew the grief he was feeling. I could get his confusion and need for everything to be just right. Order was in his blood. It ran through his veins like a current in a stream. Nothing was going to take it out of him. You could take the man out of Germany but you couldn't take Germany out of the man. He'd joked with me about that many times. I had told him I'd be in touch and I would be. Just as soon as I got my head around the emotions of it all. But that was going to be easier said than done. My emotions were beginning to resemble a volcano. I was smoldering beneath my soft surface and it was only a matter of time before the deep grumblings and rumblings became an eruption.

But long days wearing nothing more than the charcoal onesie Julia gave me for my last birthday and a set of black socks which Jamie had left in the laundry gave me the dubious luxury of being able to sleep all day or mope around occasionally on some housework. If I'd been any quicker at it I would have been mistaken for a hermit crab.

I'd made Dominic promise not to tell Julia or Josephine that I'd stopped seeing Dirk and so they both thought I was still living the high life at his place in Wavell Heights. Nothing could have been further from the truth. I was living as a low-life in my own home. I was so low that I could have made a groundhog jealous. It could have been Groundhog Day for all I knew. Every day was the same: onesie, socks, crumpets and coffee. I was totally oblivious to the world outside of my door.

Every now and then I'd pop into Julia's bedroom to check on the kids. They all looked pretty sallow in there but Barbie Doll was definitely ruling the roost from where I'd placed her on the bookshelf. She reminded me of Ursula a bit, the vacant stare and plastered smile hiding her evil desires. She could have been plotting my demise for all I knew. There wasn't much depth but there was determination in the way her hand reached out toward me. I left the room feeling certain that I was now officially insane.

I finally took a Dominic call one afternoon when I couldn't remember what day it was. I'd seen the morning news on television but I was becoming confused and was beginning to think my name was Truman. Was it good morning? Was it good afternoon? Or was it good night? I didn't know.

Maybe it had all been set up. Maybe Ursula was working her way to me through that little blonde doll. Maybe the doll was really a troll and she'd worked a doldrums spell on me.

Thinking about Ursula took me back to the root of all my problems. My age. That ache in my back wasn't from twerking. It was from tweaking. I'd tweaked it during a feeble attempt at vacuum-cleaning. When I looked in the mirror I noticed that my face was sallow. My eyes lacked depth. My brain was AWOL. I needed help desperately. And it was Dominic's voice that finally brought some sanity into my thoughts.

'Maria are you listening?'

'Hmm? Listening to what?' I replied with lackluster.

'Can I call around?'

'A round what?'

'Maria can I come over?'

'Over where?'

It took a minute but I finally got my faculties back and pretended I was lucid. 'I've been meaning to invite you over for dinner,' I murmured by mistake.

Dominic's angelic nature flew at the opportunity. I hardly had time to change from my onesie into something more comfortable before he was at my door.

He arrived in the speed of light filled with the radiance of a cherub and the exuberance of a nine-month-old Labrador and carrying a few garden-picked flowers and a bag of apples. I had to command him to sit just so I could cook and serve the dinner.

But obedience was not one of Dominic's traits. He flitted around my kitchen looking for cutlery and napkins and candles and matches, running back and forth to the dining table like a waiter. By the time we sat down I felt as if I'd gone back to being Princess Kate. Camilla was not in sight and Prince Jamie's black socks were back in the washing basket. But it was after dinner that I began to understand how seriously worried about me Dominic was.

'I could stay in Julia's room,' he mumbled under the napkin as he wiped his lips.

'Stay? Why would you want to stay?'

'You need me to stay Maria.'

I got up from the table. 'More coffee?'

'I'm fine,' he replied as he finished taking our dishes to the kitchen. 'But you're not fine Maria, let me stay with you?'

I began to stack the dishwasher, jabbed my hand with a knife, stepped to the sink.

'It's fine,' I reported before Dominic could dial the emergency hotline. Blood hadn't even been drawn.

'Let me do this.' Dominic commandeered the dish cloth. 'We don't need the dishwasher, go and sit down. Maria have you looked at yourself in the mirror lately?'

'Yes and after they cracked I ordered new ones. Seven years of bad luck times three mirrors,' I joked. 'And probably the sum total of my remaining life,' I added sullenly.

'You've lost weight,' he noted without a smidgen of frivolity.

'If I've lost weight we should be celebrating.' I picked up my glass of wine from the dining table, placed it on the coffee table and flopped onto the couch. 'Please don't worry about me Dominic.'

'If I don't worry who will?'

I let out a burst of breath. 'Is that why you worry? Because no one else will? You really do think I'm a loser.'

He swung around from where he was elbow deep in washing up bubbles. 'I didn't mean it that way, I mean Julia has left.'

'Oh yes, Julia, now that is a worry.'

'She and Jamie are doing fine.' He rinsed off the plates and cutlery and stacked them in the dish drainer.

'Fine? They are too young to take on such a commitment. They should be at home saving their money.'

He pulled the hand towel from its hook. 'Now that's being over-protective.'

'You'd know about over-protective-ness,' I slurred as I sipped the wine. 'I'm not your daughter and you're over-protective. You're so over-protective that it's a wonder you haven't left little notes on my doorstep telling me how to look after myself.'

Dominic laughed loudly.

I wanted to bottle it again. As I couldn't, I tried to keep it rolling. 'You're so over-protective that if I received a present in the mail you'd want first dibs at the bubble wrap so you could wrap me in it.'

His laughter sounded throughout my house.

'You're so over-protective that you could be the poster boy for Over-protective Friends Anonymous.'

He came into the lounge room as if he was riding the crest of a wave.

'You're so . . .' but he had plonked himself beside me and had his hand over my mouth.

'You're just trying to hide the fact that you want Julia back desperately,' he teased.

'I do miss the smell of nail polish remover and books spread across the couch.' I finished off the wine. 'But most of all I miss her hugs.'

'I can fill that need. Here give me that glass.' He took the glass from my hand and put it back onto the coffee table. 'Lie back.' He lifted my legs onto his lap and pushed my sandals from my feet.

I obliged tentatively, wiggling my backside down till I was comfortable.

Dominic grinned as he rubbed his hands together and rotated my toes. 'That's some movement, do it again.'

'Those wiggling movements are reserved for special moments,' I rebuked playfully as he held one foot and then the other and rotated my ankles slowly.

'And this is not one of those moments Maria?' He walked his thumbs back and forth over the soles of my feet.

I'd closed my eyes and was falling into the bliss of relaxation as he began to massage the balls of my feet.

'It's a moment for sure,' I replied in between sighing ahh and aww. 'But I'm not sure if it's one of those.' I giggled as he slid his hands up and down over my entire foot.

'What does it take to make it one of those moments Maria?' He glided his thumb all the way up my shin.

I inhaled deeply. 'Just massage my foot you overprotective man you,' I cooed.

It was midnight when I awoke. I know that for sure because I'd inadvertently set my phone alarm to midnight instead of midday, the time I actually wanted to be woken up. I looked across at Dominic. He was sound asleep at the other end of the couch, the foot massaging having come to its own toe-curling but sleepy end.

'Dominic,' I whispered. 'Wake up.'

He groaned and snorted like a normal man. Maybe he wasn't an angel after all. He opened his Depp eyes.

'You take Julia's room. Go on, it's fine,' I relented.

He silently helped me up from the couch, put his arm around my waist and kissed my neck.

'Let's get you to bed first.' His hot breath in my ear sent shivers down my neck.

We stumbled up the stairs, giddy from the wine and the seductive whispers and I led him to my bedroom. As I opened the door and stepped inside, a feeling of loneliness engulfed me. I hadn't noticed it as much before because except for my soiree with Barbie Doll and Ken after Julia's departure, I'd pretty much stayed downstairs where the loneliness had disappeared into the background, disguised by the television set which I'd kept on twenty-four seven just so that I didn't have to listen to the voices arguing in my head about whether it was my fault or Dirk's that it hadn't worked out between us.

Dominic must have felt me tense. He went into the room and began pulling back the bed covers.

'Don't worry, I'm not going to seduce you,' he assured me.

'That's a shame,' I murmured as I followed him in and tossed the cushions to one side.

'Did you say what I think you said?' Dominic asked quickly.

'No I didn't.' I laughed. 'But do you know what? I'd like your company and after all, we have shared a bed before, even if it was with two others.'

Dominic laughed. 'You don't have to ask twice.' He pulled his shoes and socks off.

When he dropped his pants and stood in front of me in boxers and shirt I gave a little gasp. As he unbuttoned his shirt to reveal his toned and sun-bronzed chest, the gasp turned to a shudder so I whisked off to the bathroom to do my teeth.

When I returned he was flat on his back under the covers.

I slipped under the blankets next to him fully outfitted in my paisley PJs and cozy socks. 'You know you've never told me much about yourself.'

'What would you like to know?' His voice lit the darkened room.

'Oh I don't know, just tell me stuff, pillow talk.'

'Okay let's see, I was born in British Columbia Canada to a Jamaican father and an Irish-Australian mother. Arrived in Australia at the age of seven weeks. Grew up in Brisbane in a suburb called Virginia, rah rah rah, nothing interesting.'

'It's all interesting.' I pushed myself onto my elbows and looked down at him. 'I had no idea you had Jamaican blood in you. I don't know why I had no idea, it's where you get that beautiful skin.' I snuggled back to the pillow. 'What else?'

'Met Claire when we were both teaching, we were married in our twenties, she died of leukemia two years later.'

'Oh I didn't know.'

'It was years ago, never re-married. I gave up teaching and got into IT. I spent the next ten years trying to figure out what to do with my life.'

'Have you figured it out? What to do with your life?'

'I had a son with a woman I lived with for a while, she took off with him when he was five, ten years ago now.'

'That's sad.'

'Yeah it is. Anyway I went interstate and spent some time volunteering with homeless people in Melbourne. When I moved back to Brisbane I got involved counseling young fathers who were trying to get custody of their child. It wasn't usual for a father to have a court order for a child fifteen years ago but now family law pushes for shared custody.'

I turned sideways to look at him. 'I had no idea about your background.' I rolled onto my back. I had to admit to myself that I had been very lax in getting to know this wonderful man who had come into my life.

'Tell me about you,' Dominic whispered.

'Me? Well after Julia I would've liked to have another baby but our marriage fell apart. I just got on with life after that and that somehow didn't result in re-marriage.'

'You were born in Australia?'

'Yep, born here. I have a sister, Rosemary and two brothers. I don't see any of them.'

We lay quietly for a moment and I gazed into the darkness lulled into relaxation by Dominic's company. I drifted in and out of a light sleep comforted by his gentle breathing, calmed by the warmth of his body beside mine, carried away by the connection I felt with him.

'You know how you talked about purpose?' I finally whispered between one of my naps.

'Mmm.'

'Did you mean doing things for others?'

'Not really, I meant doing something that means something to you without fear of what others think. Without losing your truth or succumbing to indifference. Kind of like what you did at work. You stood up for your truth and how you continued with Dirk because you loved him, regardless of what criticism Josephine held out.'

'I hardly think what I did with Dirk could equal what you've given society.'

Dominic turned onto his side facing me. I could feel his breath on my ear. 'We give what we are able to give. I know what you've been going through, I know what it did to you to lose your job the way you did, how devastating it's been for you.'

I slid onto my side. Our faces were barely visible in the dim glow of the street light which was squeezing its way through the curtains, but I could see enough to know we were eye to eye. Our breaths became one and when we spoke it was as if our words melted between us.

'I didn't realize it, but all this time I've been hiding my grief, behind my love for Dirk, behind my flurry of job interviews.' I reflected quietly for a moment. 'I didn't want to face it, I didn't want to cry alone, or be alone but over the past couple of weeks I've had to do both. When you spoke about purpose it touched something inside of me. At first I thought you were some kind of new-age do-gooder. I cringe at what I was thinking. I was waiting for your flaws to show.'

Dominic sighed. 'Don't worry, I have flaws, more than the average.' He laughed quietly.

'But I was convinced that it was you who was on the wrong path.' I paused. 'Now I recognize that I don't even have a path. My feeble efforts to get work were undermined by my own fears of aging. You had to go get a job for me because I couldn't do it.'

'You have to try to see life as it really is, Maria.' I could sense he was beginning to doze, he struggled with his words. 'Instead of seeing it in the way you decide it is.'

'What do you mean?'

There was silence.

'Sorry, are you asleep?' I couldn't bear the thought that he mightn't explain what he meant.

'No, I'm awake.' He wriggled to get comfortable. 'I didn't have to get you a job because you couldn't. I got you that job because I could. Simple. What you've got to understand Maria, is that life is like a tide, it washes the shores at different times for different people. It's about the journey, not the destination, unless you believe in heaven.'

'I don't know what heaven is.' I rolled onto my back. 'Do you believe in anything after death Dominic?'

'Haven't given it much thought, still trying to figure life out but I know one thing.'

I waited.

'It's all good until emotions come along and mess with our minds.'

My eyes widened. 'You amaze me Dominic, how wrong I've been about you.' I rolled back onto my side to face him. 'Hey why are we whispering?' I giggled.

'Because this is a moment,' Dominic whispered as he touched my face. 'And I want to keep this moment.' When he kissed me my entire body came alive and I had to ask myself if friendship really was what I wanted with this Jamaican-Canadian-Aussie, this *dinky-di* as Josephine had so wrongly labeled him.

I sighed. 'Let's sleep, moments are best treasured sometimes.'

He kissed the tip of my nose and slid down in the bed and planted a kiss on my belly-button that was peeping through the gap of my buttoned top.

I let out a light squeal.

'It's okay.' He lifted himself over me and kissed my forehead before flopping back to the bed beside me. 'I'm just making sure you still have what it takes. From the reaction I got I'd say you do.'

We giggled for a while before I dozed off in the sheer delight of what lay in store for me if I was ever ready.

Chapter 13

THE morning light brought with it the throb of a headache. It could have been the wine or the lack of sleep leading up to my night with Dominic. It could have been my sadness over Dirk. It could have been the extreme hunger I was feeling. Or it could have been caused by a million other things. All I knew was that it was there the moment I woke up. The heaviness of my head felt as if someone had sat on it all night while I slept and I don't think that would have been Dominic because I recall waking at one point to see his back to me and hear his snoring fill the room. I felt dull and nauseous and not at all like I'd felt as I'd dozed off to sleep with him at my side whispering about special moments. I rolled over and forced my eyes open.

The space beside me was empty. Maybe I'd dreamed the entire evening up. Maybe I'd finally gone over the edge and could now officially announce that not only was I insane but I had moved into the realm of split personality. Or even bi-location. Was my doppelganger over at Dirk's place right now living a separate life? Or was it down by the bay where it should be, pounding the footpath to get its lazy muscles working? I didn't know. All I knew was that the *me* that was in my bed was alone and confused. Not a Dominic in sight. It would have been easier to comprehend if there had been a sound, but there was nothing. Not a toilet flushing, not the sound of a fly being zipped. Nothing.

I rolled out of bed and steadied myself on my feet. I rubbed at my forehead trying to quell the throb. There's nothing quite like an empty bedroom when you're expecting to see someone in it. It almost screamed at me with its silence. It made me feel as if I was in the *Twilight Zone* only it wasn't twilight. It was . . . What was it? I fumbled for my phone among my clothes in the ensuite and couldn't find it. I remembered I had a bedside clock but that was no use, it had been turned off the last time there was a storm power-failure. There was nothing else I could do but pull myself together and open the curtains. That was a mistake. I was almost blinded by what looked like the midday sun. Was it midday? I was desperate to relieve myself and barely made it back to the bathroom where I sat in exquisite release for what seemed like an eternity.

Downstairs it was no different. The place was deserted. But clean. That was a refreshing change. That's when I saw an array of florist-created yellow roses on my coffee table. My second mistake was to say out loud, 'what the fuck?'

A voice from my back veranda answered. 'Hello?'

I dashed to the sliding door. 'Dominic you're still here.'

He looked up at me from his laptop in bemused delight. 'How are you?'

'I'm okay, looks like I slept in.'

'It does look like that.' His face glowed with amusement. 'You slept through an entire day and night, it's Tuesday.'

I closed my mouth and eased myself into a chair beside him.

He slid around to face me. 'You've been sleeping for almost two days.'

'That's impossible,' I spluttered.

'Evidently not.' Dominic laughed as he got up. 'You must have needed it. I've been here the whole time keeping a close eye on you.'

'It must be true.' I shuddered. 'I'm starving. But aren't you meant to be at work?'

'I do most of my work at home these days.' He nodded in the direction of the laptop. 'I went home and got my stuff and I've been at it since. Now let's take care of that hunger for you.' He went through to the kitchen and opened the pantry doors. 'I did an online order and I've put your groceries into your pantry, what would you like? I have croissants, there are plenty of eggs and bacon.'

'All of the above.' I rubbed my stomach. 'What about the roses? Are they from you too?'

Dominic raised his eyebrows. 'I wish they were but I'm afraid not.'

I headed to the lounge room. 'Then who?'

'Before you take a look Maria, there's something else you should know,' Dominic called after me.

I stopped in my tracks. 'There's a bomb attached to them?'

'Of sorts.' He looked at me with an expression of bewilderment. 'You had a visitor while you were playing Sleeping Beauty.'

'A visitor?'

'You go have a shower and I'll make lunch. What's it called at midday? Brunch? And I'll tell you everything.'

It was two o'clock before Dominic finished explaining everything to me. That was probably because my response reactions fluctuated between stopping to eat and drink, dealing with emotions of anger and dread, confusion and disgust, sadness and surprise. Sometimes all at once. The thought of Ursula being on my door step made me feel sick. It took several attempts by Dominic to convince me that it wasn't just a nightmare he'd had.

I couldn't help but think of how much Ursula had hurt me with her push to have me out of the team, how much she'd changed my life and left me at the mercy of my later years. Her discrimination and bullying had stolen not only my job but also my income, my future, my reputation, my very soul. And now she had actually stood at my front door? I was horrified.

By the time Dominic uttered his last comment I had eaten everything he had put in front of me and asked for more toast and coffee. And I was holding the card that came with the roses tightly in my fist unfolding it every now and again to re-read the words.

Maria please contact me, it's important. Ursula.

'Okay,' I reiterated. 'Let me go over this again. First the flowers arrive. You think they're from Dirk and want to throw them in the bin before I see them, right?'

Dominic lowered his eyes and grinned. 'Then Ursula turns up at my door? Seriously? Have I got that right?'

Dominic nodded. 'She wanted to see you. I told her you were unavailable for a couple of days. She asked if you'd received the flowers and she wanted to give you an envelope.'

'Right.' I acknowledged with a nod. 'And that's the envelope?' I was pointing to a manila envelope lying on the coffee table beside the florist's display. And it's about?'

"I questioned her as much as I could, she said it was about the Crime and Misconduct Commission. About a complaint you put in. Evidently it was lodged the week after you left.'

'I didn't do that,' I insisted.

Dominic shrugged his shoulders. 'I told her I knew nothing about it. That's all I can tell you Maria. Open it, take a look.'

I hovered my hand above the envelope. Time stood still as a million thoughts traveled across my mind. If I opened this and found that Ursula was taking me to court or suing me for I couldn't think what, it would be the end of me emotionally. I'd faced enough, been through enough, cried enough. It was time for me to get my life back. If that was ever going to be possible. The last thing I needed was contact from Ursula.

I picked up the envelope and slid my fingers under the sticky tape that held it closed. I pulled it open and pushed the envelope wide so I could peer into it. There was a letter addressed to me and signed by Ursula. I slid along the couch beside Dominic, pulled the letter out and held it for us both to read but I read aloud anyway.

'*Dear Maria,*' I announced with a puff of air. '*I'd like you to understand that my actions while you were employed at South State Legal were not actions I took without direction from senior management.*'

'Yeah right,' I mocked before going on.

'*I was under extreme pressure to manage my budget more effectively. I was given no choice but to bring my team to self-management without the assistance of an administration assistant. I can't begin to express in a letter how sorry I am for what happened as a result.*'

'Nothing like how sorry I am,' I interjected. 'But let me read on Dominic.'

'*I understand that you lodged a complaint with the CMC after you left. I have decided to go to the Chief Executive Officer with my concerns about what happened to you as a result of pressure brought to bear on me by Felix. Because of the widespread discrimination and bullying within the organization I am going to need support.*'

I looked up at Dominic. 'I didn't lodge a complaint.'

'Keep reading.'

'*I am writing to apologize for what you encountered and to ask your support. My private phone number is on this letter. I would be happy to hear from you soon. I hope you like the roses and accept them with the sincerity and good cheer with which they are meant.*'

I put the letter onto the coffee table with the envelope. Dominic raised his eyebrows and nodded to it. I picked it up and passed it to him, folded my legs under me and pulled a cushion to my chest. I felt in need of more than the support Dominic could give me. This was completely out of his league. He understood nothing of what either my previous workplace or Ursula was like.

Dominic scanned the second letter in the envelope which was a copy of my complaint to the commission. 'What are you going to do?'

I pulled myself up. 'Josephine, that's what I'm going to do, she has an answer for everything.'

Dominic went to the kitchen and came back holding my phone. 'There is one more thing.' He tossed the phone my way.

'Why not?' I sniped as I caught the phone with two hands. 'Apparently it's a chocolate day. Do I know what I'm going to get this time? Is it crunchy? Or is it soft? Please tell me it's soft.'

Dominic's eyes held an understanding gaze. 'Dirk.'

'Now that was priority mail,' I panted. 'What about Dirk? Did he turn up at my door too?'

'Not quite.' Dominic nodded toward my phone with a grin. 'Check your missed calls, I think you'll find there are about a hundred.'

I jumped to my feet in delight. 'Now it's a toss-up between Josephine and Dirk. Who should I call first?' I exhaled heavily. 'Probably best to get things out of the way.' I looked at Dominic.

'Josephine,' we said in unison.

'Let Dirk wait,' Dominic said. 'You need time to think about what you're doing with him.'

I thought I detected a slight weight towards negativism in Dominic's voice but I could have been wrong. I'd been wrong before about those types of things. My own thoughts were that I needed time to think about what I was doing with Dominic. But he was right about one thing. I still had to face Dirk and to do that I had to make the decision about whether or not I was going back to him. That decision was best made after I rid myself of Ursula.

It was as difficult as thumb-tacking jelly to a post to get Dominic to leave. He kept on sliding right back in. He didn't want me to be alone and refused to leave until Josephine arrived after work. When she was securely inside my house the two of us laughed and pushed him out and shut the door behind him only to have him turn up on the back veranda knocking on the glass door. When that hilarity died down he gathered himself up and agreed to go on the condition that I would stay in touch to let him know I was okay. Josephine's eyebrows were raised almost to her hairline at that.

'What are you going to do about him?' she gasped the moment we heard his car accelerate. 'I hope his GPS works because that man is lost in you. I bet he shows your picture around just so that he can prove he's met an angel. If he was any more in love you'd have to extricate him with dynamite. The man has lost his dignity over you Maria, you have to do something.' Josephine's words flowed from her mouth as if she was a teacher scolding a class of ten-tear-olds. Her eyes widened. 'Or have you already done it?'

I laughed. 'No, it's not like that with Dominic.'

'You want to make a bet?' She started to make coffee. 'Now what is the important thing you want to tell me about? Speak to me woman.' She poured boiling water into our mugs.

'Ursula has been here.'

Josephine's brow furrowed. 'That narcissistic perpetrator was here?'

'She wants me to support her complaint to the CEO about Felix being a bully and she probably wants me to withdraw my complaint to the Crime and Misconduct Commission. A complaint which evidently was about her.' I raised my eyebrows and shrugged.

'Evidently?' Josephine carried our two mugs into my lounge room. 'And you never told me about your complaint because?'

I followed her to the couch. 'Because I didn't lodge one.'

'Then how?'

'I don't know how, all I know is that I typed one up and threw it in the bin before I left that rat hole. Someone else must have pulled it out and lodged it. On my bloody behalf I might add.'

We looked at each other with mouths open. 'David,' we shouted.

'Oh David, David, David,' Josephine lamented. 'Poor David. Yes it was him, I remember now. He told me but I was too busy putting in my notice and finishing up to listen to that poor little junior lawyer. He put it in because he thought it was shameful what happened to you. He told me that.'

'But I hadn't signed it.'

'You probably don't have to, long as it's in writing is enough, I suppose.'

'You would think I'd receive notice from them that they are on to it, it doesn't sound right.'

'It's probably not,' Josephine replied. 'But what is right? If we wanted right we'd have left the planet a long time ago.'

'What will I do?' I asked in a mournful voice as we got comfortable at each end of the couch. 'Do you think I should support her?'

'It's true that she was under pressure. It all makes sense now that I think about it. Senior management are a savage lot, they basically forced me to do your work. And I wouldn't put anything past Felix.'

'Then I should help her?'

'Just because it's true that she was under pressure doesn't make her a nice person.' Josephine sipped her coffee. 'Or what she did to you any less despicable. And help her what? She doesn't need your help to make a complaint. If you ask me, by the look of those yellow bloody roses over there she wants help for more than making a complaint.'

'What do you mean?'

'I mean anyone can make a complaint to either the CEO or the CMC, all they do is investigate it. They've obviously started an investigation on your complaint already. But Ursula?' Josephine mused. 'Now that's a complex kettle of fish. I'd be putting out a bit of bait to see what she really wants if I were you.'

'But what could she want?'

'My guess is your undying support, saying what a wonderful person, lawyer and supervisor she is. I'll probably get my visit soon. She'll need us to help her keep face in legal circles until she can prove that she was pushed into doing what she did to you. My lawyer once told me that if you're talking about doctors they all stick together but us lawyers, he said, we will stab each other in the back no problem. She probably needs a couple of knives pulled out.'

'You mean her career might be on the line?'

'Maybe. Or maybe she could do with a friend right now, someone who understands. Lawyers don't make good friends when you need help, they make good money.' She laughed.

'I will wait till you hear from her then.'

Josephine looked down at her silenced, vibrating phone. 'And that might be right now.' My eyes fixated on the screen as she held it up for me. 'She can wait.' Josephine pocketed the phone. 'It will do her good,' she snickered and folded her arms. 'Now tell me little Miss Hold Back, what's this with you and Dominic?'

'Oh please Josie don't ask me about Dominic.' I got to my feet. 'I don't know what to say, I don't know what to do, I don't know anything.' I held my head where a dull ache had begun. It trod across my equilibrium and crowded my senses like hot school kids on sports day. 'I'm not well,' I pleaded.

'What's wrong Maria?' Josephine swung around in the couch to keep visual contact as I went to the kitchen.

'It's all catching up with me Josie. I thought I was through the pain but it's hit home.' I fumbled through cabinets looking for Panadol. 'And now I hear from Ursula, what bad timing.' I held my forehead.

'I don't think anyone could get over the way you were treated, Maria.'

'It's not just that Josie.' I threw the capsule into my mouth and gulped down a glass of water. I went back to the lounge room. 'It's Dirk.'

Josephine swung back around to face me. She remained silent as I sat on the couch beside her.

'I haven't told you yet but he ditched me.' I studied my hands in my lap. 'He told me that I'm too old.'

Josephine slammed her fist into the arm of the couch and bounded to her feet. She seemed speechless and I hadn't often seen that in Josephine.

I blinked nervously. 'Josie?'

She swung around with her back to me and punched her right fist into her left hand. She swung her arms out to the side in a gesture of helplessness, slapped her thighs and spun around to face me.

'Maria,' she implored. 'What part of dickhead do you not understand? Can you please get it through your head that that man is the biggest loser since Germany lost World War Two. That man would make Hitler look like Princess Mary.' Her voice had risen with each sentence.

I stood up and resettled myself in an armchair. Josephine's words came to rest on my timber floors. I looked about. I could almost see the words struggling for breath in the corners of my lounge room. Had I opened the back door they would have bounced right on out there and the neighbors would have thought it was another occasion to call the police who would have swooped with dogs and Taser guns and been confronted with a pint-sized, red-haired, sumo wrestler if they'd burst into my lounge room.

I adjusted the imminent volume of my voice and prepared to plead my case calmly. 'You're wrong.' I looked up at her still standing in front of the couch. 'I deserved it. It was me who deceived him about my age. I should have known better.'

Josephine shut her eyes as if to block out the sight of me. When she reopened them, they were filled with pity. 'Oh that's right,' she scoffed sarcastically as she threw her arms up in mock surrender. 'You were so wrong not to divulge your private business to him the first night you went out with him. You were so wrong not to give all, before he had a divorce to be able to give anything. How wrong you were Maria,' she pretended.

She threw herself onto the couch and thumped her tiny fist onto the arm rest. I cringed at the thought of the stuffing having little pockmarks where her fist had hit.

'You're not too old for him,' she announced as if she was a weather reporter. I could hear the words run across my mind but my thoughts were elsewhere. It's not too cold for wind. Is that what Josephine had said? It's not too cold for wind? Or was I purposely blocking out her words? 'You're too bloody good for him.' You're too bloody good for wind. Yes she was doing a weather report. I was sure of it.

'And he knows it.' Her words continued as if I was actually listening. 'He's probably found a younger woman by now. Or two. Young chicks who wear black toe-nail polish and flip-flops.' Her green eyes glared at me through her glasses and I was sure I could see a little spark of red in there.

I held a cushion tightly to my chest. 'You're not considering how I feel.'

'Maria, that's the only thing I consider. If it wasn't for how you feel about him I'd be rubbishing him.'

I rolled my eyes and exhaled. 'Josie he was just as devastated as I was that it wasn't going to work for us. He's asked me to think about it and I am.'

'Yeah well think hard and long is all I can say.' She folded her arms with a huff.

I sat silently for a moment with my face buried in the cushion. I could have sat like that forever, there was some kind of comfort not having to look at Josephine. I would much rather have stayed with being ditched because I was too old for Dirk than because I was too good. Too good only made me think how I should be supporting him through his time of grief, how I should be thinking up ways to make it work between us. It was easier to think that it was over because I was too old. Or because I had lied. If I could have privately bounded up those stairs and thrown myself into Barbie Doll's arms, I probably would have. The coldness of her hug would have been nothing compared to the emptiness I felt thinking about Dirk with someone else. Especially while I was tearing myself apart with empathy over his loneliness. But just as I was about to tell Josephine that I needed to be alone, Julia and Jamie turned up and we all fell into making plans to go down to the waterfront for fish and chips.

Later that night I stumbled into my bed with thoughts bombarding my mind like hail in a storm. Did Dominic think the same way about Dirk as Josephine did? Did Dirk still want me to come back to him? Would having contact with Ursula be like a re-run of *Get Smart,* all secret weapons and traps? It was one big thumping headache of questions with no solutions in sight. I felt that I'd fallen into a hell-hole instead of Wonderland. Life was meant to be getting easier wasn't it? Instead, a retirement village with trimmed hedges, or better still a nursing home, was beginning to sound like a perfect paradise in which to hide myself.

Chapter 14

JOSEPHINE was on the phone to me at morning-tea break the next morning.

'She says she wants our support and for you to be re-instated at South State Legal,' she told me as soon as I answered. 'But first we have to sing her praises so no one blames her for shafting you.'

'Sing to who?'

'To whom Maria,' Josephine chided. 'The legal fraternity, the powers that be, you name it we sing to them.'

'That's not going to happen.'

'Oh come on Maria, you're not going to help the woman who saw you tossed out on your ass because she didn't like you? What's wrong with you girl?'

'Josie every bone in my body cries out for revenge.'

'Now that you cannot have, too dangerous.' Josephine laughed. 'Unless you're thinking of anonymously throwing eggs at her house in the middle of the night in which case I'll help you. But don't go looking up egg-throwing on the internet in the meantime or when the police seize your computer it will be a scrambled give-away.' She laughed raucously.

'Revenge is something my childish self wants,' I commiserated. 'But it's for those who have not reached the wisdom of my true stage of life. As much as Ursula discredited me I have come to the conclusion that it is time for me to grow up and act my real age.'

'Which means?'

'Which means that I can't partake in useless and idle chatter about egg-throwing and getting back.'

'I was joking.' Josephine laughed. 'Kind of. So when did this wonderful change in you take place?'

I continued without diversion. 'I am on the threshold to the next part of my life Josie. My authenticity as a person depends on my integrity and wisdom. I have emerged from this as a woman who is whole, I am no longer the old Maria, I am evolved. From now on my decisions will be my own and I will not accept ridicule or criticism from anyone about anything in my life.'

Josephine cleared her throat and started humming a song about being a woman and roaring.

'Josie are you listening to me? What happened to me at South State Legal was more serious than I think you understand. I've been thinking about everything. I know you care but I don't think you know what this kind of thing can do to women like me. I've read about other women who have been bullied and discriminated against at this age. Bullying and unemployment in my age group is growing.'

The singing ceased. 'I know,' Josephine acquiesced.

'I'm not far off retirement age but I'm not ready for retirement. The ramifications are far-reaching. I know I've been lucky to get the new work but how can I live on a part-time income?'

'It could become . . .' Josephine began.

'But it's not about that anyway,' I continued. 'It's about the fact that others colluded against me. It's about the corruption of organizations like South State. It has the word justice as a part of its mission statement.'

'Yes it's rather misleading,' Josephine interjected.

'It purports to be providing twenty-first century HR practices but they don't even provide justice for their employees.' I knew I sounded like a rebel-rouser but I was past caring how I sounded.

'Maria I know.'

'Josie it's about justice, that's what it's about. It's not about Ursula and what she did to me. It's far more than that, it's that she could do it, that she had the power to do it. And if I'm going to do anything it's going to be to confront Ursula with the reality of that. I want her to understand what she can do to help stamp out bullying in the workplace. I want her to be aware so that others don't end up like I have.'

'Good luck with that,' Josephine ridiculed. 'I hear what you're saying but if you want my opinion. Which by the way I know you always treasure. I would leave well enough alone and stay clear of her. Send her a letter telling her to go to hell and to get back to you when it freezes over. That should give you time to wake up to yourself and realize that she's just an egocentric self-serving narcissist bent on squeezing the rest of your sanity out of you.'

'She probably is but I have to live by my truth.' There was a silent pause. 'What did you tell her Josie?'

'What I just said. But you can tell her that as well. Her brain cells are so focused on herself she won't notice being insulted twice.'

I laughed from the depths of my being. How blessed I was to have Josephine as a friend. Nothing came out of her mouth that wasn't either true or should be true.

'Josie you and I have lots in common. Our dedication to our work, our belief in truth, our commitment to fairness. I have seen you boost my daughter's morale. I've watched your vibrancy with people at work. You're a gem Josie and I value you very much.'

Josephine was silent for what seemed like ages.

'Maria,' she finally answered. 'You know how dismayed I was at the treatment they dished out to you at South State. It stunk. I felt cheated of my own integrity. I wish I had my violin here with me because I don't say this kind of stuff often. They robbed your colleagues of the best person we've ever worked with. And I only want what's best for you.'

'Thank you Josie.' There was another pause. 'But I must do what I have to do, that goes for all parts of my life.'

'I hear you,' she answered. 'What I want to say is this. Ursula has caused you grief, Dirk has put you out of his life for whatever reason his tiny little brain has thought up, don't let either of them do any further damage to you.'

'I will try to talk to Ursula. Correction. I will try to educate Ursula,' I responded. 'As for Dirk, I don't know. That's a relationship I will have to sort out for myself.'

When I hung up I was feeling stronger than I'd felt in months. I answered the knock on my front door with vigor.

'Ursula.' I gasped. 'What a surprise.'

'Hello Maria, I know I should have called. Can we talk?'

I opened the door and stood back. 'Come in.'

She followed me through to the lounge room, her flats making a little clicking sound on the timber floor. I was astonished by how much smaller she looked out of high heels and the color black. She was almost attractive in her baby-blue winter tunic, dark tights and gray scarf. She sat meekly on the couch while I made coffee. I offered her some of the Iced VoVo biscuits that Dominic had put in my grocery cupboard. She accepted.

I sat opposite her. 'Thank you for the flowers.'

She sat upright and smiled. 'You're welcome Maria, it's the least I could do.' She bowed her head as if in prayer. She cleared her throat and looked me in the eye. 'I should get straight to the point.' She moved slightly in the chair.

She was studying my face. Her gaze was one that a pathologist might use to examine a cell under a microscope. I was feeling strong. I hoped she didn't see anything sinister, it might cause me to falter.

'Before you say anything Ursula I have something to say.'

She pulled back as if she'd just seen something abnormal.

'I'm sorry, I don't mean to be rude, I just want you to understand that I've been through a fair bit over the last couple of months. I don't know if I can honestly say that I forgive you.' We both moved uncomfortably on our chairs before I continued. 'Regardless of the fact that you say you were badgered into your bullying practices by senior management, the outcome remains. You left me devastated.'

I felt a lump forming in my throat. I swallowed hard.

'I know you need my support so that you can try to rectify matters, but to be honest I believe your short term proposal won't do anyone any good but yourself.'

'Maria, no you don't understand. I want to help you get your job back, to be re-instated.'

'My job back?' I felt my face flush. 'Ursula you got me terminated, now you say you will get my job back for me?'

'Maria I'm so sorry let me explain. I am being forced from my position as well. I understand that you lodged a complaint with the CMC after you left and I will lodge my own if I can't get the CEO to listen to my concerns. Because of the widespread discrimination and bullying, I am going to need support. If you don't help me, I stand alone against that great big top-heavy organization. I won't be able to do anything for anyone on my own.'

'How do you plan . . .?' I started but was interrupted by the sound of knocking on my front door. 'Excuse me Ursula, it's like Central Station here today.'

She managed a pathetic smile as I got up.

When I opened the door Julia greeted me with her usual exuberance and bounded inside before I could say anything.

She gasped when she saw Ursula. 'Oh hi, sorry I didn't . . .'

'It's okay Julia.'

Julia looked at me with apologetic eyes.

'This is Ursula from South State Legal,' I said. Julia almost curtsied. I turned to Ursula. 'My daughter Julia.'

Ursula nodded and smiled.

Julia didn't linger, she disappeared into the kitchen with the finesse of a tight-rope walker.

I turned back to Ursula. 'You may not understand, I don't want to go back to South State.'

'Then think about me,' Ursula begged. 'I might not only lose my job because of your complaint to the CMC but my reputation is faltering. Felix is pushing me to the extreme, it will be over for me if I can't get the CEO to understand what Felix is doing and what he's done.'

'Ursula you could have stood against them for me, you could have saved my job, you had every opportunity of defending me to Joseph. Instead you wrote my demise in your false report.'

She lowered her gaze. 'Maria.' She looked at me with pleading eyes. 'Can't you think about me and what it will do to my career?'

I saw before me a frightened young woman. I had no need to make her suffer, no need to make her swallow her own medicine. But I felt nervous.

I heard the sound of knocking on the front door again and I began to wonder if it was a special day I'd forgotten about. I stood up.

'I'll get it,' Julia called as she slipped quietly to the door.

'Tell me what you want me to do Ursula and I'll think about it.'

I turned around to see Dominic standing behind me. 'Dominic.' My voice held surprise.

'Ursula this is my friend Dominic.' I was beginning to stammer, my confidence shaken by the realization that my emotions were beginning to surface. 'Dominic, Ursula was my supervisor at South State.'

Dominic twigged to my spelling out the obvious and took my hesitance on board. 'Ursula I'm glad to have this opportunity to meet you again. Maria told me what's in your letter, that you want her support. Do you think this is something that would come easy for Maria after what you put her through?'

Ursula produced a weak smile as Dominic continued. 'I've watched Maria go through hell.'

Ursula stood up and looked directly at me. It was as if Dominic wasn't in the room and hadn't just uttered the strong words he had uttered. 'Maria, Chloe-rose is supporting me but I need you to show support.'

'Chloe-rose is supporting you?' Dominic asked.

Ursula continued as if he was invisible. 'In light of your complaint to the commission Maria, the CEO is willing to have a look at what I take to him with regards to senior management bullying me.'

'Is that right?' Dominic scoffed. 'So it's really about you? You want Maria to help you when you didn't help her?'

My confidence had taken a nose dive. Gone was my roar. I was left with the twitch of a frightened rabbit.

'Maria if you come forward with an understanding attitude toward me the CEO will definitely be persuaded to see that it is Felix who has been instigating discriminatory practices. It was Felix who forced me into pushing you out.'

Dominic escorted her to the door.

'Maria you have to help me,' Ursula called.

'I'll be in touch,' I promised as Dominic closed the door behind her.

Dominic turned to face me rubbing his hands together. 'Now what's for lunch?' he asked mischievously.

Julia re-appeared from the kitchen, the uncertain look of a scared chihuahua on her face, her blue-eyed stare holding my gaze with caution. 'Was that?'

'Yep, none other than my previous supervisor. She just popped by to tell me how sorry she was that she took my job away. Oh and if I could help her keep her job by saying some nice things about her.' I inhaled deeply and sighed. 'No flies on her.'

'Oh Mum, you and your old-fashioned sayings.' Julia chuckled.

Dominic and I exchanged a grin.

Julia turned to Dominic. 'I've come to take Mum to my place for lunch.'

I was lost in thought. Could I stand by and allow senior management to do to Ursula what had been done to me? And yet by giving her my support it would seem as if I was condoning her bullying. I was stalling for time with her but I'd have to come to a decision on how to handle it sooner or later.

I was distracted by a voice in the background. 'Have you, Mum?'

'What? No, I haven't inspected Julia's new home yet,' I acknowledged ruefully. 'I've been completely self-absorbed since the day you left, Julia. In fact, Barbie Doll and I just haven't been able to get it together.' I laughed as I hugged her.

I looked over Julia's shoulder and noticed a gentle smile settle on Dominic's face. I let go of Julia, pushed hair back from her face and smiled. 'There are some kitchen items for you that I threw together a few months ago.'

I looked at Dominic. 'They're in some boxes in the garage.'

Dominic was a cloud of dust before I could finish. And before I could say *let's go*, Julia had invited him along and he was at my car waiting for me to unlock the boot. He put the boxes in and we three headed to Julia's place.

The first thing I noticed when we pulled up outside Julia's apartment was the lovely white gate and the blue slate path that led to her front courtyard. The path was lined with a hedge and Golden Cane, pebbles filled the garden beds between rows of Mondo Grass. I felt a swelling of pride, a feeling of having achieved a stage of life with Julia that was solid and good.

As we went through the gate a breeze blew at my ankles and I was reminded of the sweet moving-forward of life. It didn't seem that long since it was me who was moving into my first home away from my parents, hardly any time at all since I'd been scouring second-hand shops for furniture and odds and ends.

Beyond the gate was a courtyard with another garden of Mondo Grass and a Lilly Pilly in a corner by the fence. The glossy green leaves of the small tree seemed to be alive and welcoming as we went to the glass sliding door which was the front door. Julia pulled keys out of her pocket with so much pride that I thought her little chest might burst. Dominic and I exchanged a knowing look as we followed her inside.

'This is it. What do you think?'

'It's lovely.' I squeezed Julia's arm. 'I'd like to take some photos. Show me the rooms?'

We followed her down a short hallway where Julia stopped at each open door and with a swish of her hand announced its function.

'Bathroom and laundry.' She posed and I used my phone to snap a picture of her at the door. 'Main bedroom, second bedroom and here is our backyard.' Julia was standing at the back entrance which led onto a second tiny courtyard. 'All we need now is a barbecue,' she hinted with a wink. 'Oh and a little step ladder so I can trim those bushes.'

'Wow Julia, it's beautiful. Hold still.'

I took a picture of her at the door and beside the back fence and a few more throughout the flat. She beamed with contentment as she posed gracefully. It was as if every word I said made her glow more and more. It made me understand how important I was to her and to her sense of achievement. I took her into my arms and hugged her tightly.

'I'm so proud that if I was any prouder, I might be mistaken for a peacock,' I joked.

Julia and Dominic looked at each other and made an animated roll of their eyes.

'That is so not funny, Mum,' Julia admonished with an exaggerated tone of maturity. 'Leave the dumb jokes to Josephine.'

Dominic's laugh was contagious. I buried my head on his shoulder and laughed until it hurt.

'What's so funny?' Julia's face held an air of innocence that was almost angelic.

'It's the end to a difficult day,' I told her. 'And you make it all worthwhile.'

Chapter 15

I USED to think everything that went wrong was my fault. Leaky tap? My fault for not knowing how to change a washer. Flat tire? I must have forgotten to have the wheel balancing done. Workplace harassment? I must have looked like a victim.

It wasn't like that anymore.

Something had changed inside of me. And I liked it. It was no longer my fault that it rained when it was washing day. And even if it was my fault for some unknown universal reason, I could forgive myself for it. I had discovered that life just is. Sure some things are a result of other things not being done. But this was different. This was about me forgiving myself for what I thought was my fault and for what really was my fault. If I could forgive myself, I could forgive others. And the biggest others in my life to forgive were Ursula and Dirk.

Dirk had been in and out of my mind since the missed calls Dominic pointed out. But my relationship or lack thereof with him, had to wait. I could forgive myself for that. And it wasn't just about forgiveness with him, it was about timing and decision-making. And the time wasn't quite right because my decision had not been made. I didn't know yet where it would, or could go after forgiveness. I didn't know how I felt about Dirk anymore. Or indeed how he felt. And for the time being I was afraid to find out. My mind scanned a mental diary. Over the next couple of weeks Josephine wanted me to go into the office to give me a head-start on some training. Dominic wanted to take me camping on Moreton Island as spring would soon be in the air. Julia and Jamie were planning a house-warming party. And I had to sort things out with Ursula. The issue with her loomed large in my mind. It wasn't going to sort itself out. I had enough to help me block out thoughts of Dirk for the time being.

Ursula had got into the very heart of me. What had happened to me because of her and senior management had inspired me to think about social justice in a way that I hadn't considered before. The more I researched, the more I discovered that bullying in the workplace was rampant. Bullies were often in a position of power and targeted people like me who posed a threat in some way. That I had spoken up, that I had been prepared to question workplace practices, that I hadn't been prepared to back down were all common threads to being someone a bully would go after. Another common thread was that those bullied were intelligent and hard-working employees. That revelation was heart-warming.

That Ursula had been pushed into what she did rang true for me. She was being bullied as well. She was a threat to senior management. It was one of those down-hill things. That Ursula wanted to speak up for the truth and bring about justice made sense. But if I wanted to help her I had to trust her and that was the part I was finding difficult. With Ursula I felt like a skydiver on my first jump but without a static line. I had to free fall and there was no guarantee that I would land safely.

Josephine had made it quite clear that to trust Ursula was the equivalent of falling from a plane without a parachute. If Josephine was right, there would be no one there to break my fall. I was on my own with this one. Dominic was at my side every time I turned around but he had no experience skydiving and he was no match for someone like Ursula. And if I sustained any more emotional damage, a million Dominics wouldn't be able to heal me.

Josephine giggled over the phone when I told her about Dominic's constant presence in my life. 'Stop turning around,' she said.

'I reckon that even if I didn't turn around Dominic would be there.' I laughed. 'He's always there.'

'So he's watching out for you, right?'

I had a mouthful of toast topped with peanut butter, my evening meal. 'Right,' I mumbled. 'And what's more.' I swallowed. 'I've been enjoying it till now.'

'Till now? Then it must be time to give in.'

'To what?'

'His desires woman, do I have to teach you everything?'

'No Josephine.' I laughed and took another bite of toast. 'You do not.' I swallowed.

'What have you decided to do about Ursula?'

'My first thoughts are to find out more. Maybe I do want my job back at South State. I need full-time work Josie.'

'Getting involved with Ursula at any level is a bad idea, I told you that,' Josephine warned. 'Don't go letting your lofty ideals about changing the world influence you to think that it could actually happen.'

'Someone's got to make changes.'

'That someone does not have to be you.'

'I guess you're right. Ursula has been known for the trouble she causes. But what if she truly is trying to make a change? What if this is my chance to help that change come about?'

'It's not, end of story.'

'You're probably right.' I took the last bite of my toast. 'I'll keep away. Oh wait.' I swallowed. 'Dominic's car has just pulled up outside. I kid you not.'

'Go Maria, you need some loving. How long's it been? And you can't count the German because I'm sure he wasn't a good . . .'

I interrupted her. 'Got to go, I will call you back.' I pressed the little red phone symbol.

I pulled the door open as Dominic came up the path. He was dressed in jeans and a T-shirt with a thigh-length parka, his hands thrust into the pockets. He had the beginnings of an unshaven shadow on his face and his hair looked as if it had gone through a hypersonic wind tunnel. He pushed his fingers through it as he approached and gave me a smile that would have made a weaker woman collapse on the spot. But I was strong. I could almost hear the roar inside myself.

Dominic approached ardently, as if he had a purpose and that purpose was me. I felt a little gasp escape my lips and my roar turned into a purr. I wiped peanut butter from my mouth with the back of my hand and gave a feeble *hey*.

'Maria you're waiting for me,' he postulated.

'Not exactly,' I answered before his mouth landed on mine. I stepped back a little, jolted by the surprise of his fervor. I pushed the door wide for us to enter and hurried inside. 'Come in and have a coffee,' I suggested.

'I didn't come over for coffee Maria.'

'No, it doesn't appear so,' I shot back as I went into the kitchen and took mugs from the cupboard. 'But coffee is all I have to offer. Unless you would like the last of the Iced VoVos.' I laughed nervously.

'What is it with you?' Dominic was removing his parka. 'I know you don't hate me.'

'Oh how funny, why would you think that? You are my best friend.'

'Friends? That's how you want it Maria?'

'I didn't say that, I just meant you are a good one. Friend that is.'

'And you want it to stay that way?'

'What way?' I stirred my coffee and pushed his mug across the bench. 'Dominic you know I have heaps on my mind. I'm still getting my head around the thing with Dirk. And you know all the goings-on with Ursula. I don't know whether I'm Arthur or Martha most of the time. Isn't that a funny expression? Arthur or Martha. My mother's favorite.'

'You're Martha, I mean Maria. And I want you.'

'Want me to what? Oh sorry, want me.'

There was a moment's silence broken only by the thudding sound of the teaspoon which I dropped into the sink. I needed to regain my strength. I could feel myself succumbing to his agenda and I wasn't ready for that.

Dominic was still uncharted waters and I had yet to finish exploring the waters I had charted.

'Dominic we all want things.' I sounded like a mother speaking to her ten-year old.

'You're being unreasonable,' he grumbled as he took the mug to the lounge room and slumped into the couch.

I followed him and sat in one of the armchairs. 'I'm being unreasonable? It's you who's being unreasonable. Putting this pressure on me when I'm so clearly stressed.'

'Pressure?'

'Well yes.'

'I've done nothing but try to help you.'

'You have, I admit,' I answered thoughtfully. 'I notice you re-hung the bird bath out back. I appreciate that.' I went to the back door and peered behind the curtains into the darkness. 'My little Butcherbird has a nice drink every morning. I see you moved my rubbish bins about as well.' I went into the lounge room and sat down. 'They're not as accessible as they used to be.'

'Rubbish bins?'

'Yes, I like to be practical Dominic, I think they should be closer to the house, way up there in the back yard where you've put them.' I gave a little backwards wave. 'It's a bit too far, for convenience sake I mean.'

'I thought you'd be grateful to have the things out of sight.'

'I didn't say I wasn't grateful.'

He groaned. 'You might as well have.'

'You've moved the groceries around in the pantry when you filled the shelves too. I couldn't find the new jar of coffee the other day.'

'Maria what are you trying to tell me?'

'I don't think I'm trying to tell you anything more than what I'm saying.'

'In that case you are being ungrateful.'

'Dominic I am thankful for everything you've done for me.' I picked up my coffee. 'I'm just finding it hard that you seem to be taking over my life.'

'So you are trying to tell me something?'

I dropped my gaze. The coffee looked like muddy water and I realized I hadn't allowed the kettle to boil. I was about to tell Dominic when he interrupted my thoughts.

'You loved my affection, I know you wanted more. It's Dirk isn't it?'

I got up and stomped back into the kitchen. 'You're beginning to sound like Josephine.'

I stood at the kitchen bench and looked him in the eye. 'What is it with you and Josephine anyway Dominic?' I uttered before putting my mouth into gear.

His face lit up as if I'd put a battery in his chest and switched the *on* button. I thought he was about to start strutting around the lounge room like a Santa Clause toy. 'You think there's something going on with me and Josephine?'

I turned my back to him and busied myself in the pantry. 'Oh here they are,' I pretended as I brought forth the half empty packet of biscuits. 'They're still fresh if you'd like one.' I pulled them out and spilled coconut onto the bench. I pulled the dish cloth from the sink and began wiping as Dominic moved towards me. 'I'll get a plate.' I hurried across the room.

'You're worried about me and Josephine?' Dominic laughed.

'No, not at all, Josephine is my friend, she'd tell me if anything . . . ' I stopped as he came closer to me. I ducked under his arm as he reached toward me. I laid the biscuits on the plate and bounced back into the lounge room. 'Come on have a biscuit,' I chirped as I slumped into the armchair.

He sat on the couch opposite me. 'You'll tell me when you're ready then?

I flinched. 'Ready?'

'To make love.'

My mouth dropped open. 'Dominic how can you be so assumptive?'

'Oh I'm not being assumptive,' he asserted playfully. 'I'm being reflective. Reflecting on our beautiful night together.'

'Nothing happened on our night together,' I reminded him.

'That's not my memory.'

I cleared my throat as I searched his eyes for clues. 'And what is your memory Dominic?' I questioned warily.

'My memory is of a rich and warm interaction with a beautiful woman.'

I exhaled with relief. I must have been red-faced because I could feel heat burning my ears.

'We're going camping in a few weeks Maria, you won't want to be using two tents I hope.' He chuckled.

'Get away,' I teased. 'I have a perfectly good tent of my own and I take it that you do as well.'

He laughed that laugh again and a warm feeling of familiarity and relaxation shot through me. But I wasn't ready to explore the highs and lows of familiarity with Dominic. There were far more important things for me to consider not the least of which was Ursula. And most of my reflection was still about Dirk. It had been almost three weeks and I was beginning to miss him terribly.

'Dominic I really do have to think about the situation with Ursula, you don't mind if we call it a night do you?'

'No that's fine.' He rubbed his chin as if in thought. 'Have you decided what you are going to do about her?'

I scratched the back of my head and inhaled deeply. 'Both you and Josie say not to go near her and I think you're right. I emailed her the summary I sent to the CEO so she can see what my viewpoint was.' I again repositioned myself at the edge of the armchair. 'Other than that she's on her own. You know, at a deep level I'm still hurting because of Ursula.'

Dominic sat very still.

'And I've given a bit of thought to whether or not I want to work for South State again. And honestly? I think I'd rather sweep streets.'

Dominic raised his eyebrows.

'And as far as Ursula is concerned I am ready to forgive her but that doesn't mean I'm ready to trust her.'

'She can't be trusted,' Dominic assured me as he stood up.

I smiled and got to my feet. I laughed with a false sense of joviality. 'Don't worry Dominic I'm not going near the woman.'

But I was worried about how I was going to tell her that.

Chapter 16

'COME over,' Josephine told me when I rang her back the following night. 'David has just arrived and we're having a chat. Join us.'

'David? From South State?'

'That'd be the one.' I sensed a tone of incredulity in her voice.

I imagined David sitting all prim and proper on Josephine's couch sipping tea and nibbling on Gingernut biscuits. I hadn't seen David since my last day at South State when he had come up behind me at the desk when I was packing my things. He patted my shoulder and told me to have a nice weekend. He watched me get into the lift and made a little wave with his hand. His face carried the look of a baby hedgehog all scrunched up, peering at me through little blue eyes. He was the epitome of freshness and ephemeral innocence. I wondered how dented that innocence looked now, after he had covertly filed my complaint.

'But haven't you got work in the morning?' I asked peering over Josephine's shoulder as she opened her front door.

'You and I both do.'

I followed her in.

'I want you to come by the office and I'll do some training with you. It's really just a matter of showing you how things are done at Crime Legal. You'll be fine.'

I knew I'd be fine. And I was ready to be fine. I needed to get motivated into life again and work would be just the thing to do it for me. Now that I had the Ursula decision made, a load had been lifted from my mind but I was still thinking about Dirk and what would happen about that. He had rung again after all the missed calls he'd made and I had finally taken a call from him. And he was as remorseful as I thought he would be. His German-accented words dizzied me and I told him I'd see him soon. How soon that would be had yet to be decided. I'd hardly had time to get in touch with my feelings about him.

'David has just popped into the bathroom,' Josephine told me as I looked around. She raised her eyebrows and sent me a look.

I smiled with a feeling of apprehension. I pushed Josephine's violin along the couch and sat down. 'How are you going with the lessons?' I shook my head and waved my hand to her as she pointed to her coffee mug.

'*Schlinder's List* is almost half complete.' She beamed as she sat opposite me. 'Though I still have quite a few rusty spots to oil. But I'm onto them.'

I smiled. 'Congratulations I admire your commitment.'

Josephine leaned forward. 'If I had to guess, I'd say that nothing happened with Dominic last night. Am I right?'

'That's straight to the point,' I answered. 'Is it a rhetorical question?'

'It might be rhetorical,' she said. 'But are you being reticent? It leaves me with the question, is anything ever going to happen for you with Dominic? Or should I give up asking?

'I'd go for giving up asking, you know I'm still interested in Dirk.'

David entered the room looking like a swanky character from the Gatsby movie.

'Maria how are you?' He shoved his hands into his trouser pockets and bowed slightly from the waist.

'David it's good to see you.'

'Tell him how you are.' Josephine winked as she pulled her legs under her.

David sat in the armchair adjacent to mine, his beaming face peering at me as if I was the runt in a litter of abandoned puppies.

I hesitated. 'I'm fine.'

Josephine laughed. 'What she means David is that Ursula has been in touch with both of us to support her in a complaint against Felix.'

I gasped. 'Um, well, I guess so.'

Josephine sighed. 'David knows, why else do you think he's here?'

I let out a small fake-sounding laugh. 'David what do you know?'

David leaned across his spindly legs. 'I don't know much, only that I've heard Ursula is taking a complaint to the CEO, or further.'

'How do you know about it?' My curiosity brought a thought to my mind. Did Ursula know that David knew?

'I think it's pretty general knowledge at work. Among the Ursula supporters anyway.'

'Do you agree with what she's doing?' I inquired.

'I wanted to see what stance you're taking, Maria.'

'What does it matter what I'm doing?' I looked from David to Josephine and back. Both of them sat very still.

'David's admitted that he was the one who put the complaint through to the Crime and Misconduct Commission on your behalf Maria,' Josephine informed me.

David took a deep breath. 'That's why I wanted to get in contact. I wanted to say I'm sorry Maria. I think it's because of your complaint that Ursula feels compelled to run with hers. It's getting messy.'

'Indeed it is,' I replied. 'It doesn't appear to me that anyone else knows you put it in on my behalf though and it was my own complaint I admit.'

'Are you going to be assisting Ursula?' David asked.

'No of course not, why would I? I have nothing to gain. I don't want anything to do with her, or South State for that matter.'

'It is an in-house problem,' David agreed. 'But you were so badly affected by everything that was going on.'

'David I don't know how much you know, but for me the way things turned out almost destroyed my ability to move forward with my life. The less I hear about that organization the happier I will be.'

David stood up. He looked like a giraffe standing on two legs. Josephine bounced to her feet. If David had put one of his skinny arms straight out Josephine could have fitted underneath with some space left to hold an umbrella against the pending downpour of events that were about to rain on us.

She looked up at him towering over her. 'Thanks for dropping by David.' She gave me a look as she followed him to the front door.

'I'm glad I did,' he replied. 'I wanted to be sure that you and Maria are okay.'

Josephine laughed. 'No worries, everything is fine here.' She waved him down the path and closed the door behind her. 'Shit,' she spat as soon she turned the lock.

'What's wrong?'

'I'll tell you what's wrong, if Ursula finds out he's been here she's going to put more pressure on us to come through with support. Don't you think it was a bit fishy David turning up?'

'Kind of but I thought . . .'

She interrupted me. 'Don't think so much Maria. Listen.'

'To what?'

'To the sound of gossip in the air is what. As soon as I opened my mouth about Ursula looking for support I thought of something. I think Felix might have put David up to this.'

In my mind's eye I saw more innocence fade from David's face. 'No,' I replied in a disbelieving tone. 'David wouldn't.'

'I think he just did.'

'But Felix wouldn't.' I walked back to Josephine's lounge room. 'Would he?'

'I wouldn't put anything past that toad. Felix knows Ursula wants his job and he must know about your complaint.' I could see that Josephine's mind was ticking over like a time-bomb. 'Now I know why David put your complaint in. It wasn't about you, it was about Ursula. He's a Felix supporter, he wanted to be certain that Ursula got into trouble and of course he moves into Ursula's job.'

'Goodness your mind is a marvel Josie.'

She continued without distraction. 'Felix is probably trying to find out how much further you're going with your complaint. And.' She hit her forehead with the palm of her hand. 'How much support Ursula has. So I've just given David information that he probably wanted. Maybe David didn't know at all that Ursula was putting in her own complaint.' Josephine dropped onto the couch. The violin almost toppled to the floor but she caught it just in time. 'Oh dear I think I've just made matters for you and me worse.' She laughed as she picked up the bow and played the first few notes of Beethoven's Fifth Symphony. Dah dah dah dah!

I laughed. 'It's got nothing to do with us Josie, thank goodness. We're out of that place. The worst that can happen is that Ursula will drive us crazy.' I laughed. 'But she's too late for that. Don't worry, I'm not having anything more to do with Ursula. She can send me flowers until I have my own florist shop but it won't convince me to get involved. I've got too much on my mind to give her any more thought.'

Josephine packed her violin into its case. 'It does sound like that.' She took the violin to her bedroom. 'What's this about still being interested in Dirk?' she called. 'He treated you like mud under his feet Maria.' She came back to the lounge room. 'Why would you be considering him?'

'He's sorry.'

'And you believe him?'

'Absolutely.'

Josephine held my gaze. 'You gave your heart to that man and he tossed it back at you because it wasn't good enough for him. If you want my opinion, he will be wanting something from you.'

I looked away.

'It's getting late Maria,' Josephine spoke softly. 'Come to the office after lunch tomorrow and we'll spend the afternoon going over what your duties will be at Crime Legal. See you at two?'

I smiled and nodded.

As I made my way to my car I felt the old feelings of confusion making their way into my conscious mind. The sooner I got back into the workforce the better I would be. I wouldn't have time for matters of the heart. That was the hope anyway.

'I need you to re-write your report of the situation Maria,' Ursula informed me the next morning. We were sitting at an outdoors table in a coffee shop on the Redcliffe esplanade. She was opening a folder she'd placed in front of her.

It was nine o'clock. The early morning sun on the water looked like snow caps glistening. I adjusted my sunglasses. Breakfasters chatted at tables around us. A small child did an imitation of a sea gull while jumping up and down at the cash register. Her mother juggled a breakfast tray. All about us there was an air of holiday-making. It contrasted sharply with Ursula and me.

Ursula was dressed in her formal black court attire while I was in gym pants, pink T-shirt and runners, complete with the stale sweat of my early morning gym class. That I hadn't known that Ursula was going to call by and pick me up for breakfast was apparent. What hadn't been apparent was that she had prepared her own summary for me to sign and was now holding it in front of her as if she was a judicial assistant and I had to make a final judgement.

'You asked me for a summary and what I sent you is the way it happened,' I insisted.

'It might have been the way it happened from your point of view Maria, but it wasn't the way it happened in reality.' Ursula shoved her report in front of me. 'If we are to show Joseph what Felix is doing you have to write a report that tells the whole story.'

'But I don't know the rest of the story.'

Ursula flapped the sheet of paper at me. It was headed *Summary Report*.

And here's one I prepared beforehand, I thought to myself as pictures of Jamie Oliver danced across my mind. *Ta da! A Summary Report.* Just add your spiced-up signature and a bit of heavy-handed crying and Joseph can have it at his next morning tea.

'I can only tell what I know.' I took the report and held it. It was as fresh as bread out of a bread-maker.

Ursula's gaze was vexing. 'You must be willing to let go of a narrow-minded way of seeing things Maria. This thing is bigger than both of us. You must be prepared to stand up for the truth.'

'As I said I'm not sure if I want to assist you Ursula and I don't know what you want me to say.'

'Didn't you tell me that it was Felix who brought Joseph to see you at the morning tea?'

I nodded as I opened the sugar sachet. As Ursula continued I watched the sugar tumble into my coffee, picked up the spoon and stirred. All around me, people chatted about trivia over their lattes and cappuccinos. It seemed an inappropriate place for us to be discussing serious matters.

'Felix was trying to manipulate things,' Ursula finished.

'But what difference did it make that the CEO knew what I looked like? My report had been sent, he could have made a formal request to meet me.'

'It's their simple and single-minded attitude,' Ursula responded as she lifted her mug of cappuccino. 'It's called colluding.'

'Conspiring?'

Ursula nodded sternly. 'Felix was enormously concerned that you were making waves, he likes to do what he pleases. It all appears to meet guidelines but you can't get past the reality of it, he bullies to get his way.'

'I know.' I dropped my gaze as a rush of emotions swelled in my chest.

'It all seemed to start over the budget,' she went on. 'Our team wasn't getting enough work in for a while and it shot the figures completely out of balance.'

'A budget problem?'

'Initially.' She placed her coffee mug back on the table. 'But it went beyond work coming in. Felix could see that the work being generated by myself and Chloe-rose was above average. David was a bit slow but Felix needed to keep that junior lawyer position open. Losing an admin person was the best way to go because we could use Josephine for that in the meantime. He had plans of making your position casual so that he could change staffing arrangements at will.'

I shook my head. 'I still don't get it.'

'Bottom line, he wants to make the budget look good, which of course is understandable.' She looked me in the eye. 'But he also wants to make himself look good. By pushing me to pressure and bully you it gave him two things Maria, I looked bad and he could move me. And if you went, he could get that position re-established.' She nodded toward the report I held. 'Read that Maria.'

I looked down at the paper in my hands. 'So Felix gains what? Power?'

'Exactly,' Ursula responded smugly. 'And he gets to continue in the position he is in. It's an Acting role at the moment and I'm a threat to him.'

'This report says that I suspected that Felix was trying to undermine you. Wait up, it says that I thought he was working against me and the team.'

'That's all true Maria, think about it. You said in your own report that you couldn't go to senior management. Felix is senior management Maria,' she emphasised. 'Your report to the CEO was too wishy washy, it didn't spell it out in the way it needs spelling out.'

I laid the piece of paper onto the table and picked up my coffee mug. I looked across the road where at the far end of the Redcliffe jetty, the whale-watching boat and some smaller boats were moored. A scene couldn't have looked more sublime. It contrasted sharply with the discussion unfolding before me.

'Ursula I have to think about this before I put my signature to anything.'

'Of course, but I've arranged a meeting with Joseph for Thursday next week Maria and I would like you to be there.'

I fumbled with the paper in my hand, laid it face down on the table. 'It makes me nervous.'

'I can understand that.'

'What do you hope to achieve by that meeting?'

'I have prepared reports for Joseph. Statistical reports, staff reports, financial reports,' she listed. 'Contrary to what your friend Dominic thinks, Chloe-rose has agreed to support me in this, she's a staunch believer in justice.'

'But seriously Ursula, if Joseph colluded with Felix as you implied then the CEO himself is a bully.'

'He colluded with Felix on the understanding that Felix had identified you as a trouble-maker in the team. That your complaints went unheard was a direct result of Felix, and subsequently myself, reporting that you were nothing more than a disgruntled staff member who had failed to do her job, refused training and wanted to upset other staff.' Ursula lowered her head. 'I'm sorry Maria, I know how hurtful that sounds.'

I quelled my emotions. This was exactly what my mission was about. That they could do that meant more to me than the fact that they had done it.

Ursula picked up the report and handed it to me. 'Keep this, change it around to whatever you think might read better. I don't want you to lie and I don't want you to feel uncomfortable.'

I sighed. 'A bit late for that.'

She looked at me with a warm smile. 'I know.'

I wanted to trust her and everything she was saying told me to trust her but there was something about her demeanour. I looked into her eyes. Her gaze was beguiling, in discordance with the words she was speaking.

'Which is why it makes it even more important that you should see justice done,' she said almost with affection.

'Justice? Is there such a thing?'

'It might be that my pleas to Joseph will go unheard,' she admitted. 'But I want to give it my best shot. No different to how you tried to complain I suppose.'

I looked her in the eye. 'Yes but when I complained, you were against me.'

'I'm not against you now Maria. I will push for you to get your job back if that's what you want.'

I sniggered. 'Let me get back to you on that.'

'You have a little over a week and regardless of whether or not you want your job back, you will need to make up your mind fairly quickly as to whether or not you will attend the meeting.' She paused for a moment. 'This is your chance to make a difference Maria.'

'I want justice, I'll be there.'

'You won't regret this, you can stand proud.'

I held my head up. 'I already do that, I did nothing wrong.'

She looked away.

'I want to make sure that Joseph knows what really goes on at South State Legal,' I said. 'I will read your report Ursula and I'll let you know if there are any changes.'

Ursula's dimpled chin softened what was otherwise a fast-aging face for a young woman. She smiled with an almost impish grin and a tiny hint of delight and told me she had better get to work.

She didn't finish her coffee. Instead she paid for us both on her way out and left me sitting there looking out to the bay with only one thought in my mind. Could I really trust her?

Chapter 17

URSULA had insisted that I not confide in anyone about the upcoming meeting with the CEO. She highlighted to me that confidentiality was of the utmost importance and, in order for us to gain any footing with Joseph, it had to be maintained. And so it was that I berated myself for having mentioned thoughts of supporting Ursula to Josephine during my training session at Crime Legal. We'd been chatting about the rights and wrongs of having told David about Ursula's intentions when it just slipped to the end of my tongue and spilled out into the atmosphere. I'd tried to pull it back in when Josephine flew into a fit of worry, but it was too late. It was out there and I had to take the consequences. In the end I insisted that, as it was my decision as to whether I helped Ursula, nothing more would be said about it.

As I considered my plans I realised that everything I was going to do qualified as cringe-worthy at some level: stepping back inside of that building, going up to the CEO's floor, sitting with Ursula as her support. Only my intentions seemed to be of value. At a younger age I might have been unable to forgive Ursula but I had come to know that I had to learn the ways of the age I was rather than fight them. I doubted my presence in my age at times and I was often traveling a path of uncertainty. My longing for peace of mind and my search for wholeness would not be satisfied if I was headed in the wrong direction. I was seeking to understand myself. Maybe it wasn't understanding that I needed, maybe I needed to know myself. And what I was coming to know was that there is peace in forgiveness. Even if there isn't certainty.

I was aware of the misgivings that Dominic and Josephine had regarding Ursula. It was easy to see that their concerns were based on Ursula's past behavior toward me as well as recognition of the fragile state my emotions had been in over the past months. What I couldn't understand with Dominic and Josephine was their inability to see why I *wanted* to forge ahead in trust and why I was so willing to forgive. I resigned myself to accepting that they were entitled to their own perspectives and I mine. I pushed on with my plans to be a part of Ursula's commitment to justice.

I had taken to spending most mornings on my back veranda. Little Butcherbird was still doing his singing out there and I began leaving a bit of minced meat out for him. That's where I was sitting when Ursula called two days after our meeting. She wanted to see what changes I had made to her report. The thing was that I had decided to make no changes. I could see clearly that her handle on things was much more comprehensive than my own. Whereas I'd been attacking the snake with a stick, Ursula had used the stick more wisely. She intended to distract the snake with its own policies and was about to lift it up gently and place it where it belonged. All I had to do was help lift it up, stand back and watch it settle. She sounded happier than I'd ever known her to be and I wished that things had been different when I used to work with her. She suggested we meet for lunch the next day as she was taking a day off. I invited her over. Back verandas and butcherbirds are made for early spring lunches.

Ursula arrived dressed in jeans and a white long-sleeved top. A multi-colored scarf around her neck enhanced her complexion. Her face had filled out a little since I worked with her and the black curls which framed her forehead had been straightened into a fringe that was barely an inch long. In fact she had taken on a completely new and modern style.

'I've prepared salmon with salad for lunch,' I told her as she followed me into the kitchen.

'Wow Maria,' she chirped. 'That's my favorite.'

'Great. I kind of remember you telling us at work once that you loved it.'

'Good memory.'

'At times,' I joked as I carried our plates to the veranda.

She sat opposite me in the speckled sunlight. The overhanging bottlebrush tree blew slightly in the breeze while in contrast the umbrella tree stood sturdily at its side. My neglected lemon tree which grew beside the fence was the boldest of all. Regardless of how little attention I gave it, it produced an abundance of fruit. I went down the steps and pulled a lemon.

I laughed as I came back to the table. 'Perfect to go with our fish.' I cut it into wedges.

Ursula broke into the fish with her fork. 'Have you thought any more about wanting to be re-instated Maria?'

'I have thought about it and I'm still of two minds, I have been offered a part-time job as you probably know.'

'Mmm.' She nodded with a full mouth. 'Chloe-rose's Dad, Harold.'

'Do you know him?'

'I know the firm, they receive some funding from South State for their criminal clients, a long-standing firm.'

I laughed. 'Well I need a long-standing job.'

As she chuckled, the butcherbird landed on a chair at the end of the table.

'Be really still,' I whispered. 'He will stay there if we let him.'

Ursula froze.

I laughed. 'Not that still.'

She dropped her fork and the bird took flight.

'Oh sorry.' She wiped her mouth with the napkin. 'I couldn't help it, that was so funny. I've never seen a bird come up so close before.'

'Oh he does, he's my little pet. Do you have any pets Ursula?'

She laughed. 'You mean those furry little things that climb up onto your couch and give you fleas? Oh good grief no. My mother has two of them, *Peak-n-pees* Dad calls them.'

I gulped down the water I'd just sipped and laughed out loud. I had never imagined Ursula to have a sense of humour or, by default, her father's sense of humour.

'Where's your daughter, Maria?' Ursula inquired as she finished off her lunch.

I picked up my glass of wine. 'Julia has moved out, I'm going it alone.'

'It's nice to be alone,' she said. 'No one to untidy the place, no one leaving their boots in the doorway. I was married you know, I was very young, very stupid. Steve and I broke up ten years ago, I was twenty-five.'

'Oh that's sad.' There was a silent pause. I got to my feet. 'More wine?'

'No I'm driving but you have another.'

'Come inside Ursula, it's getting a bit cool out here. And leave the dishes, I'll get them later.'

She followed me to the lounge room where we made ourselves comfortable opposite each other.

'What could I expect if I took my old job back?'

'Oh there will be changes. Firstly I want Felix gone. His role is coming up for renewal soon. I'd want my admin assistant to be permanent, none of this casual business but that's an organisational decision. I won't have much input into it if Felix gets what he wants while he's in the position. Once we have the meeting with Joseph and I present him with the solid facts about the team, I think it will be a perfect time to introduce the idea of a permanent admin. You would then put your hand up.'

I considered for a moment. 'I'm torn, I've been through so much change that I'm not sure I would take the risk and especially if it was to be casual.'

'I understand but let's not talk about that now. Tell me more about yourself Maria.'

'Nothing much to tell. As you can see I have my own home, I have my daughter Julia and that's about it.'

'There must be more to you than that, a man maybe?'

I laughed. 'Two actually.'

'Two?' She almost choked. 'Oh, you really do have to tell me.'

I took her up on the idea of having another wine and by the time I'd finished my third I'd divulged almost my entire personal life to Ursula.

 Our laughter would have been heard all the way to the bay, I was sure. The pelicans were probably perching themselves on the light fixtures over the Houghton Highway bridge, throwing back their heads swallowing their fish and guffawing at our antics.

'I heard Josephine talk about Dirk,' Ursula said. 'You both met him when you were out one night, isn't that how it goes?'

'It does go like that, after work one night actually.'

'Wasn't there something about Josephine dating him when she came back from Europe?'

I cleared my throat. 'No it didn't happen like that, Josie's never been out with Dirk.'

'I think you should keep an eye on that best friend of yours Maria,' she stated, squinting her little brown eyes. 'I don't have a bad memory and I remember her telling me she was seeing him for a time. There were a few Friday nights she left the office all dolled up for her date with the German, as she used to call him.' She laughed.

My heart pumped vigorously within my chest and there was a slight stab in my side. I felt devastated by Ursula's suggestions but I had no intention of confiding my feelings to her. But there was no way I could contain my surprise at what she was telling me, I could feel the heat rushing to my face.

'I'm not saying anything happened between them mind you but I would certainly be keeping my ear to ground about it, especially now your relationship with him is on the line.'

I was interrupted by knocking at my front door. Time had passed quickly. It was late afternoon. Time had passed quickly. I went to the door and opened it with the swaggering stance of a tipsy woman.

'Dominic,' I said. 'How nice to see you, do come in.' I swept my hand across my body and bowed.

Dominic's eyes lit up. 'What are you up to Maria?' He did a quick scan of the lounge room and settled on Ursula. 'Hello.'

'Dominic nice to see you again.' Ursula got to her feet and picked up her scarf and bag. 'I'll go Maria. Again thank you so much for your hospitality, I've so enjoyed our day.'

'Me too,' I chirped as I followed her to the door. 'I hope you come again soon.' I bowed in a frivolous curtsy.

'I would love to,' she answered. I closed the door behind her.

I swung around and walked straight into Dominic.

'Dominic,' I drawled looking up into his face. 'I didn't see you there, come on let's have a wine.'

'You might have had enough wine Maria.' He put his hands on my arms to steady me. 'None for me.'

'Dominic,' I stuttered. 'Now tell me, isn't she a lovely lady?' I went to the lounge room.

'I don't know if she is and I don't think you should be making that assessment while you're in this state. Wait till you've sobered up a bit.' Dominic sat in an armchair.

'I am sober, I've been sober all day, just a few wines with lunch and after lunch.'

'So you and Ursula have become friends? I thought you agreed that she couldn't be trusted?'

'What would you know about Ursula, Dominic? Nothing.' I nodded emphatically. 'But I do, I have discovered that Ursula is a sweet, honest, sincere person.'

'I think you're being a bit extravagant in your tally.'

'Not at all, in fact I could say more. She is intelligent, witty and . . .' I searched my head for more adjectives. 'She's fashionable and I really love her scarf.' I concluded with a nod. 'We are the best of friends.'

'That's not what you thought the day she presented you with that rotten report. I can't understand why you've given this woman your trust. How can you forgive her?' He looked at me with consternation.

'Why not? She might be my boss again soon.'

'You've decided to apply for your old job?'

'I think so.' I sank into the couch.

'I think that's what I've decided but I'm not sure if I've decided that. If I have decided that it's a good decision isn't it Dominic? And if I haven't decided that it's a good decision too. That's what I always say.'

Dominic laughed loudly at my chicanery.

'Oh where is that bottle?' I pulled myself to my feet and feigned a search of the kitchen bench top.

'What bottle?'

'The bottle I keep your laughter in, it's around here somewhere.'

Dominic's laughter became a roar. 'You keep my laughter bottled Maria?'

'Of course I do. Doesn't everyone?' I took him by the hand, pulled him from the couch and dragged him behind me up the stairs towards my bedroom.

'Maybe I left it under my bed. Like my grandmother used to say, you can keep your laughter under my bed any time. Or was that boots?' I pretended mischievously.

He stumbled behind me humouring me all the way with his laughter. I pulled him into the bedroom and slammed the door behind us.

'Now I have you.' I snickered with my shoulders raised. I rubbed my hands together. 'We won't be having any more talk about my friend Ursula, will we now? Hee hee hee,' I chiacked.

Dominic grinned. 'You had me the first time I saw you.'

'Oh is that right?' I taunted playfully. 'We shall see.' I yanked off my top and threw it to one side with a wide swish.

'Now, now Maria,' Dominic objected skittishly. 'This is not the way to go about things.' He gently manoeuvred me to the bed and yanked back the bed covers. 'You just rest up until you're sober, then we'll see if you're so keen.'

I sat down and he lifted my legs onto the bed. I allowed my head to hit the pillow with a heavy fall and rolled over as he covered me with the blankets. He tucked me up as if I were a lost woman.

As he went out the door he called back to me. 'We might have to have a talk about things I think.'

I saluted from where I lay on my side, the comfort and warmth of my bed sucking me in. *Now isn't that a turnaround*, I thought smugly.

Chapter 18

WINE has been credited with fighting heart disease. I figured my heart must have been completely cured after my afternoon with Ursula. And I had had just enough wine to combat the effects of Dominic-itis.

When I heard Dominic reverse out of my driveway, I opened my eyes and took a deep breath. I hadn't had too much to drink. My biphasic curve had been nicely managed. And my technique for getting Dominic to leave had worked like a charm. He had proved he wouldn't take advantage of me when I was down but I had already worked that out about him. What he didn't know, or didn't want to accept about me, was that I was at my limit as to where I was prepared to go with him. What I was looking for lay elsewhere.

My heart yearned to be with Dirk. Every part of me sang a sad chorus of *Stuck on You*. But now that Ursula had made her revelation about Josephine and Dirk, I faltered in my confidence. Could he have dated on those nights Ursula said? Of course he could have. Would Josephine have lied to me about that? Of course not. We were best friends and Josephine was open and honest with me in everything. It was merely conjecture on Ursula's part. Dirk was waiting for me to decide about our future. Josephine didn't come into it at all. And I couldn't put my decision off any longer.

The problem was that I just didn't know if my relationship with Dirk could come back from where he had taken it the day he told me it was over. I made a promise to myself that as soon as the meeting with Ursula and Joseph was behind me, I would give myself a few days away and consider my future. Dirk or no Dirk, I had to get back in touch with where I wanted my life to go. I resisted the urge to stay in bed and sleep. It was only six o'clock. The night was still young. I hadn't visited Barbie Doll and Ken for days. It was time to put my head around the door and expel another sigh over the loss of my daughter.

Julia's bedroom held the stale odour of old perfume and hair products. I moved to the window and pushed it open, inhaled the fresh smell of the evening. Outside, the shadows of the day were becoming the dark spots of dusk. There was something about dusk, something still and otherworldly. It made me feel alone and isolated as I sat on the edge of Julia's bed. But it inspired me to get in touch with my emotions. They were a sad lot sitting inside of me and they ached for some understanding. And now they held a tiny bit of discordant curiosity about my best friend and Dirk.

At times, living in my empty house was torture. Sometimes I felt that life had just gone too quickly, that regardless of the fact that there had been many times I savoured, it had still managed to speed up and dump me at a time when I could feel a complete failure. There seemed to be nothing in front of me. Nothing but disaster behind me. If all I had was the tiny light of truth and the guts to do something I should have done a long time ago, then I should support Ursula and do it. Whether I could trust her was open to debate. But if I walked away now I would never find out. And I would miss the chance to honour my own integrity.

By the time the following Thursday came around the thought of meeting with Ursula and the CEO of South State Legal made me so nervous that when I awoke I felt as if I'd been bundled into a straitjacket. Maybe I'd turned into Harry Houdini in the middle of the night. But I wasn't skilled in the practice of escapology. If Dominic or Josephine had tiptoed into my room in an attempt to restrict my movements they'd been successful. Josephine was probably on her way to the authorities to have me declared dangerous. I would be added to the prohibited breeds list under class two along with dingoes, if she had her way.

When she called me wanting to know if I could come in for more training I could hear the sound of doom in her voice as she realised that I was headed to see Ursula. I breathed a sigh of relief that I was about to get on the seven-twenty train to Central, it gave me a reason to make the conversation brief. But why did I have to be fearful of Ursula? I had already lost my job. And my dignity. What else could Ursula take from me? No, this was my chance to be heard. And heard I would be. If anything, it would cement the idea of not blaming myself for everything anymore and be kind of a walk-the-talk action on my part. That's what I told myself. What I didn't bank on was the fact that nothing is ever as it appears to be. I had also underestimated how raw my emotions were.

When I arrived at Bowen Hills station Dominic called. Static on the phone cut him in and out and the only thing I could extrapolate was a discordant message the meaning of which I gathered by extrasensory means.

'Maria . . . worried . . . didn't you tell me . . . would have come . . . your emotions . . . monitor . . . don't realize . . . people . . . affected . . . angry.'

'It's going to be . . .' I answered over the top of him. The call dropped out before I could say *okay*.

The early morning commuters who sat about me on the train had looks of resignation on their faces. It reminded me of what I used to look like when I arrived at work and looked at myself in the mirror. Their unwritten rules of interaction drew my respect as they went about their routine of entering and leaving the carriage in a refined and well-established ritual. I recognised some of them and we nodded or smiled as our glances met across the carriage. Opposite me sat a man with a small backpack between his legs. He had smiled at me when he crawled across the passenger beside me and settled himself in the seat. I mindlessly studied his face for a few moments before returning to my thoughts.

What both Josephine and Dominic didn't know was that this was probably only the first of several meetings I'd have to attend before the matter might begin to look like being resolved. If indeed there was a resolution. In fact I wasn't sure if resolution was what I was seeking. Resolution for me would look like being re-instated. What I really wanted was justice. For Ursula resolution looked like exposing Felix for the bully he was. I feared it would be a long and convoluted road to either of those objectives.

The atmosphere inside the front reception area of South State was stifling. I had an overwhelming feeling of being suffocated. I waved my hand in front of my face in a feeble attempt to get oxygen. I felt heat travel up my neck and into my face and a nauseous feeling inside my stomach. I steadied myself and was about to ask the receptionist for a glass of water. The next thing I know I was on the floor with my feet raised onto a bunch of towels and several faces looking into mine calling my name.

'She's back,' someone announced.

'Maria,' I heard another voice say. 'Are you okay?'

I knew that voice. It burrowed into my brain like a beaver into its lodge. I searched my peripheral vision looking for its owner and there she was. Ursula. She was dressed in her standard black work clothes and in her hand she held a water bottle that she was holding out to me. Beside her, in front of me, was a plump beady-eyed man who I knew hung out on the first floor. His first aid badge was prominently placed on his chest with his name printed in big black letters. DICK. His mouth was moving but no sound was coming out. He looked at me through a furrowed brow. I noticed he was holding my wrist.

He stopped counting and called out in an authoritative voice. 'Give her space to breathe.'

Those milling around behind him made a beeline for the exit. Ursula moved closer with the water bottle, the receptionist served someone at the counter.

I inhaled a small gasp of air. 'I'm okay, I blacked out.'

'You fainted Maria,' the First Aid Attendant corrected. 'We're getting an ambulance for you. You've hurt your face.'

I let out a small laugh. 'Oh no, I don't need an ambulance, I'm fine.'

I held my hand to my head and felt the warm sticky feeling of blood. Ursula held the water bottle to my lips as if I was a wounded soldier on a battlefield. I fully expected her to pin a bravery medal onto my lapel. I pushed the water bottle away and lifted up onto my elbows.

'Seriously, I'm fine.'

'Just the same we'll need to let you go in an ambulance,' First Aid Attendant Dick stated. 'Policy.'

I nodded obediently and looked at Ursula. 'I'm sorry.'

'Don't be silly Maria,' she scolded. 'No need to be sorry, I can attend this meeting myself. It will only be preliminaries, I'll re-set another meeting for you. I'll be in touch.'

She pranced off leaving me sprawled out on the reception floor feeling as if I'd not only rained on her parade but had brought enough hail with me to make the ceiling crash in on her. I smiled meekly at Dick as he lifted my head and put a cushion under it.

'Lie still,' he instructed.

I didn't blink an eyelid.

'Maria I'm so sorry for what happened to you,' Ursula told me by telephone while I was in the back of the ambulance. 'I couldn't speak to you freely in front of other staff, that's why I waited till now to call you.'

'It's okay Ursula, it's not your fault.'

'I'm about to go into the meeting. Will you be free on Monday if I can get Joseph tied down to that day?'

I hesitated for a moment. 'Ursula it's proving pretty stressful. Maybe it's not a good idea for me to go ahead.'

'You want to back out?' Her voice had the alarmed sound of someone in a toilet cubicle realising that the fire drill was for real.

I squirmed. 'Not exactly, it's just Josephine's not going ahead. And she's worried I might be setting myself up for something worse than what I've already been through.'

'Maria, nothing could be worse than what you have already been through in losing your job. I can't understand where Josephine's coming from with that and I don't know how she, of all people, can say that. What could be worse than your own best friend betraying you with your boyfriend? I don't think Josephine is someone you can trust for advice.'

'She's never told me about dating Dirk.'

'Of course she hasn't but you can believe me, Josephine can't be trusted. She emailed me a photo of her and Dirk very early in the piece, I'll send it to you if you like.'

I stifled a gasp. 'A photo?'

'That's right Maria, it's all the proof you need to know that Josephine has been deceiving you all along.' She snickered. 'Pretending to be your best friend. Don't let her talk you out of doing something you believe in. You believe in what you're going to Joseph about and I believe in you.'

'I do believe in what I'm doing.' I felt renewed energy. 'Set the meeting up for Monday, I'll be there.' I nodded so hard that my forehead hit the phone. It smarted badly.

'Okay, I'll phone you at the weekend. Maybe we can catch up for coffee on Saturday afternoon if you're free?' 'As long as my head holds out I'm free.' I laughed feebly rubbing my hand across my head.

'Oh of course, get that attended to. I will call you and confirm for Saturday. Why not come to my place?'

'Sounds good,' I answered.

'This has got to be telling you something,' Dominic commiserated as he eyed the taped bandage and bruises across my forehead. He passed me an icepack.

Julia had let him in. She'd been with me since she and Jamie picked me up from the hospital at lunchtime. She'd brought pillows down from my room and plumped them up on the couch, supplied me with a selection of home-maker magazines, a glass of lemonade and the remote control. As an afterthought she tossed me a book on neuroplasticity and exercising the brain.

'Can't hurt to know these things.' She winked at me with a grin before heading to the veranda to study.

'What is this meant to be telling me?' I looked at Dominic with the most innocent look I could muster.

'That you should not be getting involved in this stupidity of Ursula's, your emotions are vulnerable.'

I sent him a look which told him not to say too much in front of Julia. She had her studies to think about. Dominic obliged by making himself comfortable at the end of the couch and taking my feet onto his lap.

'There's a bird out here driving me crazy,' Julia called.

'That's my baby, he's safe,' I called back.

Julia came through with her books hugged tightly to her chest. 'Yes but he's making such a racket, you don't mind if I go, Mum?'

'Not at all. Here give me a hug.' Julia leaned over me and put the side of her face to mine. 'Thank you for your help.' I squeezed her shoulders.

She kissed me on the cheek and shot toward the front door. 'Will you be okay for the house-warming on Sunday Mum?'

'Oh Julia, is it this weekend? I didn't forget but it's come around so quickly. Time flies when you're having a great time.' I rubbed my head sheepishly. 'Have you got everything organized?'

'It's just you guys on Sunday. Jamie and I are having our friends over on Saturday night.'

'I'll be fine, what am I to bring?'

'Food and drink, oh and a pressie would be nice. And I want those pics you took at our apartment, can you bring them?'

'Julia, there.' I pointed to the computer desk. 'Take that USB, it has my phone pics on it. You'll need time to sort them.'

Julia picked up the USB. 'I'll catch you guys later. By the way Mum there was mail for you. I left it in the kitchen somewhere, I think.'

'Thank you,' I called after her.

Dominic gave Julia a little wave and squeezed my feet, which were still in his lap. As the door closed, I bit my lip and looked at Dominic with perplexity. 'I have something on my mind.'

'After what happened to you today I'd imagine you would have a lot on your mind.'

'It's not about what happened.'

'Then what? I'm confounded by your apparent lack of discouragement with regards to Ursula.'

'It's about Josephine.'

Dominic scratched his head. 'Okay, I'm listening.'

'Be honest with me, do you know anything about her dating Dirk?'

Dominic got up and gently placed my feet onto the couch. 'Nope.' He went into the kitchen. 'Should I?' He commenced to take the coffee out of the pantry. 'Coffee?'

'No thanks. It's just a thought I had,' I lied. 'Nothing more.'

'You have so many thoughts, your mind is never at rest.' He came back to the lounge room and perched himself on the edge of the armchair. 'What have you decided to do about Dirk?'

I looked at him with tenderness as I inhaled and exhaled deeply. 'I haven't decided what to do about Dirk. I want to be with him, you know that Dominic. But I don't know if he really wants me back.' I took another deep breath.

Dominic sighed. He got up and went back to the kitchen. 'All that matters is that you're at peace.' He made coffee for himself. 'What about Ursula?'

I patted the couch beside me. 'Bring your coffee here and talk to me.'

For most of my single life I'd thought about having a relationship with a man like Dominic. Someone who was reliable, trustworthy, intelligent. The list went on.

Dominic met almost all criteria. Except for one. I wasn't in love with him. I tried to be. I thought maybe it was like chess, if you practised long enough surely you'd get it. But I never did. So maybe it was like floating. I should pretend I'm lying back going to sleep. Then I'd float down the river of life and love more easily. I decided to give it a go. I'd relax. I lifted my feet back onto Dominic's lap as he eased onto the couch with the coffee mug in his hand.

'What is it that you want to talk about?' he asked.

'If I remember correctly it was you who said we should have a talk about things,' I reminded him.

He grinned and put the mug onto the coffee table. 'Oh yes, your seductive ways.' He raised one eyebrow and gave me a look. 'How badly injured are you?'

I smiled. His hands were traveling up my legs.

'Are you badly bruised?'

'Only my forehead. Apparently when I fell I hit the side of a plastic rubbish bin.' I laughed. 'Just used to being left on the scrap heap I guess.'

His hands had reached my thighs.

'Ouch,' I cried playfully.

'Can I kiss you without you feeling pain?' He leaned over me.

I smiled. 'You can only try.'

He put his lips to mine.

'Can I come in?' Josephine called from the front door.

I pushed Dominic aside.

He slid to the end of the couch. 'Josephine, in here.'

'Help, quickly,' Josephine called as she came through.

Dominic jumped to his feet. I caught sight of Josephine balancing two large cartons of Macca fries and two cans of soft drink. Her bag, which was slung over her shoulder, was threatening to fall down her arm and knock one of the drinks flying.

'Hurry, let me put this down before I drop the lot of it.' She made her way into the kitchen with Dominic animating assistance but uncertain which item to take from her.

'Junk food,' I moaned as Dominic sat in one of the armchairs.

She laughed. 'No it's not, I didn't bring vegetables.'

'Oh ha ha, you have brought calories.'

'Okay Dominic can help me eat this stuff,' Josephine replied as she tossed her car keys onto the bench and reached into the cupboard for plates. She raised her eyebrows as she began to empty out fries. 'I'm surprised to see you here Dominic.'

Dominic and I exchanged a fleeting glance. I decided to change the subject.

'Don't put the fries onto plates,' I said. 'They are so much nicer from the carton.'

Josephine stopped. 'You're right, but I didn't count on Dominic, I only have two cartons.'

'None for me,' Dominic said.

Josephine stuffed a chip into her mouth. 'Goof,' she answered as she chewed. She brought a carton to me, put the back of her hand to her forehead and fell into the armchair in a mock faint. 'Oh good grief, look at you Maria. I told you how dangerous it was to go near Ursula but I didn't expect she'd actually beat you up.'

Dominic laughed.

Josephine persisted. 'What were you doing going into that sanguinary place anyway? Did you actually expect to return unharmed? Or even alive? You should have known they'd want blood.'

I began to laugh but stopped short. My head hurt when I moved it.

'It's only a scratch Josie, it's the bruises that hurt. I'm sorry I didn't tell you about my supporting Ursula. I went to a meeting at South State.'

Josephine had been gobbling fries. She produced an animated cough as she got to her feet. She went to the kitchen. 'Paper towel? There it is.' She brushed her hands with the towel. She glared at me. 'Maria I'm tired and I'm not up to poor jokes, tell me something serious. And intelligent.' She came back to the lounge room. She eyed Dominic. 'You knew she was doing this?'

'I . . .' Dominic began but I interrupted.

'I'm prepared to take a risk on Ursula.'

'It's one hell of a risk, you know that don't you?'

'It's true,' Dominic put in.

I folded my hands in my lap. 'My risk.' I looked at each of them in turn.

'Yes your bloody risk,' Josephine retorted. 'And after all she's done to you, you're willing to take it?'

I stood up. The carton of fries toppled from my lap. 'Shit,' I spat as I began to rummage for the ones that had fallen under the armchair. Dominic helped me pick them up. I took what I had into the kitchen and tossed them into the bin with the frenzy of a cut snake.

'Dammit Josie, is there anything I can actually do without you criticising me?' I held my hand to my forehead.

Dominic came into the kitchen and stood beside me.

'If you did sane things you'd have my wholehearted devotion,' Josephine mocked.

I swung around to face her. 'Josie this is no joking matter, I'm about to stand up for what I believe in. Even if you think I'm wrong, actually even if I am wrong, don't I deserve some support? There are never any guarantees Josie. I don't know what the outcome of this will be. I do know that it's something that integrity compels me to do.'

'There is no integrity in Ursula. I think you're seeing things in the way you want to see them.'

'And if I am? Doesn't that still deserve a friend's support?'

'I've always supported you.' Josephine went back to the lounge room. She placed the carton of fries onto the coffee table. 'So now you're telling me that I don't support you?'

'I'm not saying that exactly.' I tried to sound reflective.

'Take it easy Maria,' Dominic soothed. 'You should be lying down.'

'Then what are you trying to say? Exactly?' Josephine emphasised with a shake of her head.

I ignored Dominic's hand on my arm. 'Josie you'd be honest with me about everything wouldn't you?'

'Of course and I'm being honest about Ursula. She cannot be trusted Maria.'

'I don't know any more who can be trusted.'

Dominic eased me back to the couch.

'Oh, so now you don't trust me?'

'Josephine, I didn't say that.'

'It sounds pretty much like it to me.'

She stomped to the door. In a flash she was gone.

As Dominic and I exchanged troubled looks, Josephine came back inside.

'Where are my bloody car keys?' She strode into the kitchen. She picked up the keys and gave a huff. 'I've always supported you Maria but I get a cold shiver down my spine about Ursula.' She nodded in the direction of the kitchen counter. 'That looks like a letter from the CMC on your bench.' She marched to the door. 'If you need me call me.'

'But Josie . . .' I started.

She left without another word.

Chapter 19

'WHAT is wrong with Josephine?' I held the icepack to my head. 'If anyone should be angry it's me.'

'I don't see reason for anger at all,' Dominic concluded. 'But once you bring Ursula into the picture there's tension. Maria, do you realize what we've watched you go through because of her?'

I stretched out on the couch holding my head. 'I think I need a Panadol, Dominic.'

He was up before I could say another word and had a glass of water in front of me. He dropped two capsules into my hand.

'Thank you,' I whimpered. I swallowed hard and passed the glass back to him. He placed it on the coffee table and took up residence in the armchair.

'When I first started at South State several years ago Josephine was working at front reception.' I narrated with my eyes closed. 'We had lunch at the same time and got talking in the lunchroom. Every day at about five past twelve we'd arrive in the downstairs kitchen. Whoever got to the lunchroom first saved a table. Sometimes we had to share with others but that only made it more fun. Most days we'd sit through the first half hour of *Dr. Phil* episodes on the lunchroom television. We made bets with our sweet food about what Dr. Phil's advice was going to be.' I lifted the ice pack from my head, opened my eyes and looked across at Dominic. 'You could win half an iced bun or a sesame bar if you got it right.'

Dominic smiled.

I returned the ice pack to my forehead. 'As soon as we finished eating we'd dash outside for a quick walk and whoever we knew that was on late lunch would watch the second half of Dr. Phil and email us in the afternoon to tell us what happened.' I let out a small laugh. 'Whenever Josie and I had late lunch Josephine would email everyone about the ending. Complete with her hilarious comments.'

Dominic laughed.

'It wasn't until we began working on the same floor that tension set in between us.' I removed the icepack and pulled a Kleenex from under my pillow. 'I noticed it the first day I set foot in the admin position. Josie had been in crime for over a year. She warned me up front about Ursula being hard to work with. She told me then that Ursula couldn't be trusted.' I twisted the tissue in my hand. 'I'm sure she didn't mean anything by it but I felt as if I was meant to do something about Ursula. But what could I do? I had to fit in as best I could.'

'I agree with Josephine that Ursula can't be trusted,' Dominic said. 'But I think she's wrong to be angry at you. It's her way of trying to be protective.'

'Oh there's that word again. There must be a fine line between friendship and over-protection. Either that or you both think I'm a child.'

'It's not like that, I think it's more a defining line between trust and trustworthiness. Ursula hasn't done anything to prove herself.'

'I've come to know Ursula as a vulnerable and sensitive person. Doesn't that mean something?'

'It means something, but it doesn't mean she's trustworthy.'

'You're being so difficult Dominic. Like you know everything and I'm some kind of feeble old lady.'

'I'm not trying to be difficult. I'm trying to be analytical. If that's possible here.' Dominic leaned forward with his elbows on his knees.

'Who asked you to be ana-bloody-lytical? Can't you possibly try to see it from my perspective for a change?'

'I see a cut and bruised face.'

'Oh Dominic, I fainted okay? There was no oxygen. The air conditioners hadn't been started, that's all.' I wrapped the Kleenex firmly around my finger, unwrapped it, and wound it tight again. 'But there is something that really is playing on my mind. I want to tell you but I have to trust you not to tell Josephine.'

Dominic looked crushed.

'I'm sorry, of course I can trust you. It's about her and Dirk.'

'What you've been thinking about them?'

'Josie emailed Ursula a photo of her and Dirk together.'

Dominic grunted. 'Hmm, doesn't sound good. Josephine never mentioned it to me.'

'Nor me, and it hurts.'

'I guess it would. You need to ask Josephine about it.'

'I won't be asking Josephine anything. If it's true she would only deny it. I'll be looking at that picture first. Ursula is going to email it to me.' I smirked. 'All this garbage from Josie about not liking Dirk, what a ruse.' I wiped a tear from my eye. 'She was trying to get me out of his life.'

'Don't jump to conclusions Maria. It might be completely innocent.'

'If it was innocent why didn't she tell me? I'm sorry Dominic, but sometimes I think that you just want to take a middle road all the time. You don't seem prepared to discover the truth. You stand by with all your help and assistance but when it comes to the crunch you're all, it might be this, it might be that. Can't you be real?'

'What's real?'

'Integrity, discovering and accepting the truth. I try so hard to face the reality of situations. And I've been presented with information that my best friend and Dirk might have betrayed me. It doesn't help with you there cautioning me all the time.'

Dominic stood up. 'It's all about you isn't it Maria?'

I looked up at his beautiful face stunned by the reality he was prepared to present to me.

'About me?'

He nodded slowly. 'It's all about you and what you want and who you are. Have you ever given thought to who Josephine is? Who I am?'

My mouth dropped open. I pulled it closed quickly.

He sat down. 'I think you've spent so much of your life having to protect what you have, your home, your daughter, your job, that you've forgotten how to actually care for those who love you. I'm not going to say that Josephine is right or wrong in the way she's behaving. I'm not being her defender. And I'm not saying that Ursula is out to get you.' He re-adjusted his position on the couch. 'I just see a very sad situation evolving here. You say you're trying to see justice done by supporting Ursula but in truth what you're doing is setting up conflict between yourself and those who love you. Don't you care how Josephine feels? Or how I feel?'

My eyes were blinking rapidly as if an insect had crawled under my eyelid. I rubbed my forehead so that it wasn't noticeable, swung my legs off the couch and hung my head.

'I don't know what to say Dominic.'

'There's nothing to say, just don't let it all be about what you feel.'

'I didn't think it was. I really didn't. What I'm doing for Ursula is not about me, it's about those like me who are bullied. I don't stand to get anything out of it.'

'Standing up for others is commendable but not at the cost of friendship.'

'Dominic is it really me who is destroying the friendship? Or is it you or Josephine who can't accept what I'm doing?' I shook my head. 'It's so hard to know.'

Dominic sat beside me. 'I'd best go, you need to rest. Think things over. And talk to Josephine about Dirk.' He ran his hand down my arm and squeezed my hand. 'I support you whatever you decide.' He got up. 'Don't see me out, I'll lock the door as I leave.'

I nodded.

Ursula lived in a twelve-storey apartment block in the suburb of West End, which is approximately a thirty-five minute drive from Woody Point. When I arrived I opted to park in the street rather than the visitor parking area that Ursula had suggested in a text message. *You never know when a quick exit is necessary,* I heard Josephine's voice whisper in my mind. I laughed out loud. If Josephine knew where I was she would shudder. But she didn't know and until I was ready to confront her about Dirk she wouldn't know. But it wasn't the reason I parked on the street. Ursula's visitor's parking bay was occupied.

I half expected Ursula to be standing at her front door holding a picture of Josephine with Dirk and I found myself wondering how I would react to that. I resolved that I wouldn't react. It's not becoming of a woman to break down into a blubbering mess at the sight of her man with her best friend. No, I would hold my head high and put off my bawling and wailing until I got home.

I walked up the driveway past the neatly clipped hedges and Golden Palms and made my way around to the side. Once there I was to go in through a side entrance that would take me to an intercom center. I buzzed the fifth floor as Ursula had instructed.

When I got out of the elevator, Ursula's apartment was directly in front of me. Ursula swung the door open. 'Maria, how wonderful to see you. Please come in.'

She stood aside for me to enter. I walked into a large sunlit room with polished floors. The kitchen with sliding glass doors onto a balcony was at one end of the room and a lounge room with a large pale-blue L-shaped sofa and wall-hung plasma television set was on the opposite end.

Ursula nodded in the direction of the balcony as she closed the door behind me. 'Of course you know Chloe-rose.'

I glanced over to see that Chloe-rose had emerged from outside looking as id she'd been packaged up to sell such an apartment. She wore a bone linen jacket over a white pleated shirt and black jeans with beige ankle boots. She blew smoke toward her right shoulder and stubbed out the cigarette in a little ashtray that was on Ursula's kitchen counter.

I smiled at her. 'Chloe-rose, this is a surprise. What are you doing here?'

Ursula and Chloe-rose exchanged a quick glance.

'Hey Maria.' Chloe-rose made her way to the L-shape.

'A wine Maria?' Ursula asked. 'Or would you prefer coffee?'

'Coffee will be great.' I sat at the other end of the L.

My eyes fixated on Chloe-rose's little golden owls earrings before traveling over her hair which was hanging loosely around her shoulders. She smiled at me with the warm glow of a lipstick commercial. I resettled myself on the couch. Ursula brought coffee in a large black and white mug and placed it on the coffee table. She edged the table a bit closer and sat between Chloe-rose and me. She cleared her throat. Chloe-rose and I looked at her.

'I suppose you're wondering why I asked you here?' She folded one leg across the other.

I leaned forward to exchange a look with Chloe-rose but her gaze was averted, fixed somewhere on a spot at the edge of the coffee table. I saw her smile nervously as Ursula continued.

'The fact of the matter is that I need you both to make a new statement which can be presented to the CEO on Monday morning.'

I was none the wiser. I thought I'd already done that. I looked at Ursula with a sense of curiosity. 'Maria, Chloe-rose is our best witness to Felix's bullying.'

Chloe-rose smiled and nodded. I returned my gaze to Ursula as she continued.

'Now that the Crime and Misconduct Commission has contacted Joseph, the onus is on the organization to look at your allegations. If we can show and prove that it was Felix rather than me who was bullying, it might prevent them from digging too deep in an investigation.'

I felt a frown settle between my brows and tried to blink it away. I shifted in my seat a little. 'Ursula, why would it be a problem if they investigate further? Surely that could only be a good thing. Bullying and discrimination is an insidious reality throughout the organization.'

'That might be the case, but if you go uncovering too much they could introduce new guidelines and it will make things complex. Especially if you decide you want your job back.' She looked at Chloe-rose. 'No, if we can keep it to the point,' she looked back at me, 'a lot of problems might be avoided. All you have to do is re-word your statement so that it points the finger directly at senior management and omits all allegations against me. Chloe-rose will vouch for it.' Ursula got up.

My eyes surveyed the latte-colored cupboards and the matching blinds and came to rest on the coffee table where Ursula had just placed a large folder that she had fetched from behind the couch.

I looked up at her. 'What's that?'

'This is my evidence. Reports for Joseph. He has agreed to investigate my claims. He accepts that you and Chloe-rose will be witnesses. He's going to use my information to respond to the Crime and Misconduct Commission.'

'So what happens next?'

'Maria, what happens next is your statement, that's why we are here today.' She pulled a two-page letter from the folder. 'Please take your time to read this before you sign it.' She handed the pages to me.

'This is different to what was in the summary report,' I said.

'Oh yes, this isn't a report, this is what you are verifying to be the truth. We may have to have it sworn as an affidavit at some stage.'

I moved around in my seat as I read what she had written. I took a deep breath and exhaled. 'It seems okay to me. It's basically saying that I think Felix is the bully. I can sign that.'

'Excellent.' Ursula handed me a pen with more than a hint of enthusiasm. She folded her hands in front of her.

I signed my name at the bottom and handed pen and paper back to her. 'Now what?'

She slipped the pages back into her folder. 'On Monday morning I will meet you at the staff entrance so you don't have to go into that stifling reception area. Be there by eight-thirty to give us time to go over a few things and meet with Joseph at nine.'

I looked at Chloe-rose. 'Are you going to be there for this meeting?'

'Absolutely, I have my statement ready to go.' She glanced at Ursula before returning her gaze to me. 'But there are some things you should know Maria.'

I looked up at Ursula and back to Chloe-rose. 'What?'

'Maria,' Ursula's voice had become strained, I swung back to look at her. 'This is not going to be easy. You have to understand that we have certain guidelines to adhere to.'

'Of course.'

'And there may be some things come up that are uncomfortable.' She exchanged a glance with Chloe-rose and cleared her throat. 'There are rumours.'

'What kind of rumours?'

'Somehow it's gotten out that I've prepared a case against Felix and so now he's preparing his own case against me.'

I cleared my throat. 'What does that mean?'

'He will make accusations.'

'About me?'

'You, maybe Chloe-rose, Josephine, myself,' she replied sternly. 'We have to be prepared for whatever he might say.'

'Don't worry Ursula, I'll be ready for anything.'

She smiled. 'This will be a time for keeping confidentiality a priority. I know I can count on you Maria.'

I let a nervous laugh escape and picked up my bag. I stood up. 'Mum's the word.' I laughed again. 'I might head off now, bit of traffic being Saturday afternoon. Oh sorry, I didn't drink my coffee.' I backed towards the door. '

'Of course Maria,' Ursula replied.

'Eight-thirty Monday then.' I flicked hair back and smiled.

'Before you go Maria, that picture Josephine sent me months ago? I've emailed it to myself from work. You might want to take a peek.' Ursula walked across the room to an iPad lying on the kitchen bench. 'If you think you can trust Josephine it might give you second thoughts.'

My eyes darted to Chloe-rose and back to Ursula and I managed a weak smile. 'Sure.' I went to her. 'I'd like to see it.'

Ursula pressed a couple of screens. 'Here you go, in full color, Josephine with Dirk.' She shoved the screen in front of me.

A small gasp left my lips. I hid it behind a laugh that I pushed out immediately. 'Oh I really don't care about either Dirk or Josephine. What's it matter now? I'm over with both of them.'

'I thought you might say that.' Ursula patted my arm. 'I'm sorry it had to be me to let you in on it.' She laid her hand on my shoulder.

'That's okay. I've got to go. See ya Chloe-rose.'

Chloe-rose stood up. 'Sure Maria, see you then.'

I made my way into the elevator. As soon as the doors closed the tears that had welled in my eyes spilled over. I caught the tears with my fingertips and took in a deep breath. The sight of my best friend with Dirk had filled me with a mixture of sadness and despair. I wanted to slump into a corner of the elevator and ride up and down all day in private. Maybe by the time I got out, this terrible nightmare would have resolved itself. The bruises on my forehead began to thump as if to remind me what my cause was really all about. It was over for me and Dirk. It had been over since the night it started. I had nothing more to lose with him. And Josephine? It would have to wait, but I would have my day with her.

But why did the feeling in my stomach keep telling me something was wrong? It churned and gurgled. Something was not going down quite right. But I was resolute. Ursula leading the charge against bullying was the only way I could stand up for what I believed in. With her and Chloe-rose at my side I felt brave and strong. Everything else paled into insignificance for the moment.

Chapter 20

I OPENED the letter from the CMC as soon as I got home. As I had guessed, it was advising that my complaint had been received and that initial enquiries were being made. I tossed it back onto the kitchen bench and opened the text message that had just vibrated my phone.

Don't 4get hse-warming party tmrrow. Can u b here @ 2?

Why not make it a bit earlier? We can have lunch, I replied.

Afternoon tea. We r going 2 Jamie's mum's 4 lunch, Julia wrote.

That made it easy, I thought to myself as I headed back to the car. Some of Dominic's Iced VoVo biscuits might come in handy. I chuckled out loud. Oh if only I could keep my light-hearted attitude when Josephine arrived. I pulled the boot of my car open and eyed the little barbecue I'd bought for Julia and Jamie as a house-warming gift. That was going to stay right there in its box until I got to their apartment tomorrow afternoon. I slammed the boot closed and headed back inside.

I opened the fridge. Enough soft drink. A bottle of wine. Bread rolls and salad. And Julia's favorite banana cake from the bakery. All ready to go. I felt a sense of achievement for Julia and Jamie. The house-warming party was Julia's idea and it was a good way to bring together those who had helped her. I filled a glass with cold mineral water and headed to the lounge room with the letter from the CMC in my hand.

I had a feeling that I had sensed more than an agreement between Ursula and Chloe-rose to attend a meeting together and rally against bullying. There was some kind of vibe that I had picked up on but I didn't know what it meant. It worried me. I found it difficult to understand why Chloe-rose would have the slightest flicker of an interest in Ursula's plan to bring Felix's bullying out into the open. There was just nothing in it for her. She had her career to think about and it looked like a bright future in front of her. What was making her agree to support Ursula? Was there a tryst between the two of them that I wasn't privy to? I couldn't figure it out.

As for myself, if there had been discordance within me before, now there was a sense of urgency. Receiving that letter from the CMC put it in better perspective for me. Felix would be well aware of what I had complained about. But Felix would also be aware by now that I was supporting Ursula. He must have been wondering about that. What would he be expecting? Would he know that I was preparing a case against him? I had told David I wasn't going to be a part of it so I figured it couldn't yet be clear to Felix what I was on about. It was a hodgepodge of tiresome thoughts that invaded my mind as I sat sipping the cold lemon-flavoured mineral water and it left me feeling that the sooner the meeting was over the better for my peace of mind. Julia's house-warming party couldn't have come at a better time. It was perfect. The day before the meeting. It meant I would not be thinking about the look on Felix and Joseph's surprised and ugly faces all weekend. And I would be able to avoid disclosing too much to Josephine.

I received a message from Josephine just as I finished my drink. She was on her way over. That made me more nervous than a frightened guinea pig. I had courage to face my previous work situation but the thought of facing Josephine pressured me more than if an inflated air bag had hit my chest. I resolved to dissuade her from any personal discussions and to focus only on our plans for Julia's house-warming. Anything personal would have to be discussed once the party and the meeting were behind me.

When I heard Josephine's car pull into my driveway I took a deep breath. I greeted her at the door. She got out, went to her passenger door and started pulling out a large Cooler.

'Need any help?' I called.

'Take this,' she replied bringing the Cooler to me. She returned to the car and lifted out three bags of groceries. 'Make way, make way,' she said as she came up the footpath to the door.

I stepped inside with the Cooler and waited. After she came through I closed the door and followed her to the kitchen. She clonked the bags onto the bench.

'What have you got there?'

Josephine gave me her proudest smile. 'These are for Julia and Jamie. You're going to help me make a gift basket out of a Cooler. Got any old cardboard boxes?'

I opened my pantry and rummaged about on the bottom shelf. 'This do?' I pulled out a shoe box.

'What about some grocery bags?'

'Plenty of those.' I pulled them from the same shelf. 'I re-use them now that I've taken up saving the planet.'

Josephine smiled. 'Excellent, give me those things.' She set about scrunching up the bags and putting them into the Cooler. 'Here give me that cardboard.'

I jumped forward with it. She put the shoe box in at one side. By the time we'd arranged cans of beer, bottles of Coke, a couple of foam beer can holders, chips and other goodies into the Cooler they spilled over the top and looked set for a party.

'Now for the bow.' Josephine whipped some blue ribbon from her bag, pulled it around the Cooler and tied it. She pulled a larger bow out and taped it over the top of the knot.

I put my hand on her arm. 'This is a wonderful idea Josie, thank you so much.'

She smacked my shoulder. 'Julia deserves this and more. Now please, get me a coffee.'

I tried desperately not to allow our conversation to be tainted by news of Ursula but it was difficult given that the letter from the CMC was sitting in full view on the coffee table. We had finished our coffee before anything delicate began to emerge. Finally it must have become too much for Josephine. She nodded in the direction of the letter. 'You going ahead with it?'

'I won't back out,' I answered with tight lips.

'Hmm, I admire your guts.'

'Thank you.'

'You're quiet. I suppose I have an apology to make about walking out the other day. I'm sorry, you know how edgy Ursula makes me.'

I studied my hands in my lap.

'Is anything else wrong?' Josephine asked.

'What could be wrong?' I snapped without meaning to.

'I know you well enough to know something is.'

I stood up and carried our mugs to the kitchen. 'I'm tired. Fainting and being bruised are not my favorite past times,' I joked. 'Oh and I don't know if Julia messaged you but she said to arrive at about two tomorrow afternoon.'

'Two is good,' Josephine answered. 'Help me to the car with the Cooler?'

'Sure.'

I was half-hearted in my feelings about whether or not I should have confronted her with what Ursula had told me about her and Dirk. One part of me was reeling from a huge sense of betrayal. I was holding in my feelings until I got the meeting behind me, but the pain kept pushing at my chest as if my heart was about to burst. The other part of me focused on both Josephine and Dirk being traitors. They knew something important to me and were keeping it from me. Neither of them loved me enough to be honest. All I had to make sure of now was to be certain it didn't come out at the house-warming party. But how could it? I certainly wasn't going to say anything. And I could rely on Dominic.

Dominic came by at one-thirty Sunday afternoon and helped me pack the food into the car. As the biggest item was already in my boot we agreed to drive in my car to

Julia's place. Josephine was pulling the Cooler out of her car when we pulled up behind her. She edged out of the part-closed car door and put her hands on her hips.

She smiled. 'Good timing guys.'

'Hey,' Dominic called as he got out.

He pulled the Cooler from Josephine's car and placed it inside the gate. I waved hello and went straight to the boot. Dominic came around, took out the box with the barbecue in it, and put it on the footpath. I collected the food from my back seat and carried it to Julia's outdoors table where she'd set up an arrangement of finger-food.

'Thank you,' Julia cried as she hugged Josephine. She put her arms out to me. 'Thank you too Mum.' She kissed my cheek. 'Wow Mum, you're wearing perfume.' She winked at Josephine.

I laughed. I thought of the night Julia and Josephine and I had drunk wine together, and Josephine had phoned Dominic. A lot had changed since then.

Julia pointed to where she wanted Dominic to place the barbecue. 'We have cold beer in the fridge for you Dominic. Grab a plate everyone, I've had lunch.'

I did a quick scan inside Julia's front door. 'Where's Jamie?'

Julia made eye contact and nodded with a despondent sigh.

'Oh no. Again?'

Julia gave me a knowing look. 'After he dropped me home he took his Mum to his Grandmother's place. Now he's broken down.'

I held back a chuckle.

'It's okay,' she continued. 'His dad's picking him up.' Her large blue eyes lit up as if they were beacons. 'We can start.'

The chatter of the four of us sounded like a bunch of holidaymakers at the Sunday morning markets. In spite of my dampened feelings towards Josephine, I soaked in the wonderment of the relationships that I had built around myself and while it was a small number, I felt pride in the amount of love we shared. It made me contemplate the downside of life being made worthwhile by the love we draw from those around us. I relaxed in the joy of the moment and wouldn't allow myself to entertain thoughts of betrayal although I sensed that Josephine knew I had something on my mind.

After we'd eaten, Julia called us inside. 'I've prepared a picture tour of our apartment and a few other photos that we took before I left home.'

Josephine, Dominic and I all settled into Julia's high-backed couch.

'Get comfortable,' Julia said.

The three of us swapped amused glances as we side-bumped each other. 'We are comfortable.' I laughed. 'Show us your virtual tour.'

Julia stuck the USB into the television set and settled on the floor in front of us, remote in hand. 'Except for the ones taken at Jamie's parents' place, most of these were taken on your phone Mum,' Julia said. 'So if they're not too good that's why.' She laughed.

'Just show us.' I rolled my eyes with a grin. Dominic nudged me in the ribs.

'Okay I've started with some of me and Jamie when we first used to stay at his parents' place.'

'Oh goodness,' I commented. 'You look younger. Who's that, Julia?'

'That's Jamie's sister.'

The picture moved to the next frame.

'These are all Jamie's family. Oh here we are at the unit.'

'Oh they're the ones I took the day Dominic and I came here with you,' I said. 'You look lovely Julia. I didn't know you took one of me and Dominic standing in the doorway.' Everyone laughed at the serious expressions on our faces.

'Now here are some others that were on your phone Mum. Thought I'd toss them in for a laugh.'

Across the screen flicked a picture of Josephine in the back of an ambulance.

Josephine roared with laughter.

We all laughed loudly.

'That's the sprained ankle episode,' Josephine said. 'We could have deleted that one.' She pointed. 'There's one I took on Maria's phone from inside the ambulance.'

'Who's that in the background?' I squinted closer and let out a small gasp. 'This is the night . . .' I stopped and put my hand on Julia's shoulder. 'You haven't got any compromising pictures on there have you?'

'Do you mean the one of you and Josephine with Dominic in bed?' She beamed her most mischievous smile as she flashed the photo onto the screen.

We all screamed with laughter.

'That night was a bit of harum-scarum.' I was talking through uncontrollable laughter.

'And here's one with you two in bed with that other dude. I don't know who he is.' Julia hunched her shoulders.

I recognised him immediately. 'Josie, it's your friend Andrew. Where is Andrew these days?'

'Oh we're fuck-bud . . .' Josephine stopped. 'I mean we're friends with benefits.'

Everyone roared laughing.

'And what's this?' My mouth dropped open and my eyes widened.

I glanced at Dominic who raised his eyebrows and sent me an *I told you so* look.

I could feel my face was flushed. 'Josie, that's you and Dirk.'

'Oh no, that's almost libel to publish that,' Josephine said. 'It was taken the night we met him, remember, Maria?' She laughed. 'I came back from the ladies' room and you made a dash for it. When you got back to the table you pulled out your phone and click, before I knew what was happening, you'd taken a photo of me with the bloody German. I'll never forget that.'

I looked hard at Dominic before lowering my head into my hands.

'Don't you remember Maria?'

'Now I remember,' I answered out of the corner of my mouth. My face was continuing to heat up. I closed my eyes and exhaled deeply.

Julia had finished the photo display and was on the phone to Jamie. Dominic was beside me as still and as quiet as a baker peering into a hot oven. He knew how badly I almost got my fingers burnt. I looked into my empty hands that now lay in my lap. Maybe in them I held the key to explaining to my best friend that I had believed Ursula above her and thought she'd cheated with Dirk.

'What is it Maria?' Josephine's gaze was fixed on me from where she was sitting at my side.

I pushed hair out of my eyes and took a side-ways glance at Dominic. He jumped up from the couch and went outside where he started clearing dishes. Julia followed him out. I got up and sat on the edge of the coffee table in front of Josephine.

'Josie,' I announced with a sigh of resignation. 'I had completely forgotten I'd taken that photo of you and Dirk. I must have emailed you a copy, do you remember sending that on to Ursula?'

I could see her mind ticking over. 'I could have, it wasn't unusual for us to email photos around the office after the weekend. It was a part of the comradeship.' Josephine rolled her eyes. 'Why? What's wrong?'

I raised my head and flicked hair from my face. 'Josephine, I have to talk to you.'

We went outside while Dominic and Julia went into the kitchen to wash the dishes. Jamie was on his way and Dominic said he was keen to hear about the ongoing difficulties with his car. When Jamie arrived, Dominic and Julia greeted him on the footpath while Josephine and I were talking in the front courtyard. I was aware that Dominic was giving me the time and space I needed to divulge my almost unforgivable sin of distrust to

Josephine, and while I was thankful for the opportunity, it didn't make me feel any better about it.

I watched the smile drop from Josephine's face when I presented her with my truth. I wanted to hug her and run from her, all at the same time.

'I can't tell you how sorry I am that I thought that,' I kept repeating.

She was quiet for what seemed a long time and just when I was certain that our friendship had been destroyed forever she looked up at me from across Julia's outdoor table. 'You know what this means don't you?'

'I understand.' I lowered my head.

'Do you? Let me spell it out so there is no doubt.'

I held my breath.

'This means that Ursula is a liar, at the very least.'

'Oh,' I exhaled. I looked into her green eyes floating around behind those big black-rimmed glasses and saw a glimmer of understanding. 'You mean you forgive me?'

'Oh that? I'm disgusted that you thought I would date the German but otherwise yes, I forgive you. But it's Ursula's lies that are more revealing Maria.'

'She may not have been lying, she could have been confused about the photo.'

Josephine exhaled with a huff. 'She's a liar Maria, period. And get it through your head that you are not up to facing her. Is there another meeting that you are going to attend? Will we have to carry you out on a stretcher again?'

I moved slightly in my chair. 'Eight-thirty tomorrow morning.'

'Tomorrow morning? Ursula is certainly in a hurry isn't she. Pull out of it Maria, get out and save yourself a whole lot of heartache. Mark my words, that woman is up to no good.'

'I don't see your reasoning Josie.'

'Think about it Maria,' Josephine snapped. 'Why would Ursula care that I might have been with Dirk? I'll tell you why. She wants to make out that I can't be trusted. But why? Why did she try to turn you against me? Take warning. I have serious suspicions about Ursula and I've started a bit of my own detective work.'

Julia and Jamie bounced through the gate with Dominic and came up the path to the courtyard as I was about to question Josephine.

'Hey Jamie,' Josephine and I chorused.

Jamie smiled and bowed slightly while pushing his dark hair aside. He had matured since the days he used to visit Julia at my place. There was strength about him that I hadn't seen before. He went inside the unit.

Josephine swung around and called after him. 'We should have got you a new car for your house-warming. Either that or your own tow truck.' She laughed.

Julia jumped up and down clapping her hands. 'Jamie and I *are* getting a new car.' She squealed. 'One of Dominic's friends is selling his Subaru.' She swung around to look at Dominic who raised his eyebrows to me and smiled.

I stood up and hugged her. 'Julia, I'm so proud of you.'

'Yeah I know, proud like a peacock.' She gave me a cheeky grin.

We were all laughing when Jamie came back out to the courtyard.

'Congratulations Jamie,' I said.

He shrugged, as if getting a new car was no big deal. Instead he looked at me with a hint of curiosity. 'Are you wearing perfume Ms Valance?'

Our laughter exploded further.

Dominic came up behind me. 'There's just one more thing we have to get sorted.' I saw him wink at Julia. 'Our Moreton Island camping weekend. Better save some of that perfume for the camping trip Maria, don't you think?'

Our laughter was just the tonic I needed. I flopped onto a chair beside Josephine and looked up at Dominic unpacking the barbecue with Julia and Jamie. A settled feeling came across me. Whatever was in front of me, whatever Life sent my way, I felt sure I could accept it.

'Hoy, Dom,' Josephine called. 'What did you give Julia and Jamie for their house-warming party?'

Dominic turned around and glared at Josephine mischievously. His eyes darted from Josephine to me and back again. 'An iPod that works in the shower, want to try it?'

The laughter only increased throughout the afternoon and erased any thoughts I had of Ursula.

Chapter 21

I WAS relieved that the truth behind the photo of Josephine with Dirk had finally been revealed. While it left me with a feeling of sadness that I had been distrustful of my best friend, the knowledge that I was wrong filled me with renewed love for Dirk.

What I was disappointed in was Josephine's dismissal of Ursula's motives. While I understood that a part of that disappointment was due to Josephine not recognising my own good motives, I began to wonder if Josephine was hiding something from me. Whether there were residual feelings of distrust, I wasn't sure. I felt that she knew something I didn't know. And that thought rattled me. I was still happy to trust Ursula. In fact I was more than trustful of her. I believed in her. There was no reason I wouldn't. All that was behind me. We'd become friends.

I looked at myself in the mirror as I pulled my jacket on and straightened my skirt. My hair had grown and now flicked out at the ends of its own accord. It was a good look, my hairdresser told me. She reckoned the extra length and the darker shade of brown that I'd chosen actually highlighted my eyes and lifted my face. I certainly needed all the lift I could get. This meeting was important to me on several levels. And that was another thing that I felt dismayed about with regards to Josephine. She had not taken the time to care how important it was to me.

But one of the most significant reasons that was pushing me to stand with and trust Ursula was to become a better person. I had to forgive. I had to stop feeling sorry for myself and begin to act. I had to be the woman I wanted to be.

I moved away from the mirror and collected my things. I was heading out my front door when Dominic called.

'Maria, I'm sorry to ring you so early.' He spoke hesitantly over background noise.

'Where are you?'

'Out the front of my house. I've locked my car keys inside, and my house keys.'

'Oh no.' I glanced at the time.

'. . . in your boot,' he was saying when I returned the phone to my ear.

'What?'

'That small step stool in your boot.'

'It's for Julia, I forgot to give it to her.'

'Would you bring it over?'

'Now?' I hoped he would say no.

'Please? I'll message you the address.'

I waited for the message to arrive, pushed my phone into my pocket, and threw my car door open and slid in. Obviously it didn't stop with kids. Mothers were born with a cab license and it had to be used.

I pulled up outside Dominic's apartment in Sandgate about ten minutes later. Dominic was sitting on the footpath leaning against the fence. He jumped to his feet when he saw me and came over to my car. He pulled the door open and smiled.

'Hello there, thanks for this.'

I sighed. 'It's okay, I'm on my way to the station anyway.'

I followed Dominic as he took the step stool up the side footpath, dry leaves of winter crackling under our feet. The shade from the overhanging mango tree next door nurtured a bubble of cold air and as I moved through it I felt a shiver go across my chest. Dominic was eyeing the side of the brick building. We looked up at the window. It had a security screen. He would never be able to break in.

'Out back,' he called as he dashed around there, step stool in hand. 'The bathroom window doesn't have a security screen.' There was a moment's silence. 'Oh but it's too high, we'll have to get something to stand the stool on so we can raise it up a bit.'

I pulled my phone from my skirt pocket and glanced at the time. I'd already missed the early train and there was twenty minutes until the next one.

'Here Maria,' Dominic called.

I shoved my phone away and followed him to the back yard.

'Help me get these.' He pointed in the direction of a few scattered bricks. 'If we put these together we might be able to make a base that we could put the stool on.' He heaved a few bricks up.

I grabbed a brick. 'There's no more after this, it's not going to work Dominic.' I groaned. 'I'll have to phone Ursula, I should be there now.'

'Ursula?'

I tossed the brick and hushed him as I dialled Ursula's number.

When I hung up Dominic mumbled some kind of comment about my not having told him about the meeting.

'I don't have to tell you everything Dominic.' I smoothed my skirt and flicked hair back from my face.

'I suppose you don't.' But the look on his face spoke a thousand words.

'Don't worry. I won't faint if that's what you're thinking. You helped me feel strong, I owe it to you that I can face Ursula.'

'Hmm, I'm pretty sure that wasn't my intention.'

'Anyway she moved the meeting to eleven. And I don't know why I didn't think of this before, but why not get in my car and I'll take you to the rental agent so you can get another key.'

'They don't open for another half an hour,' Dominic replied. 'I'll take another look-see out the other side of the building first, there might be more bricks.'

I found him out the back a few minutes later sitting on the stairs. He slid his phone into his pocket as I approached and looked at me steadily. 'Don't go to that meeting Maria. I've got a bad feeling about it.'

I put my hand on my hip. 'Has Josie been in your ear?'

'Josephine did message me but she didn't say anything more than she wanted me to try to talk you out of going.' He got to his feet and stood in front of me. 'She's worried.'

I glared at him. 'You didn't really lock your keys in did you?'

'No, I mean, yes I did. This is a coincidence. And it's given me a chance to talk to you. You didn't answer your phone last night.'

'I didn't pick up because I'm tired of you and Josephine trying to orchestrate my life.' I scrunched my way back through the cold air to the front of the apartment block. Josephine's car had just pulled up out front. I stomped to the footpath. 'Oh and here we go again. It's pretty early for a visit isn't it?' I snorted.

Josephine was out of the car before Dominic could get to my side but I saw them exchange a glance.

'So it's a conspiracy? I should have known.' I headed to my car. 'Well maybe you can drive our mate Dominic to get his house keys.'

'Maria wait, I have to talk to you.'

I spun around. 'If it's about my meeting this morning or if it's about Ursula or if it's about anything remotely to do with either of those things, no.' I pulled my car door open. I turned and looked at Dominic. 'Do you know what this is about?'

The icy interactions between Dominic and me were worse than the pocket of air down the side of his house. I felt several shivers go across my chest as he looked at me.

He glanced at Josephine. 'I don't know what Josie has on her mind.'

Josephine stood in front of me. 'The last time you turned up to see Ursula you fainted Maria. You could have been far more injured than you were. You had Dominic waiting on you like you were an invalid and now you're prepared to put him through more of the same?'

'I didn't tell Dominic where I was going for that precise reason. Josephine, it seems to me that if you could keep your nose out of my business everyone would be better off.' I slipped into my car seat as Josephine slammed her car door. She started the engine and accelerated with a spin of tires.

I looked at Dominic. 'If you want a lift to your real estate people you better get in.'

He ambled to my car, step stool in hand, as if he hadn't just witnessed a high speed acceleration of emotions. 'If you could get me there, I'll wait for them to open.'

'Get in.'

Dominic held the step stool up for me to see. 'Where do you want this?'

'Put it on the back seat.'

He got in and closed the door.

I didn't say another word to him. He thanked me when I dropped him off and I headed straight to the station. I had a couple of hours before the meeting but I didn't want anything else to go wrong.

I was in the city by nine-thirty. I felt exasperated and overwhelmed. I spent until ten in the public toilets of Central Station vying for the mirror so I could tidy myself and remove bits of leaves and brick dust from my skirt. The early morning commuters dashed in and out. Toilets flushed almost continuously. Women on their way out flicked their wet hands and dropped them into the hand-dryer where the air and the sound were like the wake turbulence of a 747 taking off. Some of the younger women jostled each other for mirror space and applied make-up, fixing lip gloss before stepping through their own rabbit hole to their world of work.

And for the entire time I had to fight back angry thoughts about Josephine and her increasing dog-eat-dog approach to my life. If I was going to succeed at anything I set out to do, it looked like I had to take on the same dogged attitude. If I was to believe in myself and stand up for those beliefs I couldn't let opinions and quarrels hold me back. I pulled my shoulders down, held my head high and took one last glance at the complicated look of fear and determination that was written all over my face. I strutted off to the South State Legal building in Adelaide Street.

I arrived at the staff entrance at ten-thirty and straightened my skirt and jacket one last time. I had labored over the decision to wear my red jacket for power, or my black jacket for professionalism. I'd gone with black. Red was a little too powerful. I wanted to stand behind Ursula, not in front of her. This was not a time to be the center of attention but a time to be strong. I peeked down at my heels. Not too high. Certainly could have done with a bit more polish especially after Dominic's leaf litter. But okay. I moved about trying to address my posture, gave in and edged up against the wall. And waited.

Each time the door opened I thought it would be Ursula and, every time it turned out to be another staff member, I let out a little sigh of exasperation. I was nervous but I was sure I wouldn't faint again. Apart from my anger, which was beginning to abate, I was feeling almost emotionally stable. I stood confidently, albeit somewhat nervously. I hadn't yet seen anyone I knew.

Everyone seemed to be a new staff member. That was a little unnerving.

At ten forty-five Ursula pulled the door open and said hello. There was an air of decisiveness about her but also a wall of tension. She was the old Ursula, the one who had the ability to drive fear into my heart. I felt my confidence shrink and fall away like the label off a soup can. I was exposed for the chicken I really was. Chicken and leek. I felt a sudden urge for a ladies' room. Josephine's warning went through my mind. Something was dreadfully wrong. I only had to look at Ursula's scowl to see that. I cleared my throat, inhaled deeply and performed mental plastic surgery on my face. Julia Roberts couldn't have smiled more broadly.

'Good morning Ursula, sorry about the delay.'

'I'm just glad you're here Maria. Come through.' She held the door wide for me. 'I told Joseph we'd be up in fifteen minutes. I've booked a room for us to conference in before the meeting.' She led me up a colorless hallway. 'I'll have to get you a visitor's pass.'

I nodded and pointed in the direction of the ladies' room. I made a quick exit and when I returned I followed her into a room that was furnished with a desk, a telephone and two chairs. She disappeared for a few minutes during which time I read posters on the wall about emergency exits and fire wardens. The emergency exits were familiar to me. The fire wardens with their red or yellow helmets were all new faces.

Ursula returned with a book to sign and a visitor's pass to stick on my lapel. I pushed it on and smoothed it out. Labelled at last. All that had to happen now was to be boxed up and shipped out. I sighed inwardly.

I signed the book and Ursula returned it to someone waiting at the door. She closed the door firmly. Holding herself upright as if she might be about to walk a straight line in order to prove her sobriety, Ursula went to the other side of the desk and sat in the high-backed chair. She indicated with a flick of her hand for me to sit opposite her. I eased into the chair and edged it closer to the desk.

I looked at the young woman sitting opposite me as she opened her folder and thumbed through documents. Gone was the good-natured chatting of our coffee get-togethers. Gone was Ursula's charming casual attire, comfortable ballet flats and spring scarf. Before me was the same Ursula I had worked under, the same Ursula who had sent the scathing and untrue account to HR regarding my work standards. I shuddered at the thought that I might be mistaken in my belief that she was a changed woman ready to defend and stand united with me for a common cause. I began to jitter in my seat.

'So,' she saluted. 'Thanks for coming along today Maria.' She still hadn't made eye contact. 'I know that when we first agreed to have a meeting with the CEO you had the understanding that we would present him with a revised statement about how things occurred when you were working at South State Legal.'

I nodded agreement. She hadn't straightened her fringe. It was a row of little black curls across her forehead. I had to adjust my glance to focus on what she was saying.

'You will recall that while you were employed here there were several times you accused me of bullying.' She looked up at me with her narrowed brown eyes that almost disappeared underneath her frown. 'And that since then I have explained to you that it was in fact senior management who had instigated that bullying.'

I nodded and moved closer to the edge of the seat. I peered at the papers she had placed in front of her. She pulled them away from me. I retreated in my chair.

'I have here firstly, the job description under which you operated when you were in the role of administrative assistant.'

I nodded and flashed the Julia Roberts smile.

'I also have a copy of your complaint to the CMC.'

'Ursula, I probably should inform you.' I scratched my leg. 'Strictly speaking I didn't actually lodge that complaint.'

She glared at me. 'What do you mean?'

'I mean, I wrote it.' I smiled and nodded. 'But I tossed it in the bin. Someone else has put that in on my behalf.'

'Hmm, probably a bit late to tell me that.' She flicked through more paperwork. 'It's been accepted as yours and you've signed the statement.'

I nodded but she ignored me.

'I also have here a statement you may wish to read and sign in which you request to be re-instated.'

'But I hadn't . . .'

'Maria, I know we didn't get onto that side of things but given the circumstances, it might be the best way to go. It will distract them from too deep an investigation.'

'Do you want me to sign it now?'

'No need. First up we will discuss the bullying. We'll get onto re-instatement at our next meeting.' She looked at me with a fixed stare. 'Is there anything else?'

I blinked and held my breath for a moment. 'Not that I'm aware of.'

'Maria this will not be easy.' She glared at me with contempt. 'You need to follow my lead throughout, is that understood?'

I disengaged from her stare. 'Sure.' I nodded as I studied my hands in my lap.

'If there is anything further we need to discuss we will call the meeting to a stop and have a conference. Do you follow?'

I looked at her and nodded.

Ursula stood up and went to the door that she opened slightly. She put her head around it and whispered to someone before pulling the door wide open.

I looked up to see Chloe-rose standing there with a face like a porcelain doll. It was fresh, it was pretty, it glowed with painted love but it was rigid. She didn't speak to me. I tried to make eye contact but she fixed her stare straight ahead.

'Let's go,' Ursula commanded.

We followed her down the hallway to the elevator.

Chapter 22

'SO UM, I'd just like to open up the conversation about the items we have for discussion,' Ursula announced as we sat around the CEO's conference table.

Opposite me was Felix. He sat hunched over a thick file fiddling with the corner of it as if he was trying to lift the edges of an adhesive label stuck to an apple.

His double chin was firmly held in. He hadn't looked at me when I arrived. Instead he had flopped his soft jelly hand into mine in a feeble attempt to welcome me and had taken a seat before completely releasing his cold grip.

Beside Felix was David. He looked almost embarrassed to be there, as if someone had told him his job was on the line if he didn't show. He glanced at me slyly out of the side of his eye. Opposite David was Joseph. His blue eyes sparkled with welcome for everyone. As CEO he made the perfect host regardless of the fact that we were there to discuss a serious work issue. He offered coffee and made feeble jokes about how the coffee machine he'd ordered for his staff was the most treasured article on the entire floor. Chloe-rose was beside him. She flicked her long hair back from her shoulders occasionally with an air of self-confidence and smiled sweetly at all of Joseph's wisecracks about the coffee machine. Ursula was beside her, looking professional and intelligent but exceedingly nervous. And I beside Ursula shook inside of my unpolished shoes as I tried to remember why on earth I was there.

'Joseph as you are aware this meeting was instigated as an outcome of a complaint that Maria Valance made to the CMC,' Ursula began.

I nodded and scratched my neck. David bit his lip.

Felix leaned his arm across the table, placed his other hand firmly onto his knee. 'Before we go any further.' He heaved his body forward in the chair. 'I have something to say.' He flicked the file open. 'We've all read Ursula's report. I would like it to be noted that while the complaint was written by Maria it was not lodged by her. So let's be clear on that, I don't know how legitimate it is.' He raised his eyebrows. 'But whatever way you look at it, Maria has left the organisation and as far as I'm aware she has not applied to be re-instated.' He slammed the file closed. 'That's enough. I'd like to move on to more pressing matters.'

Everyone fidgeted in their chairs.

'What matters are you bringing to the table Felix?' Joseph inquired.

Felix moved his heavy frame back further in the chair. His belly hung over his pants and the buttons of his pale blue shirt pulled tightly.

He glared at Ursula. 'I have brought with me the entire financial figures for the time I have been manager of the Criminal Law Unit.'

'Excuse me Joseph,' Ursula interrupted. 'This is not about finances, this is about workplace-relation issues.' She glared at Felix before making eye contact with everyone around the table. She directed her next words to

Joseph. 'It may well be correct that we have to look at finances, but only to discuss how the budget was used as an excuse to condone bullying in order to minimise staff.'

'Wait on,' Joseph said. He made firm eye contact with Ursula. 'How have financial matters brought about bullying?' He let out a small puff of air that was almost a laugh. 'We've budgeted for an administration assistant in the team.' He looked at me. 'I was under the impression that you left of your own accord Maria?'

He so obviously had not read my complaints or any documentation. I rubbed my chin and was about to speak when Ursula spoke for me.

'Joseph I want to highlight the tactics Felix used for meeting budget. Those tactics finally brought about Maria's resignation. That's the basis of this meeting.'

Felix interrupted. 'With all due respect Joseph, I don't know why Maria's here at all. The CMC will investigate her claims if they see fit.'

'Chloe-rose and Maria are here as my support and witnesses,' Ursula said. Her voice had risen slightly.

Felix picked up his file and dropped it heavily onto the table. 'Witness to what? From what I can see you are dragging Maria in to make a statement that she could have made when she wrote to the CMC. She didn't make it because that wasn't her sentiment.'

'That's not entirely true Joseph', Ursula responded.

Joseph re-positioned himself in his chair. 'Look, can we please take a moment to put down the points for discussion? Have you got anything to say Maria?'

I sat open-mouthed. My mind was like the blank white board on the CEO's wall. There was nothing I could have begun to draw or even scribble on it that would have made any sense. I looked at Ursula. She didn't flinch but stared straight ahead waiting for me to say something. But I didn't know what to say.

'Um.' I cleared my throat. 'It's true that when I was working here I was bullied, I wrote you a letter with regard to that Joseph.'

Joseph flicked through a bunch of papers in front of him.

'The thing is that at the time I was under a lot of stress. All I could see was Ursula and the attitude she was adopting toward me. I knew Felix was pushing her but I forgot to mention that in my complaint.'

'What are you trying to say?' Felix asked. 'Are you making accusations against me?

I repositioned myself in the chair and cleared my throat.

Felix made a snorting kind of sound that was like a pig foraging for food. 'You are no longer an employee. Are you wanting your old job back?'

'Not at this point.'

Felix looked at Joseph. 'Then there's no issue to sort out.'

'Re-instatement is not what you're here about today then?' Joseph reiterated.

I shook my head from side to side. My mouth was dry. I wished that I'd spent more time preparing something to say. Well, any time preparing. The truth was that I had relied completely on Ursula.

'All right then,' Joseph concluded. 'It seems to me that we have a couple of things going on here. Felix what's the point behind your financial report at this time?'

I scanned each face. Everyone was looking at Felix waiting for him to answer. I fixed my gaze on Ursula's hands that were twisting and bending a paper clip on her lap beside me, her elbows making little jabbing movements into my arm.

'I have evidence to suggest that Ursula has been . . .' Felix began.

I can't recall what was actually said after that. I remember hearing sirens outside and seeing heads turn to look through the window while Felix was speaking. I was spellbound when Joseph was interrupted by his secretary who knocked at the door. She looked straight-faced and stern. There was a moment when Joseph excused himself from the room and we all sat in silence waiting for his return. I remember Ursula and Chloe-rose whispering frantically to each other as if something terrible was about to happen. From there on it's pretty much a blur.

What I do remember is that when Joseph appeared at the door again, Josephine was behind him with two police officers. I was lost in complete dumbfounded silence. My first thought was that something must have happened to Julia and my heart leaped to my throat. But in a split-second I knew it wasn't about Julia at all, it was about Ursula. But Ursula had dashed out the side door into the hallway as soon as Josephine appeared. Ursula had fled. Without thinking I bounded after her.

I was a few yards behind her when she opened the staff door and pushed past a couple of lawyers as they were entering the building.

I was further behind when she ran up the street towards Anzac Square. Moments before she got to the stairs to the Shrine of Remembrance I called to her. I thought she'd stop and wait for me. I wasn't trying to harm her. I had no idea why she was running but whatever was wrong, I wanted to help. Instead she climbed the stairs in a frantic rush looking back every now and again towards me. I slowed down, thinking I would turn back but as I swung around I saw that the police were chasing us. I turned in Ursula's direction and ran after her again. At the bottom of the stairs I came to a dead halt.

'Ursula!' I screamed. Her heel had caught on a step. She slipped. I don't know if I'll ever forget the agonising moment I watched her fall and topple backwards, the feelings of despair I felt inside of me and how my own voice rose in a crescendo of screams as it registered in my mind that the thud I had heard was Ursula's head hitting the steps.

I ran up the stairs to her side. She lay still and motionless, sprawled out like a puppet dropped from a giant's hands, her head twisted in such a way that could only mean a broken neck.

Pulling my phone from my skirt pocket I dialled the emergency number with the same surreal consciousness that I had felt ever since I gave chase. The police and passers-by stood around me. No one spoke. It was as if I had become the leader and I was in charge. I held the phone as the operator asked me to check for vital signs.

'Check her neck for a pulse, is she breathing? Is she moving?'

'No, no, no,' was all I could answer.

'Don't move her, keep people clear. Get someone to direct the ambulance on arrival.'

Most of the passers-by had moved away by the time I became cognizant of my surroundings. I looked up. Joseph was there with two policemen. Josephine stood beside them. Josephine and I exchanged a look that I will always remember. Ursula wasn't going to make it.

I wanted to go in the ambulance with Ursula but Joseph and Felix insisted it was their responsibility. Instead I walked back to the office building. Someone let me in the staff entrance and I went up to get my bag. Josephine was behind me at one point but we didn't speak. When I came downstairs she was waiting. I went to the police car with her and David.

As we piled into the back seat, Josephine commented that Chloe-rose had been taken in for questioning in a separate police car. Her father had been questioned in Redcliffe earlier in the morning. I imagined Harold's upside-down smile would have been appropriate for the occasion but I didn't say anything. None of us said anything more. I felt as if I was in a warped time zone. Everything had stopped. Josephine peered out the window as we drove. I glanced across at David and thought I saw a tear. His face looked like a twisted and sad Cabbage Patch doll.

I arrived at the police station in a state of confusion. By the time I had answered their many questions about what I could remember and listened to David's uncontrollable sobbing, I was less than prepared for Josephine's account of the story. I was weary and my head ached as if a decade of premenstrual tension had awoken and decided to strike in one day. Fraud. That's what Josephine was saying in fast, almost indecipherable speech. The word echoed in my mind like thunder. Fraud. Fraud. Fraud.

'I became aware that there were inconsistencies at Crime Legal,' Josephine said as she composed herself. 'The first thing I noticed was that Harold got our friend Dominic in to update the data base. That seemed innocent enough but soon after that I became aware that Harold had made up files for non-existent clients. It didn't take me long to see what he was doing.'

'What was he doing?' the Interviewing Officer asked.

'He was applying to South State Legal for government funding for those bogus clients. Large amounts were being transferred across to Crime Legal regularly, larger than the normal amount of funding would be. I presumed that Ursula was manipulating funds at South State's end but I had no proof of that.' Josephine stopped momentarily and looked at me. 'When Ursula got in touch with Maria and me trying to gain our support it just didn't add up. I think they . . .'

'They?' the Interviewing Officer asked.

'Ursula, Chloe-rose and her father, Harold.'

'Go on.'

Josephine looked at me. 'I think they hoped that by focusing on Felix as the instigator of bullying, they could re-direct the organization's response to Maria's complaint and prevent further investigation of Ursula.' She looked back at the Interviewing Officer. 'When Ursula couldn't get me to support her, she tried to discredit me.'

Josephine said she felt she had no choice but to move quickly as she didn't know what Ursula's next move might be. She said she spent the morning pulling up client files and printing out financial records. Josephine had tried to set it up so that I didn't attend the meeting and I wouldn't be there when it all blew up. She stopped and looked at me again at that point.

'I thought that the meeting itself would be further evidence of Ursula trying to manipulate the situation with Felix. I didn't say anything to Maria for fear that Ursula would suspect I was on to it. Maria trusted Ursula.' She dropped her gaze. 'I didn't want anyone to get hurt.'

I just hung my head and cried. There was nothing else I could do. David offered to drive me home afterwards but I refused. I wanted to be alone. I ached to be alone. I had no idea where Josephine went. And at the time I was still so stunned that I didn't care.

Chapter 23

MY house greeted me with the cold, dark silence of a morgue. I kicked my shoes across the room and threw my bag after them with all the strength I could muster. The bag hit the far wall and fell with a thud to the floor spilling its guts and the fragile privacy it held within it. My compact case burst open and sent little chips of compressed powder all over the floor. The mirror inside the case shattered.

I pulled at my hair as if it was the reason all this chaotic lunacy had propelled itself my way and finally I broke down sobbing and slumped onto the lounge room floor in the dark. If I could have stayed there forever I would have felt strangely satisfied. There's something about crying alone in a dark room, stretched out on a cold hard floor. You can let loose all your inhibitions, all your anger, sadness, despair. You can throw away the reality of your own existence in there. I didn't want to answer the door to Dominic when I heard him outside calling me. I wanted to be alone. Totally. Forever. Alone. Why didn't he know that? I let him call until he knew I was not going to answer. Then I went back to crying.

I observed several missed calls on my phone over the next couple of days. Julia had been the only person I had spoken to and that was only briefly to let her know I was okay but was in mourning. That was after Josephine had left a recorded message confirming what I already knew. Ursula was dead. Josephine's voice sounded hollow and cold, not at all like the friend I used to know. She said the funeral was on Friday and gave me the details. I must have listened to the message at least ten times and each time I shook my head over and over as I sobbed at what was happening and what I was hearing. I couldn't believe how things had worked out. But I'd be at that funeral. I believed in Ursula. She was a strong, defiant young woman who should have known better. But we'd become friends. I would honour that.

It was days before I could pull a blind open and let a bit of sunshine in. The world outside had transformed into an alien land. No longer did I feel the urge to listen to the butcherbird, no longer did I want to sit on my veranda and drink coffee. I stood at the back door watching the umbrella tree stand tall as if standing tall was really the only option in the face of despair. Ursula's voice rang in my ears as I remembered seeing her sitting at my table and laughing about her father's pet name for her mother's dogs. I re-lived over and over again the moment I watched her tumble down the stairs.

If I could have re-wound time to when we were sitting in the meeting I would have done that. I would have jumped to my feet and stopped her from running, pleaded with her to face the sad reality of her errors. But I couldn't do that.

I was sorry for Ursula. I was sorry for Josephine. My heart sang the sad tune of Josephine's violin and in my mind's eye I saw her playing as if she was in some great orchestra. I prepared for Ursula's funeral as if a great loss had happened to the world. My world.

Dominic was waiting for me outside St Francis of Assisi Church after the Requiem Mass. He stood tall in a dark suit and crisp blue shirt, his hands clasped in front as I walked toward him. My heart melted at the knowledge of the love he held for me and if I wavered at all as I approached him it was because of my own self-doubt, not because I wasn't grateful for his love.

He reached out. I gave him my hand. 'Maria,' was all he whispered. It was enough. Had he said any more it would have been verbose. Just greet me, I thought. Say no more. There is nothing to say.

Josephine stepped up from behind him. We exchanged a look that didn't need words. I ran to her and we held each other like the sisters we felt we were. Pushed apart by our different beliefs, pushed together again by the tragedy. That's how I saw it.

We three drove to the cemetery together and stood side-by-side holding hands as the coffin was lowered into the ground. One of Ursula's nieces, held tightly by her mother, tossed a rose on top of the coffin as it began to go down. As I watched her I could almost see the colored arm floaties and the sparkling water that had glistened in Ursula's photos on her desk. In her eyes I saw the controlled determination that she would take with her into her own future. A tear dropped from my eye as I thought about the young woman who loved her nieces so much that she had crowded her professional desk with pictures of them. I wondered at the fear that Ursula must have hidden within, the fear that drove her to deceive and run rather than stand up and face her truth.

As the priest finalized prayers over the coffin he added one more gesture. 'I'd like to read a verse from Two Corinthians, chapter twelve, verses nine and ten,' he announced with charisma. 'I'm not sure how many of you are aware that Ursula was a wonderful example to the young people in our parish. She contributed to religious education classes at her nieces' school every week. She told me once that this was her favorite passage. He looked down at the Bible he held in his hands and began to read. 'My grace is all you need for my power is greatest when you are weak. I am most happy then, to be proud of my weaknesses, in order to feel the protection of Christ's power over me.' He looked up before continuing. 'For when I am weak, then I am strong.' He closed the book and bowed his head.

I pulled a Kleenex from my bag and held it to my nose. I was certainly feeling weak.

The three of us turned from the graveside and sauntered back to Dominic's car. There weren't any words that we could say to one another that would explain the sense of finality that seemed to pass between us. It wasn't just about Ursula. A time of our lives had come to an end. It was as if one of the arm floaties had burst in our faces and we were left with the lasting sting of something gone wrong. In the blink of an eyelid life had changed.

There was no banter as we drove back to the church, only a shared feeling of loss. Dominic dropped Josephine to her car first. My car was around the corner. He left the engine running when he pulled up. He patted my knee before I got out. I waved as he drove off.

It was one forty-seven in the morning eight days after Ursula's funeral that I woke to discover that I'd gone to sleep with the light on. I pulled myself out of bed, slipped my feet into socks, threw a rug around my shoulders and with a pillow under my arm trudged downstairs to the back door. I flicked the outside light on over the veranda and peered around the curtains. It was the only place I might find serenity. I slid the door open and stepped outside.

The cold, dark shadows of night crept around me as if they were ghosts of days gone by. The moon struggled through gray streaks of cloud to assert itself. I slipped into the chair at which I'd sat opposite Ursula only two weeks earlier, pulled the rug tighter around me, crossed one leg over the other and rested my head on my pillow against the back of the chair.

The best laid plans don't always have the most favorable outcomes. That was an understatement. But it went through my mind repeatedly as I sat there in the darkness. That was when I first became fully conscious of what I had been carrying underneath the facade. I was lonely. Miserably, desperately, unashamedly lonely. I'd become what no one was meant to be. An island. Unattended. Unregulated. Every *un* word that is unimaginable.

Worse than lonely. It was also true that I had become bitter. I'd become like the lemon tree in my back yard: out of place, wild, thorny and unkempt. There was a possibility of making lemonade but the likelihood was the same as my making time to pick the lemons and squeeze them. Negligible.

As I thought back over the events leading up to that final meeting with Ursula it appeared to me that each of us had been set on our own self-centered path. I didn't need to look up any of Julia's psychology books to come up with that conclusion. It was as plain as the make-up on Chloe-rose's nose. Chloe-rose, who should have a brilliant future in front of her, was now facing fraud charges. My heart went out to her and withdrew from her almost in the same moment. She and Ursula had used me to try to cover their own plot. And I had been too focused on what I wanted to realize it.

But each of us had had something personal to gain through our interactions. I thought I was standing up for justice. Maybe at a deep level I had wanted to be re-instated. There could have been a part of me that had wanted revenge. Or it could have been that I thought I had not contributed anything of value in my life and it had to be done before it was too late. Before I got too old.

Josephine gained recognition for unraveling what she had suspected. I wondered if maybe that was all she had ever wanted. Recognition. Maybe for Josephine it had been about being needed I wondered if that was what had been behind her dislike of Dirk, her one-night stands, her friends-with-benefits. Just a great big need to be accepted and loved for who she was.

As for Dominic, he had been parenting me with the protectiveness and yearning of a parent whose only child had been taken from him. His motives were loving but misguided.

I questioned myself at length about all of those thoughts. The answers floated around in my head searching for a place to rest like leaves blowing along the ground after a storm.

I imagined that nothing would change at South State Legal. Felix would go on unchallenged now that Ursula was gone. David would be able to apply for Ursula's position once he gained experience. Joseph would fail to see the breeding ground for the belligerence in the organisation. There would be whispering in the corridors, gossip over the lunchroom table during the *Dr. Phil* ads but no one would ever really know what happened to Ursula, or to Maria Valance for that matter, and when questions were asked shoulders would be shrugged.

I didn't understand why these thoughts presented themselves the way they did. Maybe I was becoming bitter after all. Maybe I hadn't learned anything or indeed if I had, I'd learned that Life cannot be structured within neatly framed walls and that at times even if you felt that you didn't have the strength to go on, strength was there waiting for you in the deepest recesses of your being. The priest's words rang in my ears, *my power is greatest when you are weak*. I sure could have used some of that power.

But I knew where my loneliness came from. I missed Dominic. I missed the love he gave me. I missed being the child for him. I'd been looking to him to be protected. But now there was nothing for him to protect. Now we stood either face to face as two adults who were going to create a healthy relationship together or there was nothing for us.

Parenting each other was definitely a *no-no* in all of my relationship books. I knew that much. And in my mind I heard Dr. Phil say *do y'all get this?* But it didn't matter what Dr. Phil said or how much Dominic loved me, my heart was still with Dirk.

I drew my legs up and dozed with thoughts of the past months flicking across my mind like Julia's slide show across the television screen. It wasn't only about missing Dominic or loving Dirk. It was about the entire hurt and emotional turmoil of the months behind me. Instead of allowing myself to heal I'd demanded of myself to cope. There was a huge difference. Healing does not come from coping.

It was the breaking of dawn and the first stirrings of the creatures of the day that awoke me. I pushed myself out from the table and stumbled up the stairs back to bed. I woke again at seven-thirty. I felt a little fresher so I went downstairs, put the kettle on and went ahead with preparing myself breakfast.

Twenty minutes later I felt almost alive and decided to set myself up with my laptop and breakfast on the back veranda where soon the butcherbird would gallivant at the end of the table and whistle its captivating song. I knew what I had to do. I had to move into the stage of life where I nurtured not only my emotions but also my spirituality. Hadn't I known that all along? Hadn't that been the basis of the inspiration which had been calling me? It was the time of my life where it wasn't enough to look forward. I had to look back and assess. It wasn't about living in the past. It was about bringing into the present the lessons of my past so I could meet the future with wisdom and hopefulness. I pulled my laptop open and logged into my email account. I wanted to write what I was feeling. Speaking the words didn't seem appropriate.

I was in the middle of composing an email to Josephine when I heard someone knocking at my side gate. I eased myself up, pulled my robe around my waist and tied the belt. I stepped gingerly down the steps past the umbrella tree and around the lemon tree.

I opened the gate and put my head around. A man wearing a yellow luminescent jacket peered into my face.

He smiled. 'Hallor,' he said.

My eyes dropped to the shovel and measuring tape he was holding in one hand before returning to examine his face.

'Ve vill be vorking on the footpath for one hour, your car cannot coom out. You will need to use this one?'

The familiarity of his accent threw me. I felt myself flush with excitement as a slither of light entered my mind. I must have stood silently scrutinizing his face for a moment before I heard him clear his throat. I looked into his swimming-pool-blue eyes and thought I might drown. I was sure I saw a light in there which suggested he'd read my thoughts. If I did a quick back-paddle I might get out undetected. I averted my gaze and dismissed my thoughts quickly.

'I will be here all morning,' I told him as my hand went to my chin. 'No need for me to use the car.' My fingers smoothed across my lips as I stared into the distance. I was lost in the rush of thoughts going through my mind.

'Goot,' I heard him reply.

I composed myself and noted the clutter of equipment waiting on the footpath. I scanned the road where another yellow jacket was marking out the shape of the gutter to be repaired. I closed the gate, leaned against it and caught my breath before retracing my steps to the veranda.

As I passed the lemon tree a noisy miner objected to my intrusion with the clacking of its beak. It spread its wings, threatening me to dare come near it. I plonked myself onto the garden swing and instantly became aware of the trickle of memories beginning to take shape in my mind. I hadn't finished things with Dirk. It was right there under the surface. The voice. The emotions. The love. All of it, there waiting for me to pluck it out and do something with it. It was Dirk I missed.

Several other birds joined the noisy miner but I ignored their pleas to vacate and found myself staring into the lemon tree. I will never forget the feeling of so many memories shooting into my mind. It was like lightning across a dark sky. My senses were zapped into ignition, my eyes widened, my hearing became attuned. It was as if a symphony of emotion had overtaken me as thoughts of Dirk and I together came back to me.

The noise of the birds escalated with each of my thoughts to the point where I felt mentally backed into a corner by them. I was a predator. I had to move or they would never rest. That's when I saw it beside the fence, an injured bird lying on its side, probably dead. While the opposition dive-bombed and sounded warning screeches at me I got up and slowly moved toward it searching for any signs of life. There were none. I returned to the swing and closed my eyes rocking back and forth as I thought about the beginnings and endings of life.

Before I knew what had happened I became lost in my own world. The idle chatter between the two workmen on the other side of the fence and the noise of their jack hammers cutting concrete mixed with the death ritual of the birds and became a cacophony of confusion in my mind. I was listening to a perfect orchestration of the previous months of my life. Friendly chatter. Work. Confusion. Death. A down-hill slide. I blinked my eyes open and I knew. There was one more thing to do before I could begin to have closure. Before I could heal and move forward. I had to see Dirk.

Almost at the same moment that I came to that conclusion the knocking on the fence re-commenced and my thoughts were brought back to my surroundings. I pulled the robe to my chest and stumbled up the path to the gate.

'This one is finished for now,' the German road worker announced. 'But ve vill return tomorrow to do this one some more.'

I nodded. 'Thank you.'

As the latch on the gate closed I noticed that the birds had become silent. But the sound of the German accent lingered in my mind. Yes. It was time to sort things out with Dirk.

Chapter 24

I STRUGGLED with my thoughts for most of the day. But the truth was that regardless of my doubts, I was excited about seeing Dirk and I couldn't help but think he had been wrong that we couldn't make a life together. My notion that love was the most important thing in a relationship was certainly gone. I'd learnt that trust and loyalty, communication and understanding were the elements needed to succeed. I'd begun to understand the way walls can keep others out. Or yourself in. I'd recognised that I'd built them with every relationship I had. But if I could tear those walls down and live my relationship with Dirk in a more responsible way, it could work. I knew it could.

It was late afternoon when I showered and dressed in my new white-with-black-swirls spring dress. I pulled on my multi-coloured jacket, my favorite red Diana Ferrari sling-backs and a bracelet that I hadn't worn in months.

As I walked out of my bedroom I stopped. I went back and sprayed my neck with a touch of the Red Door perfume that had been so popular at the house-warming afternoon. Excitement ran through my veins and pumped my heart to a flutter. It had been at least six weeks since I'd seen Dirk. And now I knew with my whole being that I could make it work with him. I knew what I'd always known. He was the man with whom I would spend the rest of my life.

It was dusk when I turned into Dirk's driveway. He was in the yard raking leaves. I eased to a stop and watched him for a moment recalling the first time I ever visited his house. The grass had been dry. The shrubs with their bare branches looked forlorn. In contrast, after the summer rain Dirk used to present me with a choreographic display when I arrived, flitting from one bush to another showing me the results of his efforts to bring the overgrowth under control. The amount of tears I cried in the shower before I dressed for my reunion with Dirk was almost as much as the amount of rain we had during the early weeks we were together. The days behind me and the time without Dirk had been washed away. I couldn't believe how happy I felt.

I parked in his driveway and got out of the car. I stood in the shadows for a moment and watched as he returned the rake to the shed. I was familiar with his gait, every muscle he moved, every turn of his head, every step. Everything was starting to come together for me although it was still a little confusing. But as I gazed at him I was certain that he was the man I wanted to be with.

Dirk closed the door of the shed and turned to look at me. I couldn't predict how he was going to greet me. So much had changed between us. Our eyes met and I could tell he'd been drinking. There was a softness in the look he gave me that otherwise would have been locked away. No choreography today, he took purposeful steps towards me and we momentarily stood face to face before he pulled me into an embrace.

I didn't know whether to laugh or cry, so I did neither. I just breathed in his warmth, luxuriated in the familiar touch of his skin, the strength of his arms around me. I closed my eyes and abandoned any thoughts I'd ever had of leaving him. I wanted to be in his arms forever. I inhaled deeply before loosening myself free.

He smiled. 'Would you like to come in Aussie Girl?' The blueness of his eyes seemed to have changed. They were now aquamarine with warm circles of dark blue and they looked into the depths of me with tenderness.

I beamed. 'Thank you mein Deutscher Mann.'

The kitchen greeted me with its usual cleanliness and lack of color. Nothing had changed except that the note I'd written in German was no longer on the fridge.

I kicked my shoes off and stood listening to the sounds of silence knowing that buried beneath all the order were the giggles and laughter of the days we had shared, nibbling on salami and toast for breakfast, making hot wine with cinnamon, and having long discussions about the sounds of the English language compared to those of the German language. In some ways all of it seemed foreign to me now. It was like a great big sink hole had opened up and taken the life we had together and had sunk it to the bottom of the earth never to be seen again. But we could begin anew.

Dirk washed dirt off his feet and dried himself in the laundry. 'Would you like juice?' he asked as he came in.

I was startled back to the present. 'Oh yes please.'

He poured juice for me, a beer for himself. I found myself staring into the thick orange juice on the table in front of me and I became aware of how cold I felt. I pulled my jacket closer and buttoned it up before sitting down. Dirk sat opposite me.

I picked up the glass and sipped. 'How's your father?' I returned the glass to the table.

Dirk's eyebrows lifted a little before falling into a slight frown. He sighed. 'He is not so bad but he misses my mother.' He gulped down a mouthful of beer.

'He's alone.' I shuffled my feet, looked around at the bare walls. 'Will you return to Germany?'

'I have been thinking all the times while I have not seen you Aussie Girl and I have not thought to go back to Germany yet.' Dirk looked down. 'My father will be okay.' He looked back at me and his face lit up as if he'd remembered something. 'He is getting a bicycle.' He chuckled. 'But I do not know if he can ride the bicycle.' We both softened with sighs of fondness. 'But I have another idea.'

'An idea?'

'See what you think.' Dirk got up and leaned against the kitchen bench facing me, beer in hand. 'We buy a house together, we live together, share the costs.' He guzzled the beer. 'What do you think?'

I must have looked gob smacked. My heart held a tingle of excitement that I knew would explode if I gave it space. I could hardly find words to respond. All the thoughts I'd had about settling down, moving in with Dirk, downsizing, came together like pieces of a Simpsons' jigsaw puzzle. But there was something missing. And it wasn't Homer. It was Marg.

I scanned the kitchen, let my eyes come to rest on the fridge. It looked so bare without my handwritten note. Its absence spoke more than its presence could have. I wasn't important to Dirk. He'd told me that in this very kitchen. Too old, he'd said. Too different. Memories of Josephine asking me if he'd ever asked for money played across my mind. *What does he want from you?* And now a thought pushed through and I could hear Josephine's voice, *he doesn't want money, he wants a house.*

'What do you think Aussie girl?'

I stopped gazing at the fridge and looked at him. 'Buy a house and live together?'

'But we have to leave this suburb, I like the one in Ipswich.'

'Ipswich?' I must have sounded shocked but he didn't seem to notice. 'Why not stay in Wavell Heights? I mean, what about Julia? She lives in Brighton, it's nowhere near Ipswich.'

'You must leave Julia. If we do this you must focus only on me. If we are together then you must only do things with me.'

My face must have revealed my thoughts but it was obvious he wasn't reading them. He stumbled to the sink. I was struck by his state of drunkenness. I'd never seen him trip and stumble before. I'd almost forgotten how much he'd begun to drink. He turned to face me and I was gripped by the depth of loneliness I saw inside of him. My heart yearned to reach out to him and solve all his problems but hadn't I learned enough to know that you can't do that for anyone?

I shook my head slowly. 'Dirk, the last time I was here you told me that we don't have a future together. You told me it wouldn't work for us. You said so many hurtful things, I was heart-broken. How can you go from that to living together? What about working things out?'

'Yaaa,' he drawled. 'Apologize me, but I have thought about this one because.' He paused as he always did after the word *because,* but my usual feelings of tenderness were absent.

'I think this idea is a better one. I make mistake last time. We buy a house together is goot idea.' He stood behind me and pulled my hair into his hands, twisted it gently. I turned to face him and brought his hands to a stop in mine.

'No.' I held his gaze.

I let go of his hands. By the time I got to my feet I was fighting back tears.

'I can't understand your thinking.' I strained to speak, my voice had disappeared along with my confidence. I loved this man with all my heart. Every fiber of my being wanted to be with him. But I knew now above all knowing, that this was not right for me.

That's when I remembered it, that wisp of light that had come upon me the morning in Dirk's bedroom. It swept across my mind's eye as if it was a spiritual guide and I heard it whisper to me like an internal voice. I hesitated but pushed away the clear question that it had brought into my mind. I gathered my keys.

'I have to go Dirk,' I told him. 'I have an appointment.' I found composure in my false justification.

As I turned to go to the door he winced. He came to me and took me into an embrace, swayed with me to the music playing on a radio somewhere in the house. I hadn't heard the music until then. All I'd heard was the memories of our past. I rested my head on his shoulder and caught a sob about to escape my throat.

'I can't go through the emotional turmoil this relationship gives me Dirk.' I pushed back from him and looked him in the eye. 'I came here because I thought we might be able to make it work. I truly believed that if I changed, everything would be okay. But now I see it's not only about me changing.' I broke my gaze and fiddled with my car keys. 'I have to say goodbye Dirk.' I looked at him. 'For the last time.'

'Nor.' He held me closer.

'I wanted to tell you something.'

He tightened his embrace, held me so tightly that I thought I might not breathe.

'I cannot say goodbye,' he said.

I'd lost the battle against my emotions and without permission tears were running down my cheeks onto his T-shirt. He pushed my hair back, kissed the side of my face in between his words.

'I love you. You must know that. You must. I will always love you,' he said.

'I know, yes, in your own way you do love me.' I pushed back from him and met his gaze firmly. 'But I also know that the timing is wrong for us. The entire thing is out of place. It's like we were only ever meant to inspire each other to love. Not to be in love.'

He resumed stroking my hair and continued to sway with me to the music.

'I am so sorry.' I tasted my own tears when I spoke. I searched for a Kleenex in my jacket pocket and wiped my face. 'I am so very sorry.' I dabbed my eyes. 'Please, I must go.'

'What is it that you would tell me?' He cupped my face in his hands.

I searched his eyes. In there I saw the complexity of his background, the pain of the history that he held within. I imagined I saw the eyes of the young mother who had watched the Wall go up but who had still managed to raise her son with love.

I saw the man I felt so much compassion for, the man I fell in love with. And in his eyes I saw the definite certainty that unless I lived as he wanted to, as he needed to, I could not have a future with him. Everything that had changed within me would have fallen by the wayside if I agreed to live with this man who was so unwilling to change. The experience of the mist of light that swept over me the last morning we were together had slipped from my mind. I'd almost forgotten that I was going to tell him about it.

'What is it?' he asked dropping his hands to hold mine. He clasped them in front of his chest. 'What are you going to tell to me?'

'It's nothing really. No,' I corrected myself. 'It is something. Many things have happened in the weeks since I've seen you, I couldn't begin to tell you but the last time I was here I had a strange experience. A type of intuition. A knowing if you can understand what I mean?'

'Tell me more about this,' he whispered.

I continued, although I had a feeling that I was composing an epilogue. 'Before you told me about your mother's death, that very morning I had been thinking about her living behind the Berlin Wall. As I looked at the photo in your bedroom something came over me. I felt enormous peace.' I searched his eyes and placed my hands firmly on his chest. 'Your mother is at peace Dirk, I felt how much she loves you.' He lowered his gaze, took a deep breath as I continued. 'And the love I have felt for you is the deepest and most healing love I have ever experienced, it's changed me forever.'

'How is this?' he asked as he enfolded his arms around me.

'I thought I was self-centered but now I realize that I empathized deeply with someone outside of myself. And it was because of that, that I came to know my own good qualities. I had confidence to do things I believed in. I have never had such positive feelings about myself before.'

He leaned back and looked at me with such sweetness that I thought I would melt in his arms. 'Is this true?'

I moved away from him. 'Somehow by loving you I was inspired to stand up for truth. I was inspired to forgive and trust.' I lowered my head. 'Even though that trust was not returned.'

'You have wonderful qualities,' he said as he recaptured my hands. 'Maria, you are the best person of my life.'

'Deutscher Mann,' I said with tenderness, 'everything about our time together inspired me. You, your mother, that photograph, everything Dirk. I have loved you with all my heart.'

'Why my mother?'

'When I looked at her in that photo it was almost like she represented womanhood and motherhood. Think of it Dirk, she had no choice but to raise her family behind a wall. You were born there, you knew nothing else but she was imprisoned there. Yet she still raised you and loved you in the best way she could. It gave me courage thinking about that. It enriched my own thoughts of how I mother and how I love. And it encouraged me to stand up for myself even though my own emotions were a wall.'

'It was not easy for us behind the Wall,' he said as if he hadn't heard my own personal break-through. 'We had only one thing in our minds. To be free. And when the Wall came down.' He raised his eyebrows. 'It was hard too.' He nodded solemnly. 'We all went our separate ways. We were not close after that.'

'Walls are built to keep people out,' I said. 'Or in. They separate people. And when they tumble, they separate even those who love each other.' My mind went to Ursula and to the way she'd built her walls. I thought of Dominic and how I locked him out. I thought of Josephine and her inability to commit in a relationship. Walls. All of it. I looked back at Dirk.

'It's part of the reason it won't work for us,' I told him. 'You're not ready to be free Dirk, not really. You still need the boundaries that the Wall gave you and at the same time you still strive to be free. It's why you get close to me and then push me away. It's the same for me in some ways.' I turned to leave.

'I too,' Dirk announced with a decisive tone. He was still holding one of my hands. I turned back to face him and searched his eyes for meaning. 'I too have felt the love and for me it will be forever also,' he pledged.

I brushed his lips with a kiss, let my hand drop from his touch and went down the back steps.

'And where is the cat tonight Dirk?' Again I sought normality with which to compose myself. 'She is usually here to greet us.' I scanned the back yard.

Dirk followed me down the steps and with gentle hands turned me around to face him.

'I am sorry I did not tell you.' He cupped my face in his hands, kissed me and spoke with his lips still brushing my skin. 'The cat, she is dead. I saw the cat on the road, she is dead. I dig the hole beside the fence, under the tree.' He encircled me with his arms.

I buried my face in his shoulder. Feelings of despair that I had been desperate to hold back burst from deep within me and replenished the tears in my eyes. An overwhelming love for Dirk washed over me and filled my entire being. It bubbled up and began to pour out of me. My whole body was shaking. I muffled my sobs on his shoulder.

'I am so sorry Maria.' He held me until my breathing returned to normal, until the sobs were no longer sobs but breaths I took in rhythm with my heart. For an hour he held me like that, maybe for an eternity, our eternity, all trace of time dropped from my conscience mind. But in reality it was more likely only minutes until I raised my head from his shoulder, released his arms from around me and took his hands into mine.

'This is not a good day for me,' he whispered. 'And for you also. Are you okay?'

I took a deep breath and nodded confirmation. 'But I must go.'

Dirk walked with me to my car and waited as he always did as I reversed out of the driveway. That it was our final goodbye seemed to make no difference. He followed the car to the footpath, waited while I changed from reverse into first, waved as I accelerated and drove down the road. That it was no different that last time we were together made me cry all the more because suddenly what should have been different, was ritualistic and out of place.

As I drove home trying to keep my eyes clear from tears, trying not to hear our words play over and over in my head, trying earnestly to put them out of my mind and release the magnetic pull I felt which was telling me to go back to him, I remembered the words of inspiration that had spoken to me. I was sure I could feel the soft mist of light come upon me and I heard a tender whisper. *Behind the Wall is a spark of light. Hold it fast, hold it tight.*

I came to a stop at a red light and looked down. My feet were bare. My favorite shoes were still at Dirk's back door.

Chapter 25

I'D ALWAYS imagined that I would grow old gracefully. Trouble is that I never gave much thought to what that actually meant. And as I mulled things over on my way home I realized that it was just one of those clichés which no one really bothers to question. Much like the stereotype of the aged woman. I had become aware that aging was a developmental stage of life no less than what adolescence was. And while there were commonalities, it was different for everyone. I had to find my place in it in my own way. I looked down at my bare feet. I could never grow old gracefully. Growing old, or older, was not about gracefulness. Gracefulness could be an attribute of a mature woman, but it wasn't one of my attributes.

As I drove I found myself taking the turn that led to Dominic's place. Going to see Dominic was the last thing I had imagined I'd do after saying goodbye to Dirk. But I needed a friend. It wasn't selfish or self-centered. It was one of the benefits that came with being friends. And Dominic needed my friendship as well. I stopped and messaged him and asked if it was okay to come over, I'd be there in five minutes. He messaged right back with an upper case *YES*.

Dominic stood at his front door on the top step under the light waiting for me. As I came up the path from my car a look passed between us and I knew he could read where I'd been. I nodded and presented a weak smile. He swung his arms out to me and pulled me close.

'I know,' he soothed. 'I know.'

Sobs shook my chest as my eyes filled with tears. 'How can you know? You know me so well?'

'I know because I know myself so well.' He took my hand. 'Let's take a walk.' He looked down at my bare feet. 'Where are your shoes?'

I shrugged my shoulders and led him down the street. We rounded a corner and Dominic took us up a side street. We strolled down the middle of it towards the beach. I rested my head on his shoulder momentarily as we walked.

'Dominic, it was so painful to say goodbye.'

'Dirk?'

I nodded. 'I'll never forget him.' I stood in front of Dominic and brought him to a pause. 'And I will never stop loving him, you have to know that.'

'No reason you would need to.' He eased me back into a stroll.

'I didn't go there to say goodbye Dominic. I was going back to him. I wanted to be with him forever. I guess that's hard for you to hear?'

'A little.'

'Our time together was unique.' I looked down and kicked a little stone along the road using the sole of my foot. 'But it's over.'

Dominic remained silent.

'Oh, I feel so angry about it.'

'Why angry?'

'It's like everything that has happened over the past year. I feel like I've been caught up in a whirlwind of emotion. At first I couldn't understand why it couldn't work with Dirk.'

'Why couldn't it?' He pulled me to the footpath. I felt the cool softness of the grass beneath my feet. A dog barked at the fence. Dominic hushed it.

'You know what Dominic? I thought I knew why it couldn't work but I don't think I really do.' I stepped in front of him. 'He inspired me to love.'

Dominic leaned in and put his arms around me. 'I understand perfectly, it's what you've done for me. Inspired me to love.'

I moved away. I wasn't ready to commit to Dominic.

'There was something about that inspiration to love, Dominic. I was also inspired to accept.'

'Accept what?'

'Life, I guess. I heard the question clearly in my mind. Do you accept? It was amazing. As I drove home I tried to accept the finality of my goodbye to Dirk. I tried to accept the loss while I remembered how much I had gained in loving him. But I knew it was more than that. I have to accept everything about myself and my life. Everything that has happened.'

Dominic took my hand. 'Come on, I'm getting hungry, let me show you my bachelor pad.' He led me back the way we had come and we walked silently until we got back to his unit.

'There it is,' he announced as we stepped inside.

'One room?'

'Not really.' He laughed. 'I have a bathroom.'

'It's a studio apartment, I had no idea. It's gorgeous. So where's your bed?'

'Ta da.' Dominic swished his hand toward the couch. 'Sit down and try it. It's a fold-out.'

I eased onto the couch.

'You do realize you are in my bed now, don't you?'

I patted the couch. 'Ooh, now haven't you wanted that for a while?'

His laughter rang through the room and filled my senses with relief. I bottled it in my mind for another day.

Acknowledgments

MY ideas for story writing depend on a good coffee, best sipped in a coffee shop with friends. I've had many conversations where story dust has been left sprinkled all over the table. For me, that's where ideas for stories come from. They are the dust of what might have happened or could have happened in real life, but didn't happen at all. Stories are in the whispers and the gossip, the hopes and heartaches and they long to be set free with renewed love. Finally a guiding hand helped me wave a magic wand over the story dust. There are many people I want to thank for supporting me when fairy lights went out or the questions I asked didn't have answers. Not least are my German friends without whom there would have been no accent. There are a few names I have to mention because of their contributions but to everyone who supported me, thank you with all my heart.

Roz
Gabrielle
Francis
Andrea
Carmel
Ann
Lucy
Matt
Michelle
Kai
Paul
Trish
Bernie
Maureen
Paula
Christine
Dr Matt
Bent Banana Books
Redcliffe Book Club

About the author

Christina Debi was born and raised in Queensland, Australia, and lives in the Moreton Bay Region. *When Life Walks on Bare Soles* is her first novel.

If you have any questions for Christina or you would like to be on her mailing list for news and previews of sequels to *When Life Walks on Bare Soles* email christinadebi.author@gmail.com

www.ingramcontent.com/pod-product-compliance
Lightning Source LLC
Chambersburg PA
CBHW071057250626
47159CB00002B/495